ISLAND MAGIC

by
Loraine Barnett

MARRON PUBLISHERS, INC.

INTRODUCING
LORAINE BARNETT

Loraine Barnett, Barbadian, migrated to the U.S. in 1977. She is an editor and writer who has worked in publishing for the past seven years. This publishing of her first romance novel is a dream come true and owed all to the grace of God and the support of dedicated family and friends. She lives in Queens, New York, with her husband and baby son.

ROMANCE IN BLACK
MARRON PUBLISHERS, INC.
P. O. Box 756
Yonkers, NY 10703

ISBN 1-879263-00-9

All characters in this book are fictitious. Any resemblance to actual persons, living or dead, is purely coincidental.

Photo: Charles A. Barnett

Printed in the United States of America

October 1990

∂ ∂ ∂ ∂

To Dorothy Barnett

My wonderful mother. Hats off to you and my love always. You're irreplaceable and we're inseparable.

To Steve

Your love and undying support made all this possible. You are the ideal husband and I love you.

∂ ∂ ∂ ∂

AUTHOR'S NOTE

Island Magic is the fictional account of the lives of two lovers: Alan Hussein, a Trinidadian, and Rhonda Baptiste, a Barbadian. The novel provides a sense of West Indian culture. (The term West Indian is used to describe people whose origins stem from the Caribbean.) However, while writing this book, I realized that this is a mere taste and does not fully explore the extent of the cultural variety found even among the various islands themselves. For a somewhat truer understanding of the differences between each island's culture, one would have to live among its people and study their history.

The book also encompasses communities in New York that are heavily populated with people from the Caribbean, and communities in Barbados. The use of descriptive narrative and dialect gives one the opportunity to visualize and hear the characters as they interact with each other and their environment.

Therefore, special note must be made in relation to the use of dialect in this novel. The dialect used here—a combination of archaic English and Africanisms—tries to capture the rhythm and patterns of speech of the characters without alienating those readers unfamiliar with these dialects. Standard grammatical rules of the English language had to be broken in many cases to get as close as possible to the actual spoken word or thought.

In particular, I must point out that the word "ain't" (am not, is not, are not, have not, has not), which is grammatically incorrect, is pronounced differently by different characters; the pronunciation also varies according to the sentence or degree of emphasis in the sentence. For example, "ain't" is sometimes pronounced "'en" by Barbadians.

Lastly, I would like to add that although West Indians speak incorrectly according to standard English rules, they are not illiterate by any means. In fact, West Indians are reputed to be some of the most literate people in the world. They are quite capable of communicating both orally and through the written word in standard English when it's necessary, or when they so choose. Throughout the book there are words and phrases that may be unknown. For brief explanations of these words and terms, please see the glossary at the end of this book. Also, for those readers unfamiliar with Barbados and Trinidad and Tobago, there are short descriptions of the islands below.

Barbados

Barbados, the most easterly of the Caribbean islands, is 166 square miles. Made of coral stone formations, the terrain is hilly, not mountainous, and the island is well known for its beautiful serene beaches and pleasant tropical climate.

Bridgetown, picturesque and rich in history, is the capital of Barbados. Bounded on one side by a deep water harbor, the city of Bridgetown is the center of commercial activity and is noted for its shopping malls and boutiques.

The population of 250,000 is made up of all races and creeds, but people of African descent make up the majority. Barbadians, or Bajans, as they are commonly and affectionately called, thrive under a two-party democratic political system and an economy primarily made up of tourism, agriculture, light manufacturing and financial services.

In Barbados, English is the official language and education is free up to the university level. The literacy rate in Barbados, over 90 percent, is considered one of the highest in the world.

In terms of religion, the people are predominantly Anglican, about 70 percent, and Roman Catholics, Methodists and Moravians account for the remaining 30 percent.

Trinidad and Tobago

The Republic of Trinidad and Tobago is a unitary state made up of two islands. Trinidad, 1,864 square miles, is the southernmost in the chain of Caribbean islands and lies seven miles off the coast of Venezuela in South America. Tobago, 116 square miles, lies 21 miles north-east of Trinidad. Like Barbados, Trinidad has a tropical climate.

The capital of Trinidad and Tobago is the city of Port-of-Spain. San Fernando is the republic's second largest town. Port-of-Spain is the commercial center of the republic and offers a rare mixture of ancient, medieval and modern architecture. It is bounded on one side by a deep water harbor and on the other side by a botanic garden.

The population of Trinidad and Tobago is estimated at 1,168,227 and is made up of diverse ethnic groups. People of African and East Indian descent represent 80 percent and the remaining 20 percent comprises people of mixed African, East Indian, Chinese and other ancestry.

English is the principal and official language, and adult literacy is over 98 percent. The national education program provides free education at the primary and secondary school levels and in some faculties of the local campus of the University of the West Indies.

The people of Trinidad and Tobago thrive under parliamentary democratic rule and an economy that has the petroleum industry at its head. The economy also depends on agriculture, financial services and construction industries.

Culturally, Trinidad and Tobago is well-known as the birth place of steelpans and steelbands and for its colorful and exciting carnival.

The multi-ethnic background of Trinidad and Tobago is reflected in the islands' main religions–Christian, Hindu and Moslem—and people participate in a series of colorful religious ceremonies on special holidays throughout the year.

CHAPTER ❧ ONE

Damn these trains! They're never on time, never clean, always jammed with people. New York must have the worse subway system in the world. Rhonda frowned, knowing that somehow she had to dispel the feeling of doom threatening to overwhelm her. She burned her hand on the toaster oven that morning, ruined a new pair of pantyhose, and talked to her mother. Snatches of that conversation replayed in her head as she waited on the crowded platform.

"Hello," Rhonda croaked.

"Hello, you ain't get up yet. It's seven o'clock."

"No, Ma. I don't have to go in till ten o'clock. How are you?"

"Alright. But muh eyes acting up again. These glasses don't seem to do any good. Should I get a next pair?"

"But you just got those three weeks ago, Ma."

"Yeah. I know, but maybe they make a mistake with the prescription or something. Working at that damn machine all day long ain't no sweet bread, yuh know."

"Ma. You know you could get a different job that ain't so hard on yuh eyes. Besides, with the money I give you and what you saved, you really don't have to work that hard."

"Now, what am I going to to do at this age? You know since your father ran out on us, things tough. Things rough for a woman without a man around."

"OK, Ma, OK. Go and get yuh eyes checked. Let me know what the doctor say. Alright?"

"I wish I knew where I was gonna get the money to see a doctor, with the light bill coming in soon."

"Don't worry about the light bill, Ma. I gotta go. Talk to you later, OK?"

"Later. When is later? You always running me off the phone. Good-bye," she said abruptly, hanging up the phone.

"Bye, Ma," Rhonda groaned into the silent receiver.

The loud rumble of an oncoming train brought Rhonda from her musing. Its approach whipped up a cooling, but funky breeze in the sweltering underworld. Rhonda, like many others, stood waiting, wiping beads of perspiration from her brow and upper lip. A stocky man standing next to her looked very uncomfortable. Streams of perspiration ran down his face, despite his constant mopping with a large white handkerchief. His white short-sleeve shirt stuck to his back in a big wet patch; two wide dark spots stained the underarms.

The graffiti-decorated No. 4 train screeched into the Franklin Avenue station, flinging passengers into each other. Globs of commuters shuffled forward to block train doors, heedless of the cautionary yellow strip painted about two feet away from the edge of the platform floor. Like robots, they were so accustomed to the early morning routine that the acrid odor of urine, oil and grime went unnoticed; as did chipped, dingy tiles that lined the station's walls; the cracked and peeling dark blue paint that no longer covered ceiling or the rows of equidistant steel columns; and the littered platform floor. The two silver parallel rails on which the train ran was the only place where light could be reflected in twin beams in the dark, dank underground.

Stumbling along with the rest of the mob, Rhonda finally made it to the doors, only to feel a wild yank at the handbag at her side. Spinning around, she shouted, "Hey," and made a futile grab, but the snatcher darted away into the crowd, taking Rhonda's handbag with him. Suddenly, a hand reached up from within the crowd and gripped the snatcher's collar, stopping his escape. Slowly, Rhonda pushed her way back through the crowd toward the two opponents—faced off in confrontation.

"Where yuh think yuh going," the stranger said, practically lifting the snatcher off his feet.

"Yo, man, be cool," said the snatcher defiantly.

"Why all yuh like to thief so," the stranger said, his face hard.

A crowd gathered around the scene as the train rolled out of the station. Rhonda stood in the forefront, her attention riveted on the teenager who had snatched her purse. The snatcher stood about five-foot-eight. A faded black and red checkered shirt and a washed-out blue jeans hung on a lank coffee-colored frame, while high-top sneakers, once bright white, covered feet firmly planted about two feet apart. Close-cropped hair added to the youthfulness of the hairless face. He was no more than fifteen, yet hostile, angry, black eyes spoke of harsh experiences way beyond his age. Wide nostrils flared in pride and agitation, and his lips curved downward in disdain and disregard.

As the stranger's grip tightened painfully, the snatcher dropped the handbag. A fearful plea for release, clearly visible in his eyes, replaced an initial look of daring, but he dared not make a peep, for the stranger's strangle-hold was cutting into his windpipe.

Rhonda's attention focused on the stranger, immediately noting his superior height, dark blue suit, stark white shirt and blue silk tie. A riot of short curly hair added boyishness to strong masculine features.

The stranger relaxed his hold slowly. His eyes dared the snatcher to make another stupid mistake. "Why don't you find a way to make a honest living and stop stealing hard-earned money from yuh brothers and sisters." Anger, disappointment and sympathy all meshed in the stranger's tone as he shook his head in regret.

The stranger released the youngster, and the young man backed off, then made a mad dash through the crowd toward the exit.

After silently watching the teenager make his escape, he bent down and retrieved Rhonda's handbag.

Rhonda's relief was so great that she quickly searched for a way to reward her newfound hero. She moved forward and looked up at her rescuer, profuse thanks on her lips. But up close, the full impact of this strange man's presence overwhelmed her, and dry lips just formed an "O" and nothing emerged.

The stranger frowned down at her from his six-foot height, as if he thought her stupidity was at fault for having had her handbag snatched. Thick eyebrows knitted over light brown eyes that immediately brought to mind the popular expression "bedroom eyes," but which at this time mirrored no thoughts of the bedroom whatsoever. They were frozen chips of brown stone. His dignified African nose flared with annoyance. Unlike the hard eyes, his spice-colored skin breathed warmth and sensuality. Rhonda's hands twitched with the unexplainable and surprising desire to run her fingers over the curly hair that clouded his head.

Handing her handbag over, he muttered, "All yuh women should only carry things yuh can handle or leave the damn things home."

His low grumble was barely audible, but Rhonda detected his Trinidadian accent and his anger.

"Thank yo. . . ."

Before she could finish thanking him, he was moving rapidly toward the exit, his long strides incongruous in such a crowd.

Well. He didn't have to be so rude, Rhonda thought while gripping her handbag. She slowly turned around as the next train rode into the station, and tried to refocus on her upcoming day, for once on board, the feeling of doom returned. Today. Today was the scheduled announcement. She would learn today if her career was either going to accelerate or remain on its stagnant course. Michael Ramdeen, her employer and the publisher of *West Indian World*, was going to name a new managing editor. As Assistant Managing Editor, and presently, Acting Managing Editor of *West Indian World*, a magazine for West Indians living in the U.S., Rhonda had a strong chance of landing the position. Heaven knows, she had worked hard enough for it. This unsettling feeling she was experiencing probably stemmed from those whispers she had heard about the publisher bringing in an outside editor. *No sense worrying about it until it happens*, Rhonda tried to rationalize.

Gazing out the window, deep in thought, Rhonda didn't notice as the train stops of Eastern Parkway, Grand Army Plaza or Atlantic Avenue flashed by. Some sixth sense stirred her as the train came into the Nevins Street station. She exited and headed down Flatbush Avenue to the offices of TradeWinds Enterprises.

The summer sun was already heating up downtown Brooklyn. Rhonda was only one of many early-morning commuters walking briskly to work. She carried a black briefcase in her left hand and now held the tan handbag hanging from her shoulder with an extra firm grip. On close inspection, the glisten of the light oil sheen conditioner she had put on her low-cut black hair after shampooing that morning could be detected. Her beige cotton suit and gold blouse highlighted the richness of her brown skin. The sharp crisp taps of her shoe heels against the pavement were in tune with the gravity of her thoughts. A tightness settled upon the normally lush full lips as Rhonda got closer to the office.

Located at the corner of Dekalb and Flatbush avenues, Trade-Winds Enterprises comprised of a dance theater, a drama theater and a publishing house, the latter being six years old. The ten-year old company was the most talked about in artistic circles in regards to Caribbean culture. Its drama theater produced million-dollar hits in the last two seasons and the demand for its dance company, already on tour in Europe, was phenomenal. The publishing segment focused on nonfiction and children's books, while *West Indian World* magazine was created to test the waters for lighter material.

Rhonda entered the building and climbed the stairs to the second floor. While passing through the glass doors, her eyes immediately went to Judy's circular station on the right. But Judy, the receptionist, wasn't there. *Must have gone to the lunch room for coffee*, Rhonda thought, visualizing Judy, patting her big Afro into place, while earnestly making that first cup of coffee.

Making her way across the grey-carpeted floor, past soft pink walls and the four desks of the editorial assistants and copyeditors, Rhonda headed for her office. Soon, the adjoining managing editor's office would be occupied by someone else. She hoped and prayed it would be her.

Rhonda sat at her desk, a frown still on her face. The deadline for the October issue was a month away, and the galleys weren't in her hands yet.

The buzzing of her telephone brought her out of her reverie. "Michael here. Rhonda, would you come up please?"

Rhonda climbed the stairs to the third floor where the offices of management and the art department were situated. Upon reaching Michael's door, she hesitated, knocked, and entered at his request.

Michael Ramdeen was noted for his stern, no-nonsense attitude. Although he wasn't tall—about five-feet-seven—his slender build, straight black hair salted with grey, intense black eyes, and cupid's bow lips all combined to create one handsome devil. And this Trinidadian devil of East Indian descent was ruthless in his business transactions.

"How are yuh?" he asked from behind his huge mahogany desk, as he indicated she should sit, which she did.

The pink and grey decor was repeated in this room as well, but the effect was more luxurious. Exotic hand painted metal vases and handcrafted wall prints from the East graced the floor and walls. For once Rhonda's eyes weren't drawn to her favorite print: A field of colorful butterflies.

"I wasn't chosen, was I?" Rhonda ignored Michael's greeting, not out of rudeness; that wasn't her style. But she just couldn't hold back the desire to know immediately what the future entailed. She wanted that promotion so badly, and she had worked long and hard to achieve this dream. She deserved it. Phrasing the question in negative terms was her way of preparing herself for the worse, but it was also her hope that a positive answer would be returned.

"No. We decided to go for an outsider with more experience and exposure. It had nothing to do with your work."

A lump formed in her gut and in her throat. She shouldn't have been surprised. She'd been preparing herself for the rejection for days. But the news still shook Rhonda. In typical TradeWinds' style they had pulled the rug from under her.

"Who is he and when is he starting?" she asked. Rhonda wanted to sound firm, but her throat refused to do her bidding. The words crackled.

"Who says it's a he?" Michael tried to tease her in order to lighten the atmosphere. But she wasn't in the mood for teasing today.

"Alright. Alright. It's Alan Hussein. Personnel is still working on final arrangements. I'm not sure when he's starting."

"That's it?"

"Rhonda. Look. Don't take it so hard. Hussein is an excellent editor and publisher. He has a knack for knowing just what brings in the bucks. *West Indian World* is doing OK, but it can do a lot better. You know that. And he's a nice guy to work with. You'll see."

"Well. . . I guess that's it. . . Talk to you later."

She got up and left, not seeing the look of sympathy Michael gave her retreating back. He'd heard the crack in her voice when she had asked about her new boss and he felt some remorse. Her question indicated she thought it was the old boys' chauvinistic network operating again. But it wasn't. Alan was the man for the job. Rhonda was still green, not hard enough. And when it came to TradeWinds he was a businessman, first and foremost. He liked and respected Rhonda, but she wasn't seasoned enough to handle that kind of responsibility.

Michael shook his head and focused on the file of budget allocations laying in front of him. He couldn't afford the feelings of guilt nagging at him.

Rhonda returned to her desk and sank her head dejectedly onto clammy hands, her elbows on the desk. Staring into space, she tried to put a handle on her emotions without too much success. *Nice guy to work with, my butt. Probably some pigheaded baboon. They don't know when they have something valuable. They treat good people like crap. I should really quit and leave them high and dry,* she thought resentfully.

Rhonda spent the rest of the day just trying to focus, torn between hot rage and tears of disappointment. As far as she was concerned the day had already ended, just like it began—a total disaster. And all she wanted to do was shut herself up in her bedroom. She didn't want to talk to anyone. Luckily, or out of sympathy, not many people disturbed her that day. And when she got home in the evening, she drank a cup of herb tea took a shower and buried herself under her pillow and comforter. Eventually, sleep replaced the misery and tears, and she didn't move until the alarm went off the following morning.

Upon arriving at the office the next day, Rhonda detected a certain tension, as if the entire office was sitting on a crater of excitement that was about to explode.

"Hi, Judy. Wuh happen? Why everybody so quiet?"

"He's here."

"Who's here?"

"The new managing editor. He starting today."

"What! Nobody told me? Of all the low down. . . ."

Judy, a fellow Barbadian, tried to warn Rhonda with her already huge hazel eyes. But Rhonda was too upset, and since her back faced the main office entrance, she couldn't see the cause of Judy's agitation.

"Excuse me. I'm looking for Rhonda Baptiste. Could you tell me where to find her?" A baritone voice, obviously male and slightly familiar halted Rhonda's colorful expletives.

That voice. . . Oh no. . . No. . . God, yuh couldn't be so cruel.

She snapped around, almost colliding with the stranger who had rescued her handbag only yesterday. Once again, she was speechless. A light gray suit replaced the blue one he had worn yesterday, and the effect was just as devastating. Without anger hardening his face he was even more attractive. *This has to stop*, she said to herself. *What's the matter with me?* Clearing her throat and forcing some authority into a shaky voice, she bluffed, "I'm Rhonda Baptiste. What can I do for you?" Extending his right hand, the stranger said, "I'm Alan Hussein, the new managing editor. Michael told me you're the best person to start me off." Alan's eyes betrayed no recognition—he was cool, businesslike, and expressionless.

She was aware that all the eyes in the outer office were upon them. She knew she had to remain as calm as possible, and behave like the professional she always prided herself as being. What she didn't know was that her eyes betrayed the emotions tumbling within.

Similarly, Alan was shocked by the wave of feeling that swept over him when he looked into Rhonda's stormy eyes, where hostility ran neck and neck with an effort at self control. Since helping her to retrieve her handbag yesterday, her face had mysteriously stayed with him, but he couldn't for the life of him figure out why. After all, at thirty-four, he wasn't a woman-hungry school boy. Now, her dark brown eyes, with their curled lashes, locked with his own, and he suspected that he would had an interesting battle on his hands.

Within seconds, he absorbed the details of her features that he had missed yesterday. She was about five-foot-eight and short-cropped hair molded her skull like a velvet cap, adding rather than detracting from her femininity. Her small nose looked vulnerable and childlike. Full tempting lips added to her face's softness, and he could tell that any attempt at sternness would never reach them. The upper lip and the outer rim of the lower lip were darker, but a soft pinkish tinge colored the inner portion of that bottom lip. He had an overwhelming desire to reach down and press his lips to hers, lightly.

"Come with me," she said, abruptly.

As Rhonda turned, Alan focused on the picture she made in the cream form-fitting short-sleeve dress that hugged the waist with a broad belt made from the same material. The dress' cut drew attention to her slender torso and slightly larger lower body. Alan's eyes travelled downward and were trapped by the dance of her high protruding rear-end. The raised bottom of a "Jep," came immediately to mind. He had been stung by those vicious wasps a few times. *Hope she ain't like no Jep*, he thought humorously.

Sprawling back on the chair Rhonda offered, Alan surveyed the office, noting that everything on the desk was neatly stacked and labeled for easy access. Though immaculate, the room emitted a warmth that could only come from the occupant's special touch. A vase of red and white carnations with a lush bundle of fern and baby's breath stood on the cream file cabinet. Light from the window streamed in, and with the flowers, softened the harshness of the office decor. Framed photographs of the magazine's colorful covers awakened the light grey walls.

"Mr. Hussein. Welcome to *West Indian World.* I hope you enjoy working with us. I'm here to answer any questions you have," she smiled, with difficulty, hoping he wouldn't see through the facade.

He listened to the drawl of her Bajan accent, noting her deliberate use of proper, polite English. He liked the timbre of her voice: low, throaty.

"No body else ain't try to strangle yuh with yuh bag?"

He relaxed, ignoring her proper English routine. He knew when and where to use it. She was family, despite her airs.

All along, Rhonda was praying that he didn't remember her or that if he did, he would realize it later, after she had had time to adjust to his presence in the office.

Rhonda smiled feebly, "I didn't get a chance to thank you yesterday. Thank you very much."

He acknowledged her gratitude with a slight nod, still absorbing the atmosphere of her office. "Hmm, nice office," he said more to himself than to her. Alan could feel the tension and animosity enveloping the room and getting thicker every minute. He didn't know how to handle it, since he didn't know why it existed—but understood that he couldn't progress any further until he identified his obstacles.

"Are there any pressing questions you want answered before we get started on the magazine, the staff, the facilities, etcetera." Rhonda prompted.

Alan bristled at her tone, and wanted to say, *"Get off your high horse, woman,"* but suppressed the urge. Instead he decided to cut to the chase with, "Why don't you want me here?"

"What?" Rhonda's insides jerked with the accuracy and unexpectedness of his question.

"I said, 'Why don't you want me here?"

"I don't know what you are talking about."

Alan pulled forward from his sprawled position. With his elbows on the arms of the chair and his fingers linked, he leaned forward and fixed Rhonda with direct brown eyes that were the color of moist tea leaves.

"Don't act stupid. You know what I talking about. I don't like people who tell lies, especially to me."

Rhonda pulled her eyes away to stare at her fingernails briefly, avoiding the piercing stare. This wasn't going at all the way she planned. She had geared herself for a cool businesslike encounter. She certainly hadn't expected to see him again, especially in this capacity, and she didn't expect anyone with so brusque a manner. But this time she had no intention of letting him make a fool of her, so she decided to stick to her original tactic.

"I repeat: I don't know what you are talking about. Perhaps you're misreading me somehow. What I feel at the moment is shock. I wasn't warned of your arrival, so I'm not prepared." Rhonda sat back, trying to retreat from the power of the waves emanating from the man.

"I doubt that," he said, and rocked back to his previous sitting position.

Alan knew she was snowing him, but he also knew that he would get nothing out of her right then. After all, they were strangers, weren't they?

"You, no doubt, know the intricacies of the publishing business, so the important thing right now is to familiarize yourself with our immediate projects and our style. Did you have a tour?"

"No. I just saw my office," Alan said, with a hint of boredom.

"Alright. We can tour the office and meet people a little later on. The issue that's mailing in two months is in the finishing stages" she excused her lie internally, "so what you'll be working on right away is the next two issues. We have a three month lead time."

What followed was an indepth discussion on the themes, articles and layouts of the next two issues. Alan's pertinent, probing questions almost caught Rhonda off guard a few times, and were she not a stickler for details, she would have fallen victim to his merciless evaluation.

His initial tactic was to mislead his prey with apparent nonchalance, for although he would flick the thumbs of his linked hands to rub his forehead absently, she was not fooled, for Rhonda knew the telltale sign of total awareness: His eyes never once left her face.

Before the meeting concluded, Alan Hussein had earned Rhonda's professional respect. He was an expert in his field and she would learn a great deal from him. But at the same time, all she could feel emotionally was the anger and resentment churning inside her. *They had no right to bring in a stranger.*

The magazine was faring extremely well, with the market increasing rapidly. She knew she had done a remarkable job of collating the copy and getting clean, impressive issues on the stands ahead of schedule. Besides, she had really been the managing editor, since David was never around to do his job. She was glad they had fired him. He was a pain to work for, and a drunkard to boot. The job should have been hers, for she had worked hard and long for it, in the office and at home. She had worked her way up from editorial assistant, being one of the last original staff members left who started out when the magazine had been launched. She had grown with it, and had helped it to grow. *It just wasn't fair having to show someone else the ropes.*

Alan who was in the middle of discussing an idea for the December issue, saw Rhonda's withdrawal and knew she hadn't heard a word he had said. He continued talking, but focused on the expressions flitting across her face. She even started to nibble on a forefinger, and Alan watched the movement of her lips in complete fascination.

There it is again. That resentful, angry look in her eyes. What the hell is wrong with this woman?

He stopped abruptly, but Rhonda didn't notice. He then baited, "How about a naked woman wearing only a Santa Claus hat for the December cover?"

"What!" Rhonda snapped back to the present. "What did you say?"

"I said how about that tour now. I think we exhausted the topic of the magazine enough for the day. Besides, I prefer to get all the crap out of the way the first day anyway."

"Fine. Let's go." She was embarrassed, but didn't know how to correct this first bad impression.

They got up and headed toward the door. At his outstretched hand indicating "after you," Rhonda opened the door and stepped out into the hall. Again Alan's eyes were drawn to movement of Rhonda's buttocks.

I am going to have a hard time hiding my fascination with that part of her anatomy, he sighed.

ᘒ ᘒ ᘒ ᘒ

Rhonda opened her eyes to the grayness of her room, noting that the rain was pouring down as the weather man had surprisingly predicted. *Weekends were meant for bright warm days, not dreary days like this one,* she sighed. Even waking up to the familiar, merry sound of calypso playing on WLIB wasn't going to do it today. She could tell. Days like these made her yearn for Barbados. Oh, how she missed home at times.

Often, as a young girl, Rhonda would sit in the yard under an ackee tree, reading or writing as young blossoms fell on her hair and onto her book. The breeze had been mild and cool as the sun beat down. Under the shade, she had enjoyed the air's surrounding warmth and revelled in it. Through the wooden back door would come clanking sounds of her mother moving around in the kitchen, and she'd feel at peace. As a teenager, she had always hated rainy days because they interfered with fun. She smiled in remembrance of those Saturdays when the sky threatened rain, and how often she was close to the brink of tears as a result. The thought of not being able to go to the Vista Cinema with her best friend, Sandra (who was also sixteen) would nearly devastate her. It was hard enough to get permission to go, but to contend with the weather, too, was more than Rhonda could bear, for the Vista was the key to a young girl's romantic fantasies. It was the cleanest and only air conditioned cinema nearby, and the most handsome boys were there. Of course, that was the real attraction to the Cinema. Rhonda grimaced as she recalled all the times she all but told a boy outright, *"I like you. Would you please pay me some attention? A kiss later wouldn't hurt either."*

Her reason for venturing over to the Vista Cinema was a closely guarded secret because her mother would have skinned her alive is she knew that the word "boy" was even in Rhonda's vocabulary. But for all her mother's strict rules, Rhonda loved and admired her mother. After all, she was the only parent she had, for her father had left them when she was just a baby. Her mother never explained why, but she knew. The boys and girls on her street often taunted her about her father: their mothers had whispered that her mother wasn't enough woman for him. That was why Miss Milly's granddaughter was her half-sister. But Rhonda often wondered just how many women were enough for her father, since so many other women had children for him.

Rhonda and her mother shared good and largely bad times together. Yet, being together never seemed enough for her mother, Rhonda thought. She was always dropping remarks like, "If you was a boy I wouldn't have to worry about you so much," or "If you was a boy, I wouldn't have to work so hard." Rhonda remembered how hard she tried to be everything her mother wanted her to be. She was strong, athletic. She won many trophies for running. She was the handy man around the house, doing everything from carpentry to masonry. She tried, but Ma never seemed satisfied.

Deborah Baptiste molded her daughter into the independent woman she was today. Now she was in control of her life and she had learned from her upbringing. One thing was crystal clear to Rhonda: No man, at no time, was going to walk out on her. She wasn't going to give him the chance. *No man is going to walk all over me either*, she vowed silently.

❧ ❧ ❧ ❧

Alan Hussein was also observing the weather from the bedroom window of his house, but with gladness rather than regret. He found it just the kind of day to take a long, long sleep—it was Saturday and there was no work to rush to; no need to trigger the automatic cycle of the weekday ritual. Instead, he allowed the trickling of the raindrops rolling down window panes to transport him back in time to Granny and the house in which he was raised.

When Granny died, a large part of him went with her. They understood each other, she with her old ways and he respecting those ways but longing to try new ones. He didn't try to hold back tears when she left him, for the pain had been too deep. Crying was the only way to ease the restriction of his grief.

Yes. Days like these in Trinidad were welcomed blessings, especially where he grew up in San Fernando. Long leaves of sugar cane trembled in ecstasy as raindrops pummelled their leanness. The pea trees and dasheen bushes seemed to quiver with pleasure as clear drops cooled their hot, limp leaves. The rising heat from the earth blended with the cool falling rain, and a fragrant moisture filled the air. The pigs in the pens grunted excitedly, longing for a chance to roll in the mud.

And he could remember Granny scurrying after chickens and ducks to put them in their coops before the yard flooded. *Granny, how I love and miss you,* Alan thought longingly. She had taught him a great deal about loving, living and hardship. She had felt no regret when her daughter, Eleanor, had left him in her care. She had believed that she had done everything possible to instill love, loyalty and a sense of responsibility in Eleanor, and raising Alan had meant as much to her as raising her two daughters ever did.

He recalled the year he was twelve, and the quarrels his grandmother and mother had waged over him. Grandpa stayed out of them, leaving his wife to handle his "hardened" daughter. Eleanor's stubborn determination to live life in her way despite her parents' advice was the cause of many quarrels. Eleanor wanted to take him to Port-of-Spain to live with her. She was renting a room from a friend and was working full-time so she could take care of him now, she argued, but Granny always won in the end. *"Oh no,"* Granny would say, *"Not for you to leave him for somebody else to take care of when you partying and spreeing all weekend long. Oh no. He staying right here."*

He was torn during those quarrels. He could not give up the familiar warmth of his grandmother's country life, but he was intrigued with the unfamiliar mystery of town existence. Even at twelve he had realized that one day he would have to make a choice. However, that choice had been made for him by fate, long before he was ready. It was made the day Granny died. At seventeen Alan had found himself alone, for Grandpa had died two years earlier.

His mother took him from San Fernando to Port-of-Spain, but when he was old enough to live on his own, he would return to the simplicity of country life and the welcome memories of Granny and those loving years. Living town life was too complicated for him at times. San Fernando had the magic of healing and invigorating his spirit. It was always there when he needed it. *Home.*

Lately, he experienced the aching need to return there with growing frequency. He felt unhappy, restless. But now wasn't the time to contemplate a trip to Trinidad, for he couldn't just walk out on his responsibilities. He'd just started a new job. A burst of thunder broke Alan's reverie and he once again focused on the trickling rain drops, allowing them to seductively hypnotize him with warm memories of home.

Soon he drifted into a deep, calm sleep and dreamed of Granny running after him with a tamarind whip, ready to beat him for eating the guava cheese she had hidden under her bed. It had been saved to send to Auntie Janice in England, and in his dream, his home loomed familiar and warm: Nine concrete pillars raised the house about eight feet off the ground. It had been built with wood and concrete, and painted cream and white. A sloping galvanized roof was the steel pan for the musical raindrops that often lulled him to sleep, and ventilated bricks lined the tops of walls and joined the ceiling. Its three bedrooms, living room and kitchen was a playground for Alan "Batman" Hussein and his batmobile when he couldn't play outside under the house. An indescribable joy rushed through Alan as he breathed deeply in sleep, for there was nothing as welcoming and as loving as home.

As the dream progressed, the mischievous boy of his youth tripped over two ducks "threading" as he ran around the house the second time, and Granny started laughing, almost forgetting how she was going to blaze his behind.

♨ ♨ ♨ ♨

Rhonda, in exasperation, flung cotton sheets to the other side of bed. *Forget it. I'm not staying in here another minute, rain or no rain.* She had breakfast, took a shower, dressed, and grabbing a shopping cart, slammed out of the apartment. She spent the morning grocery shopping and doing all the errands she never seemed to get done during the week.

In the afternoon, after her shopping spree, she decided to pamper herself for a change. She soaked in a tub of warm bubbles and periodically massaged every part of her body within reach. The thoughts she tried to avoid all day crowded her brain, each demanding supremacy.

Alan Hussein's question came back to haunt her once more: *"Why don't you want me here?"* he had asked. *Because you represent everything that I have fought against all my life. It is hard being a woman, but a woman in journalism, a woman in a top position on a well-know publication is too much for the male chauvinist world to accept. I have proven myself, time and time again. What did they want? Blood? I hate all men for their domination everything: politics, business, our lives. I don't want you around because you're the most attractive man I've seen in a long time, and you stir senses within me I'd rather keep dead. I know you are going to cause havoc in my life and I will have to fight you all the way, buddy.*

Rhonda eased her body out of the tub. As she patted her skin dry, she examined her body in the mirror. She had done it so many times in her teenage years that it was almost habitual for her to find fault. She objectively examined her small raisin-nipple breasts that pouted proudly, and stroked the curve of her small waist which topped flared, rounded hips and tapered down into long, firm thighs. The battle scars of youth that marked her brown legs give them "character," she felt as she smiled to herself. She wasn't bad at all, in fact, quite sexy really. Unfortunately, there was no one to appreciate her body—no mate and no lover. *Ah, well. It's just as well anyway. I don't need a man messing up my apartment and playing with my mind—and certainly not a man like Alan Hussein,* she decided. For the balance of the evening, Rhonda curled up in bed and relaxed with a book.

CHAPTER ᴥ TWO

*I*t's already eight o'clock. I should really go home and sleep. But Alan knew that sleep would elude him for hours during the night, and it had been this way for the past week. His first two weeks on the job had passed fairly quickly, and on a Friday night like tonight he should be home resting or preparing to party with Eddie and some other partners. They were planning to lime at Tilden that Friday night.

He leaned over to look at the working folders of some back issues of *West Indian World* laying on his desk. He decided against leaving right away and settled down to find out how the magazine really got started. It would surely keep his mind occupied, away from thoughts of restlessness and dissatisfaction with life.

Rhonda had left photocopied material on the magazine to read at his leisure. *She is really a thoughtful person,* he said to himself. *So organized. Attractive too. Why the hell am I wasting time thinking about her? She hates my guts and doesn't even know me.*

Alan tried to shift his thoughts away from Rhonda because thinking about her aroused feelings he would rather keep buried. He tried to maintain uncomplicated relationships—it was alright to have a fling every now and again with a woman who wasn't interested in forcing marriage and commitment onto you, but that just never seemed to work out. Inevitably, he would wind up ending affairs cruelly. *Too much trouble. It was always too much trouble,* he concluded. It didn't matter that Rhonda stirred feelings of warmth, protection, and the automatic desire that was there from the very beginning. "Alright. Cut it out. *West Indian World.* That's what you're here for—remember," he chided himself aloud, his voice hoarse and vibrant in the empty room. The hum of the florescent light was the only audible sound, except for the occasional squeak of Alan's chair as he moved.

As he moved to pick up a folder, another file grazed his bare arm. He had hung his jacket and tie in the closet around 6:30 when almost everyone had left. Then he had opened two buttons at the neck of his white shirt, and rolled the sleeves up above the elbows. Before he opened the folder, he sat back in the chair and absently stroked his chest, rustling the scattered hair that curled on the muscular golden surface. Moving his hand from his hair, Alan proceeded to massage his forehead, admitting he was having difficulty focusing on the issues in front of him. He took a deep breath and expelled the air in a long sigh, his cheeks puffed with the effort. With gritted teeth and a throbbing muscle along the jawline, Alan opened the folder, making one last attempt to tackle the back issues.

The magazine, he noticed, was geared toward the West Indian community in New York, and was born out of a much needed desire to represent these culturally vibrant people journalistically. Initially, the magazine focused more on West Indian politics and economic affairs and played down general interest articles. The financial statements for these issues at that time showed that the magazine barely broke even. Gradually, the emphasis shifted: There was an increase in short stories and the introduction of a poetry section featuring budding writers. Even though the magazine was popular and sales were good, Alan knew it could be better.

In its present form, the magazine needed equilibrium and was bordering too much on sensationalism and muckraking. The graphics he liked. The logo was perfect. It immediately transported the reader into a world of sea and sun, a world of much missed beauty. The letters' design mirrored the sloping movement of water, evoking calm peacefulness. The text was serif, stylish, not too harsh and sterile. The photography was good, but lacked creativity. I'*m going to talk to the photographers*, he decided, *first thing tomorrow, or as soon as possible. We definitely need more ads. The articles are too crammed, needs breaking up more.*

When he had finished digesting as much as he could, he rocked all the way back in the chair and rubbed his aching eyes with both hands. He decided that the magazine could benefit from some changes, but he had a strong feeling he would have to fight Rhonda over most of these ideas. But he intended to win every fight, regardless of what it took.

One of the major changes he wanted to implement was more extensive coverage of the smaller islands in the West Indies, like Bermuda, Antigua, and St. Lucia. Presently, the focus was almost solely on Jamaica, Barbados, Trinidad, Guyana, and Grenada.

Alan felt a surge of adrenaline flow as he considered the task ahead. *Good,* he thought as the corners of his mouth playfully lifted, *this is what I'm looking for—what I needed. The sweet rush of challenge.*

Although Alan owned a weekly newspaper called *The People's Voice* in Trinidad, he had yearned for the thrill of being actively involved in the editorial process of raising a publication to superior levels. The *People's Voice* was a successful paper that no longer needed him on a permanent basis and the challenge had been missing. His editorial staff was exceptional and his partner had practically run him out of the country. "Go take a break," Sebastian Morgan had said. "We can get along very well without you. As a matter of fact, we could use a break from the nitpicking."

So he left on an indefinite leave of absence and now he was back in the heat of publishing again. *West Indian World* had potential and he intended to tap it to the fullest.

꿿 꿿 꿿 꿿

As Rhonda sat editing a freelance article on the upsurge of fashion designers in Barbados, Alan called her into his office. She frowned in annoyance for the article was badly written and would need a great deal of work, but the diamond was there. She didn't care for the interruption or his tone of voice. After three weeks of working under him, she was already desperate for a vacation. She entered the adjoining office and sat down. Alan did not acknowledge her presence, instead he remained engrossed in the material before him.

Without preamble, sharp reprimanding words were voiced: "There's an article here on bauxite mining in Guyana. Some of the information isn't right. I called to double check some figures and they were wrong. You edited this, didn't you?" No one would have guessed from his tone or expressionless gaze that he mentally chronicled the charming picture she made in her brown suit, cream shirt and brown and black checkered bow tie while she sat before him.

"Yes, but. . . ."

"No buts. This stuff should be clean by the time it gets to me."

He paused. She could tell that he was annoyed, for a muscle throbbed along a rigid jaw.

"Now this is another story."

He indicated the second article in front of him.

"You wrote this, right?" he asked.

"Yes," she answered.

"The damn thing has no life. For something this personal, this real, you treat it like a lab report."

Rhonda's stomach quivered. She was nervous and slightly apprehensive. Sure she had a hard time dealing with criticism, but there was more to it than that. *I don't like being on his bad side,* she realized.

"'Illegitimacy in Barbados is the norm more than the exception. Statistics show that over seventy percent of households are made up of three or more illegitimate children and the numbers continue to rise. . . .' And it goes on and on in a condescending, superficial tone," he said, flipping the pages in irritation.

Rhonda just sat very still, frozen in rigid silence. *Already he's laying down the law. Lord, please just let him stay away from this article—this particular issue. I'll just die if he. . .*

"Your parents married?" he asked abruptly.

Rhonda looked at him stunned.

"Don't know your father, do you?" he fired the second question before she could respond to the first.

"Take this and rewrite it like you really know what you're talking about."

He handed the article back to her and returned his attention to the stack of articles on his desk. She had just been dismissed, and rudely to boot. On her way back to her office, Rhonda couldn't control the myriad of emotions coursing through her. She was angry, embarrassed, hurt, and she felt inadequate. Part of her admitted that he was right about the article: It lacked feeling. But, feeling meant digging far into places she'd rather leave alone; old painful memories of the past threatened to surge out of a rusted Pandora's box. She sat still behind her desk, unable to return to the fashion designers article because she wasn't ready to face anything at the moment. Suddenly, the telephone rang.

"Call an editorial meeting for three o'clock tomorrow. Oh, and let everybody know I *mean* three o'clock," Alan demanded.

The editorial meeting started at three o'clock promptly in the conference room, regardless of who was missing. Rhonda almost felt sorry for those who weren't there. This was the second editorial meeting Alan had called—the first was an introduction to the staff and he prevailed as Mr. Niceguy on that occasion. But she had a feeling Alan wouldn't be in a mood for excuses or niceties this time around.

"There are a number of things that I want to discuss today, but foremost on the list is the question of accuracy. I know that you are well aware of the importance of truth and accuracy in any story. It is only when you've done your homework that you can proceed with any writing. Now, if in the future, the accuracy of any story is questionable by the time that story reaches my hands, I will not hesitate to get rid of who wrote it. I don't care who you are, or how long you've been here. I will not tolerate any slackness from any of you. The next thing I refuse to tolerate is late stories. You've all been told, time and time again that meeting the deadline is of the utmost importance. In the two weeks that I've been here, I've seen writers hurrying to finish stories at the last minute, editors screaming for those stories and the whole place in chaos."

Alan stood throughout the entire meeting. His hands spoke just as precisely as his mouth, gesticulating and moving from hips to side pockets and then back to hips. The dialect was gone, his face cast in iron. Everyone sat with bowed heads like recalcitrant school children. The rest of the meeting revolved around general editorial business, and you could hear a pin drop by the time Alan concluded the meeting.

The next day Alan called her, demanding that she cancel any lunch arrangements she already had in order to have lunch with him. Rhonda, who had previously scheduled an interview with the captain of the West Indies cricket team, refused his demand, explaining her reason.

"Lady, maybe you're forgetting who you're talking to. There are some things we have to talk about and one of them is that article you're doing."

"I'm sorry, Mr. Hussein," she said formally. "I had hell trying to get this interview and I'm not going to cancel it now. And I really couldn't care less about who you are."

"I see."

The sound on the other end of the telephone line was dead for a while. She could hear his breathing, but she dared not breathe herself. Her insides were quivering with uncertainty.

"What about dinner tonight?"

"I don't think I could arrange that," Rhonda answered quickly.

"Oh no? I'm willing to compromise—why not you? I got the impression your job was the most important thing in your life. It seems I was wrong."

Rhonda knew he was blatantly daring her. He fought nasty. *I'll just take him on and teach him a few choice lessons of my very own*, she resolved.

"Alright," Rhonda responded, finally.

"I'll pick you up at seven. Be ready. I hate late females... And when we go out, leave that starch attitude of yours home."

Rhonda didn't know how to respond to that, so instead, she gave him her address and said "OK" to his, "See you later."

ᔐ ᔐ ᔐ ᔐ

Rhonda was on time and he was pleasantly surprised. When he had buzzed her on the intercom in the apartment building's hallway, she had responded almost immediately, telling him she would be right down. Alan noted that the building was kept pretty clean and although the corner of Franklin Avenue and Eastern Parkway wasn't the greatest of neighborhoods, it was close to one of his favorite places: Prospect Park and the Brooklyn Botanic Gardens. He also was a frequent visitor to the adjoining Brooklyn Museum.

Many people claimed that Brooklyn was the second home and heart of many West Indian peoples, and gazing at the vibrant energy that was found on just this one street on a summer evening, Alan could not argue the point. For everywhere he looked, activity played out the community's enjoyment of the freedom that was granted by the summer's warmth; for it was said that no one hated winter more than a transplanted West Indian.

As Alan waited for Rhonda to arrive, he turned to look out the scratched glass of the metal-framed door onto the street. Three young "brothers" were hanging out in front of the building. One of the teenagers was showing off recently learned dance steps to his friends. With hands stretched to the sides, thumbs and pinkies pointed outwards, and the other digits folded toward the palms, the young man dipped and gyrated his hips to an imaginary beat and ended the step in a smooth pivot and full turn. He extended a right hand to receive his brothers' approval and laughing they took turns slapping the outstretched hand.

The clip clop of someone's shoe heels hitting the marble floor made Alan turn around. Rhonda was heading towards the door in a simple sleeveless black dress that outlined every one of her curves, right down to the knee. *I can't wait to see this number from behind*, he speculated. *This woman is turning you into a sex maniac, Alan boy.*

Alan opened the door for Rhonda with his right hand, and as she came out to stand in front of him, he drew his left hand from his back and handed her a single red rose.

"A beautiful flower for a beautiful lady," he whispered, his smile white, infectious, his eyes soft in appreciation of her.

Rhonda took the rose in surprise. *So there is another side to him, hmm. Won't take much for me to get used to this.*

"Thank you, sir." Rhonda smiled and gave in to the impulse to kiss him on the cheek, where a smattering of tiny dark moles lay. He was irresistible in an olive-green cotton shirt and white cotton pants. The column of his exposed throat and the naked V of his chest were invitations to rude lips.

Her warm lips stunned him momentarily. Their softness held a promise he wanted to thoroughly explore. He presented a bended elbow for her to place her arm into and they walked down the few steps to the car. The warm summer night signaled excitement, as a rare, caressing breeze wafted over their clothes and stroked their faces while they climbed into the car.

Alan had used the need to talk over business as an excuse to explore this new lady in his life. He was inexplicably drawn to this independent, complex woman, and he couldn't understand his total lack of objectivity. It was not like him to be out of control.

In the past three weeks, he had observed her professionalism and talent as an editor and as a writer. In that short time, she had fully gained his respect. He had also noticed that she was popular, for her colleagues genuinely liked her and when together at a few of the office lunches, he had seen her relaxed and easy going. Unfortunately, these reflections had triggered an undesirable observation: she was seldom that way in his presence. In fact, she had never seemed totally relaxed around him, and it bothered him. Even more interesting was the challenge she presented. She didn't cower when he spoke or tried sugar to get around him. He knew he could be intimidating, but it was necessary in his business. Rhonda was direct, for the most part, and he liked and admired this rare quality.

Conversation in the car was minimal, as it usually is when people go out on a first date together. They talked about *West Indian World*, since it was the only thing they communicated on quite comfortably.

After a long drive from Brooklyn, over the Whitestone Bridge and through the Bronx, Alan pulled up in front of a cozy seafood restaurant located on City Island. Stepping into the dimly lit interior, Rhonda noted the intimate square tables that were made of the same solid dark wood as the overhead beams. Each table was blessed with a large peacock rattan chair on one end and a sturdy wood one at the other. Alan seated her in the simpler, more modest chair and crossed over to slide into his throne. A lone candle flickered, casting shadows on his face, and intensifying its stern and sharp planes.

"What's your fancy, my lady?" he asked, waving his hands before her face. "Now, why is it that whenever we're together you go off into dreamland? You have the most puzzling expressions on your face and I can't figure it out."

"There's nothing to figure out. I love lobster and shrimp," she added.

He got the waiter's attention and ordered broiled lobster for himself, while she ordered Lobster Marinara; her taste buds beginning to salivate at the thought of the tender lobster in a rich, tangy tomato sauce. The couple settled into a uncomfortable quiet, each absorbed in his or her own thoughts. After their salads were served, all that could be heard at the table was the rhythmic crunch of lettuce and cucumbers.

"Why do you dislike me?" Alan asked suddenly.

"I'm sure I answered that question once before."

"No. You avoided that question once before. Is it because I was hired and you weren't promoted? Don't answer. I can see that I'm right. And for God's sake, relax. You don't have to be so uppity with me."

Rhonda said nothing. She just stared at her salad.

"If you weren't so hardheaded you'd realize that if you were totally qualified for the position, you would get it."

Still she was silent.

"Listen. Tonight isn't going to work unless we relax and get to know one another. Let's forget about the job for a while. Deal?"

Rhonda hesitated. Then slowly lifting her head, she looked at him. His eyes were focused directly on her, intent, conciliatory, so brown, soft. Her stomach lurched, sending a quiver into her abdomen. *God. He sure knows how to get what he wants.*

"Deal," Rhonda answered.

"Good," he murmured, triumphant. "Now tell me about yourself," he demanded.

"I'd rather not," she stated abruptly.

Rhonda felt guilty about her terse remark, but she knew she had to do something to quell her quaking stomach. He was too handsome, too potent. Telling him about her personal experiences, thoughts and feelings would only make her vulnerable, and she didn't want that.

He decided not to pursue the issue. Instead, he watched her face as it went through its mysterious changes.

"You've disappeared again," he said.

"Oh. I'm sorry. Where were we?"

"I was going over that material on the magazine you gave me the other day. I think we need more hard news, especially on the smaller islands," he announced. It was easier to talk shop after all.

"They went that route already. It didn't work."

"Now they've gone too far to the other side. You don't want it to turn into a garbage like *Top Class* do you?" He sat back in the chair, finally at home with her and the topic.

"No. But people could get hard news from newspapers every day. And half the time that stuff one-sided and depressing anyway."

He noticed her slip into dialect, her Barbadian accent heavier, musical. She had leaned forward, both elbows on the table. His gaze was drawn to the soft curves of her breasts, made more visible by her new position. He quickly returned his eyes to her face, afraid that she might think he was leering at her breasts like a lecher.

"People have to learn to face facts. If we give them indepth, unbiased information that forces them to think for themselves, they'll thank us in the end. Our people need to take more responsibility for their actions. If they get the right type of information they can make better decisions about things like voting."

Alan went on and on, making his point. Rhonda shook her right foot, which was crossed over the left one under the table. He sounded like her history teacher in secondary school—opinionated; and she had hated Mr. Boyce.

"Alan. Alan. Alright. Alright. Yuh make yuh point. But people read magazines to relax. They don't want to read 'bout politics all the time."

"I ain't saying we shouldn't run stuff like the article you wrote—which, by the way, was as boring as hell—but it must be believable."

They spent the rest of the evening arguing, sometimes heatedly, sometimes not. He was forceful, domineering and definitely male. He was definitely not a weak man—he knew his job and Rhonda had to give him credit for that, even if she didn't agree with all the things he said. However, the bottom line was that some changes were going to be implemented right away. The conversation never did turn to her article about illegitimacy, and for that Rhonda was relieved. It was getting late and they were both tired. When he asked if she was ready to go at about eleven o'clock, she simply nodded a response. He paid the bill and they made their way toward the exit. He guided her through the restaurant, his hand warm on her right elbow. At his touch, a stream of fire coursed up her arm and she wanted to snatch her arm from his grasp. But that would have been too dramatic, too childish. *He would only laugh*, she decided.

Alan insisted on walking her to her door when they reached the apartment building. She wasn't foolish enough to object, especially since he had saved her from a purse snatcher once before. He watched as she fumbled with her keys, and when she finally got the door opened, he entered first, without invitation. Somehow knowing instinctively where to find the light switch, he flooded the room with light and proceeded to check the apartment. Rhonda was torn between amazement at his presumptuousness and an appreciation for his concern. *There is a heart behind that steel*, she noted. *He just hides it very well.*

Alan wasn't sure what prompted him to check out the apartment—maybe it was the association with saving her handbag. Rhonda was stimulating his protective streak and no one had done that in a long time, not even Nadine, his sometime girlfriend of convenience. Nadine could take care of herself; she really didn't need one man to protect or even to love her. She was so busy playing the field, that he had to book a date with her far in advance. Sometimes he didn't even bother because he hated the feeling of being one amongst many.

As he walked through the living room, he observed two large batik prints and two African masks on the warm beige walls. The figures and colors lept out from the cotton prints: One depicted a market scene with bright reds, crisp greens, brilliant yellows and earthy browns; the other a mother and child in brown and white. Good *work*, he thought, making a mental note to ask her where she purchased the African artwork.

An area rug, four large pillows and a couch covered in black and white stripped material complimented the natural color of the polished wood floor. The living room looked inviting, but somehow he got the impression that no one had sat on the pillows or on the couch recently.

He peaked into her kitchen on the right. Nothing outstanding there. No one either—just your basic kitchen furnishings. He was more interested in her bedroom. After all, robbers hid under beds and in closets.

Upon entering the bedroom, Alan stood for a moment near the full-size carpenter's bed and inhaled the smell of the room. Traces of her perfume and natural scent hung in the air. *No wonder the living room feels so empty; she lives in this room,* he realized. The stereo, the TV, and the bookcase were all in this portion of the apartment. Her dressing table was neatly arranged and surprisingly didn't have as wide an array of cosmetics as he was accustomed to seeing in other women's apartments.

Rhonda Baptiste was more into paper. Stacks of it filled three compartments of the medium-sized bookcase and were spilling onto others. He liked the soft gray color of the walls, one of which had a poster-size photograph of a bright red hibiscus flower. White curtains hung from two windows on opposite sides of her bed. Curiously, his eyes shifted toward the comforter patterned with a burgundy and pink floral design. *Now what she doing with a bedspread in the height of summer?* he wondered. *Yeah,* he nodded to himself, *she needs a man to keep her warm.* Visions of Rhonda and he lying entangled on the bed flashed through his head. He mentally shook himself and returned to the task of checking the room for intruders. He checked the windows for loose latches, under the bed and in the closet. No one. He didn't think there would be, but one could never be sure.

Finally, Alan went next door to the bathroom, located just outside the bedroom to the left. "Hmm, nice," he said aloud. He recorded the clean sweet smell of potpourri and the inviting softness of the light blue decor. As he pulled back the blue and white shower curtain, he got further testimony of her cleanliness. *Good,* he observed. Alan maintained a perverse appreciation of cleanliness, which was almost typically characteristic of the West Indian male.

When Alan was satisfied, he returned to find Rhonda at the door, a look of amazement on her face.

"Wuh happen?" he asked.

"Nothing," she replied.

"One day you'll get tired of lying to me. Yuh gonna be alright?"

"Yes. Thanks for dinner."

He made no attempt to go through the door and she did nothing to encourage him. They just looked at each other. The tension held at bay all evening surfaced—engulfing them both. Rhonda felt as if someone had reached in and grabbed her insides in one firm grip. Alan was drawn to her, magnetically, and like the second time he saw her, he wanted to kiss her. Only now the feeling was stronger, more powerful. He reached out, stroked her cheek with his forefinger, and whispered, "Goodnight."

Rhonda didn't answer. She couldn't. She was caught in a sensual web spun so tight that escape would have been futile. Alan's brown eyes, shiny, soft with desire, held hers, and weakened her resistance. Involuntarily, she swayed closer to him. He reached out to steady her. His hands, warm on her shoulders, began a slow primitive dance along her naked arms and then back to her shoulders. His grip then tightened as he pulled her to him. He gently sucked in her lips in a deep kiss. Rhonda's lips were soft, warm, and the shock of her tongue touching his sent rivulets of sensation throughout his body. Rhonda, overwhelmed by the power of Alan's touch and scent, clung to him, for fear that she might fall—so weak were her knees.

What am I doing? she thought. But no answer came. She just wanted Alan to kiss and caress her, forever if possible. But reality and sanity returned. Alan grasped her shoulders, breaking the kiss and putting her away from him. Unknowingly, Rhonda whimpered a protest and reluctantly opened her eyes. Alan's ragged breathing and flared nostrils mirrored the sexual agitation in his eyes. His eyes burned into hers, lowering for a moment to caress her lips, then back to up to her heated gaze, which mirrored the conflict within her. He released her and once again whispered, "Goodnight."

The spell was broken. Rhonda visibly released a breath she hadn't known she was holding. She double-locked the door after whispering goodnight to his retreating back. Recapturing the moment that had just passed, she wondered if she had imagined all of it. But her throbbing lips confirmed the truth: she hadn't. Hugging herself, she shivered at the memory of his touch and her uncontrollable response to it. *I hate him. Why did he have to kiss me so damn well?*

Outside Rhonda's door, Alan stood in amazement, the tip of his forefinger tracing the outline of his full, heated lips. He'd been kissed in his time... *But wow... this kiss...* his mind marveled, it usually took a lot more than this to get him as hot under the collar as he was right now. *Something tells me I had better tread easy*, he reflected. *This woman is dangerous.*

The following morning, Rhonda went to work early and closed her door under the guise of deadline pressure. The truth was, she was afraid to face Alan. Fortunately, she didn't have to worry, for when he opened her door after a brief knock at around eleven o'clock, he treated her with the usual professional formality. He handed her a stack of edited copy for her to answer queries and clean up. Rhonda suppressed the surge of disappointment that threatened to overwhelm her when he showed no sign of having experienced the taste and texture of her lips.

On his way out the door, he casually mentioned filling in for staff reporter by flying to Jamaica in the evening to cover a Caribbean Commerce conference. She was brusquely instructed to "woman" the ship until he returned.

Rhonda was momentarily stunned by the news. What if she had a major problem? She felt insecure, for she was already pro-grammed to rely on his judgement in the short weeks he had been in charge.

You'd handle it like you did when David was off somewhere nursing a hangover, she said to herself, trying to stave off panic. "Have a safe trip and thanks a lot," she muttered aloud. "Oh, I won't see you until I get back from my trip—I'm covering the Sun Splash. Remember?"

"Oh, well... yes... You can update me when you get back," Alan threw over his shoulder as he waltzed through her door.

Alan was gone for a week and during his absence, everything ran smoothly, for a change. He was due back on Monday, but on Friday evening she was flying out of JFK Airport to Barbados on a ten o'clock plane. Originally, she had rejoiced at being able to spend a week there, combining business with pleasure. She had managed to arrange the plum assignment of covering the Musical Sun Splash, a special concert featuring performers from all over the Caribbean. The concert, a one-time affair, was arranged to raise funds for polio victims. Rhonda had decided it was the perfect time to take that long-over-due vacation. However, that was before Alan Hussein had barged into her life. Rhonda reluctantly admitted that she was going to miss him for the upcoming week, for he had become a daily fix.

CHAPTER ❧ THREE

*A*fter completing the tedious embarkment process of air travel, Rhonda sat in her economy-class seat on the wide-bodied plane destined for Barbados. Tears began to slowly gather as memories flowed over her and brought along with them the sadness of the past. As always, whenever Rhonda got on a plane, she recalled her first trip to America, at twenty years old, full of dreams of the land of opportunities and wealth. . .

It was her first flying experience and she had been excited and apprehensive at the same time. Remedies for aching ears and nausea from friends and family had been foremost in her mind. She had two packs of gum for the ears and a prayer for the upset stomach. But she had no upset stomach and the ear ache was equivalent to the annoyance of getting water in your ears from swimming.

Rhonda's aunt had met her at the airport. She had not seen her niece in five years and couldn't control the tears of joy that ran down her cheeks. Rhonda was her favorite niece and so much like the daughter she couldn't have that she hadn't been able to resist smothering her with love. Deborah had never appreciated the treasure she had in her daughter, Sheila Baptiste muttered to herself many times. Deborah was blind to the fire and strength Rhonda had within her, or the tenderness and warmth she nurtured for the people she loved. The man who could accept and respect these qualities would be the right man for her niece.

Outside the airport, a crisp gust of February air had rocked Rhonda. She was shocked by the cold and swore she was in Greenland. Her fingers, ears, nose, everything uncovered seemed to freeze instantly. She had no idea then that winters in New York would be much, much worse.

"Cold, huh?" Aunt Sheila, smiled, still wiping her eyes.

"Not you. You don't even have on a coat. How can you stand this cold?" Rhonda said, struggling into the coat her aunt had brought for her.

"You get accustomed. Wait 'till winter and then complain."

"I don't think I'll ever get accustomed," Rhonda said, a quiver in her voice.

She watched her aunt as they waited for the taxi driver to load the suitcases. Auntie Sheila hadn't changed much in the five years they were apart. Sheila Baptiste was a big woman. She stood five-feet-nine with stout broad shoulders and wide curvaceous hips. She was the rich dark color of mauby bark and her lively brown eyes and quick smiling lips were a challenge to many men. But once they got a taste of her tongue's sting, they didn't wait around for Sheila to put weight behind her words, and she would, too. Her hair was pulled back in the familiar plait that was wrapped and pinned in a bun. Rhonda smiled as she watched the plait, remembering the many Saturdays she got fifty cents for making that plait. Even now, she thought it was worth more; that head of hair was hard to handle.

Soon they were on route to Brooklyn and Rhonda's second lasting impression of America was formed: brown, murky, dull. The apartment houses were brown. The street lights emitted an orange-brown glow. This wasn't at all what she had pictured. Garbage and broken glass littered the streets. Lord, she had never seen so much broken glass in all her life. Where did it all come from?

Rhonda had marvelled at the width of the streets, the numerous cars and most of all, the height of the buildings. At home in Barbados, two-storey homes were few and denoted some financial security. Apartment buildings were rare and they were usually one storey high for most people lived in houses, however modest. Everything looked strange and she felt even more than strange. It felt unreal and her mind kept going back to Grantley Adams International Airport, where her friends and relatives all kissed her good-bye and wished her good luck, just five hours previously.

The one bedroom apartment her aunt occupied on New Jersey Avenue had overlooked a park. "Park? Is that what they call a park?" she recalled asking. "Where's the grass?" There was hardly any green anywhere. That's why everything was so brown and dull-looking. No leaves anywhere. Barbados had not prepared her for leafless trees.

Double-locked away from the world, Sheila showered Rhonda with questions about everyone. This went on until four o'clock in the morning, when Rhonda's answers were reduced to steady breathing and gentle snores. . .

Now, she was returning to Barbados, six years later. It was the first time since her arrival in America and Peter's death. Tears clouded her eyes. She had been thinking about him regularly recently, recalling the fun they had and the anguish of his death. They had met at an excursion going to St. Philip, where he sat in the seat beside her in the other aisle and kept sneaking her looks and shy smiles.

Rhonda, an innocent girl of twenty, had ignored the curious stranger. He was too good-looking: Smooth ebony skin covered a slender frame. His Afro was low and neatly trimmed. Long straight lashes complemented big dark eyes that shone with mischief. Guys like that had a lot of girlfriends and she wasn't interested in being added to any list.

On the beach, he tried to talk to her. Rhonda was cold, unfriendly. But he persisted until he made her laugh with some silly joke. The beginning of a friendship was forged.

Peter Francis had been a twenty-four and a third-year law student at Cave Hill, University of the West Indies. Living with his parents and three sisters, he had been accustomed to being catered to and pampered; many times this pandering became a bone of contention in their relationship. He desired this ingrained courtesy from Rhonda unconditionally, and there were times she refused him. He expected Rhonda to wait until she had spoken to him before she made any plans for almost everything. She had rebelled, and though he was amused by her rebellion, at times it had inspired his anger. Their friendship, though stormy, had grown.

When they had discovered they were both going to UWI, they met daily and were inseparable. Surprisingly, he didn't have as many girlfriends as she had thought. In fact, some girl had left him for some other guy about six months before he had met Rhonda, and he wasn't that eager to jump back into a relationship. He had planned to put more time into studying, as exams were coming up. That was fine with Rhonda because even though he was fun and a dear friend, the idea of an intimate relationship scared her.

But Peter had ended up spending most of his time with Rhonda and she did nothing to discourage him. Outside of Sandra, he had been her best friend and his kisses were pure heaven. Gradually, their friendship had blossomed into love.

Rhonda smiled and the tears in her eyes wavered on the outer rim of a eyelid as she remembered the day they made love for the first time. His parents and sisters were vacationing in Canada and Peter invited her over one evening for dinner. The house was too quiet, he had said; he needed company, someone to eat with. She'd agreed, and after a meal of baked potatoes and stewed beef with carrots that he barely managed not to ruin, they had gone to his room to look at old photo albums.

She had liked his room. It was small and cozy. The single bed was usually covered in crisp white sheets and he was tidy, for a man. His books were shelved neatly on the bookcase, and posters of his favorite cricket and soccer stars were arranged on the wall.

They laid side by side across the bed looking at pictures of his family and friends, and as she closed the final album, she had turned to tell him she was ready to go home.

"No. Not yet. Stay a little longer."

"I shouldn't. You know Ma will carry on if I come home too late."

"Please," he had begged and added a gentle kiss to his plea. He had started kissing her face, her neck; his hand had sneaked under her black T-shirt to caress her breasts, and soon she was forgetting about rushing home. When his hand reached for the button at the waist of her blue jeans, she reached out and grabbed it. They had never gone this far before and she was afraid.

"No, Peter," she had said.

"Please," he had pleaded once more. "I won't hurt you, I promise."

"You have Durex?" she asked after a moment's hesitation. It was inevitable.

"Yes. Don't worry. I'll take care of you. Trust me. . . "

He had got up and located a small packet from a dressing table drawer and placed it under a pillow. They resumed their lovemaking and Rhonda had allowed him to remove all her clothing after he had taken off his red T-shirt and black jeans. She had been shy, but curiosity got the better of her and she stared boldly at his naked body, his manhood alive and throbbing. Panic had started to set in again, and she watched him fearfully.

Peter returned to coaxing Rhonda's tense body. She relaxed enough for him to attempt an entry. When he did, she had stiffened.

"Rhonda, you have to relax."

"I can't."

"Try."

He had made a second attempt as he continued to kiss her deeply and massage her back. She dug her fingernails into his arms, when she had at first felt the pain.

"This hurts, Peter," she said. "Peter, please."

"You have to relax. Please. . . Try. . . For me."

And she had tried, just for him. But that first experience was far from ecstatic. But it had gotten better.

Rhonda's thoughts drifted slowly to the day Peter had proposed. It had been a clear, cloudless day and they were lying on the grass under the mango tree in back yard of his family's home. "Wouldn't you like to be my wife. I'm a good catch. In two years, I'll be a fancy lawyer, making endless money. And I'm good-looking so you won't have to worry about making ugly children."

She had laughed and slapped his hand playfully.

"I'm serious. I love you and I want to marry you." He had stopped smiling and fixed her with big, black serious eyes. "Will you?"

"Yes," she replied. She had loved him, and being his wife spelled pure happiness.

They were engaged a week after the proposal. Her mother had made quite a fuss, but she found out the hard way she and her daughter were cut from the same cloth. Both were strong willed, independent women.

"Yuh young," her mother had yelled. "There is so much yuh have to do with yuh life before yuh stay home having some man babies, for him to leave yuh for some other woman."

Rhonda had faced Deborah Baptiste with tears in her eyes. Risking the wrath of a back-hand slap, she declared, "Just because it happened to you don't mean it gon' happen to me."

Her mother had stared at her in shock.

"Go ahead," she said. "Yuh make yuh bed, yuh lie in it. Don't come running to me when things ain't working out."

That was her mother's blessing. For days, she was cold, a frown characterizing the normally stern face. The black hair pulled back in its usual pony comb added to the hardness of her mother's disposition. Whenever their eyes met Rhonda was often forced to look away from the fierceness in her mother's brown eyes.

Peter Francis, her first love, was killed in a car accident one month after their joyful engagement. In two weeks Rhonda lost ten pounds and her mother decided to send her to live in America with Sheila. Her daughter was dwindling away from grief and there was nothing she could do to console her. Eventually Deborah Baptiste would join her daughter in America for it was getting harder and harder to make a decent living in Barbados.

ta ta ta ta

"Ladies and gentlemen, please fasten your seat belts and prepare for landing."

"Are you all right?" A stewardess asked, alarmed at the tears trickling down Rhonda's cheeks.

"Yes. Yes. Thank you. I'm OK."

Very little had changed. They had renovated areas of the airport, but it still felt like home. The warm tropical air was intoxicating. The rich greens, yellows and maroons of the croton plants spoke of bright sunny days and gentle rain.

As she walked from the airplane toward the wide concrete building with its decorative port holes and glass doors, she saw Sandra waving at her in excitement. Beside her was one of the cutest little boys she had ever seen. His chocolate colored eyes were huge, and he frowned in concentration as he searched the crowd.

Before Rhonda could reach her, Sandra darted forward, dragging her son with her, and enveloped Rhonda in a bear hug.

"Wait. Wait. Girl, you trying to kill me or what?" Rhonda cried out, more in joy than pain.

They stood back, looking to see what damage had been done in the six years they were apart. Sandra had put on about thirty pounds, but her honey colored skin glowed in good health. She still wore her hair pulled back in one pony comb.

"When you gon' get married, get a baby and get fat like me?" Sandra asked.

"Never."

"Wuh you mean never? You was always skinny anyway."

"Mummy?" A small voice demanded attention.

"This is Shawn. Shawn, this is my best friend, Rhonda. Say hello."

"Hello, Honda."

"Rhonda, not Honda, Shawn," Sandra corrected.

"Honda."

"Forget it. He'll get it right eventually."

The two women and boy left the airport, chattering all the way. Poor little Shawn couldn't get a word in, not even to ask for some ice cream. But he liked the new lady who smiled and squeezed his hands softly.

It felt good to walk down the Bayland's familiar narrow streets lined with houses that didn't all look alike. Built with either sloping flat top roofs or peak roofs, these houses all had distinct personalities: The Collymores' house on the east side of Sandra's was recently built with a flat galvanized roof and had louvers instead of long windows that opened vertically at the middle. It was painted white with green trims and its veranda, decorated with pots of various plants, was the perfect place to relax after a long day's work.

Mrs. Blackman's house on the west side had never been painted, and its peak roof of wooden shingles needed repair. The old lady lived alone and had no one but neighbors to care for her.

Sandra's house was similar to the Collymores', without the veranda, and was painted grey with pink trims. The big breadfruit tree in the back yard was a good substitute for the ackee tree in her old home.

Once they were settled in, Sandra demanded to know everything about New York, all at once. The next few days were spent roaming old haunts and catching up on the gossip and dreams which had changed over the years.

ð ð ð ð

Rhonda practically lived on the private beach behind the Hilton Hotel and was enjoying every minute of it. On the far left of her usual spot, one could see tall almond and coconut trees standing on a undulating hill of grass whose blades were thick and cushiony.

Below the trees and bordering the stretch of beach, a wide row of the sea-grape vine with its clustered, broad, rounded leaves and bunches of purple fruit beckoned. Rhonda usually ate her way through a bunch of those salt-sweet grapes every day on her way to her favorite spot.

Rhonda would sit on that spot, located a little to the right of the jetty on the pearly sand for hours, just looking across the sea and breathing in its heady fresh-fish fragrance. Occasionally, she'd pass a tongue across dry lips, liking the salt that the sea's spray deposited there. She marvelled at the shades of blue green observed at varying levels: About fifteen feet away the water's hue was a very pale green; at another fifteen feet it changed to an aquamarine; and finally it would then deepened to dark blue just hundreds of yards away. Once you stepped into the water and looked down, however, it was crystal clear, and dark feet stood out against the firm coral-white surface of the sand; the shimmer of the sun's trapped light dancing on them.

A few days into her vacation, as Rhonda sat sifting pinkish-peach sand through her fingers, a shadow fell in front of her. Slowly, she raised her head, her eyes questioning the dark eyes of a beautifully built man in white trunks looming above her.

"Hi," he said, his voice deep and husky.

"Hi," she answered.

Rhonda continued to look at him unabashed. He met her stare for stare. *What is this*, she thought, *a staring contest? I'm too old for this*.

"Yes?" Rhonda raised her eyebrows.

"May I sit down?" the stranger asked.

"Sure."

Rhonda continued to sift sand through her fingers, her eyes focused on the gentle blue green water ahead, her lungs inhaling the pungent aroma of the sea air. She felt the man's eyes on her body. Looking around, she encountered admiration shining from his eyes, and detected the beginnings of a smile touching the corners of his lips. *Nice lips*, she thought.

"You have an unusual face. . . but it's pretty, in a weird way," he announced suddenly.

"Huh?"

"I'm sorry. I always saying the first thing on my mind. My name is Richard Manning. Wuh is yours?"

"Rhonda."

"Simple. Goes with an unusual face."

Rhonda couldn't help but smile at his compliment. *So I have a pretty-in-a-weird-way face. Never heard that one before.*

"You lift weights?"

"I see you say the first thing on your mind, too. No. I own a construction firm. My job and a little exercise keep my body in good shape," he explained sheepishly.

"I see."

"You don't talk much, do you?"

"Sometimes. Depends on who I talking to," Rhonda answered.

The stranger looked away, hiding the sting her remark had caused. *This one has a sharp tongue, but her eyes. . .Oh, they tell the truth. She's not completely immune to me. Alright. We'll play it her way.* There was no way he was going to let this long-legged beauty slip through his fingers. He wanted to explore those curves so lusciously outlined in the one piece black swimsuit she was wearing.

Rhonda wondered about the man sitting beside her. Strangely enough, she wasn't afraid of him. She wasn't in the habit of picking up strange men, especially on the beach. In the Caribbean, some beachcombers were reputed to be gigolos, preying on lonely, widowed or single women. But he didn't seem the type. He was handsome in a rugged way, dark, with hair as tightly curled and almost as short as hers. His muscular frame was impressive, sexy. But she suspected he wasn't really her type. What was her type, anyway? She wasn't a connoisseur of men. Just Peter. Compared to Peter? They were like chalk and cheese. Just like he would be compared to Alan. *I wonder what Alan is doing now?*

Rhonda?"

"Umm."

"How about a swim?"

A swim would be perfect. It will take my mind off Peter and Alan.

"Race you to the water," she said.

"I'll give you a length," he quipped.

He was sorry. He never caught up with her. When they could talk easily, Richard allowed his surprise and admiration to show.

"Where'd you learn to run like that?"

"Right here."

"On the beach?"

"Mostly. But I meant right here in Barbados. This is the first time I've been back from America in six years."

"How long you staying?"

"Well. Half my visit is over. I have three days left."

Richard's eyes flew open slightly, followed by a hooded, vague expression that marked his disappointment. *Three days! Richard, my friend you sure are unlucky with this woman. Three days to convince this fine specimen here that you were the perfect match for her.* What a conquest she would be—there was something exciting and irresistible about this woman with crystal drops of water glistening on her eye lashes. And he had a serious weakness for this particular type of light-skinned woman.

He hesitated before asking, "How about spending those three days with me?"

"I can't. I'm here on an assignment."

"What kind of assignment?"

"A writing assignment. I work for a magazine."

"I see... I have a friend that works as a photographer for one of those black magazines. Maybe I can introduce you, so... when can I see you?"

He's persistent, Rhonda realized without annoyance. *What's the sense of letting all this all go to waste? I might as well have some fun. Heavens knows, I haven't had some real fun in long time. I need to learn how to relax and have a good time and he looks the type that can show me a good time. He's handsome enough. Intelligent. I hope he isn't pushy about getting his women into bed. I'd better settle that now.*

"I hope you ain't have no designs on my virtue?" she asked with a grin.

"Virtue?"

"Yes. Virtue. Seriously. I have no intention of jumping into bed with you. In fact, I may never see you again after this week."

"Does that mean you going to go out with me?"

"I guess so."

"Yippee," he murmured softly. And she laughed.

He was reluctant to leave after their initial conversation so they ended up spending the rest of the afternoon talking and swimming. He invited her to supper at the hotel, where he was visiting some friends and she said yes. She felt self conscious about going into the swanky Hilton in shorts and slippers, but he told her not to worry about it.

"Those tourists walk around in whatever they feel like, so what you worried about?" he had said.

They had a wonderful time and she was glad she had followed her instincts to give it a chance. He introduced her to his photographer friend who worked for *Top Class* magazine, and Rhonda did well in keeping her opinions regarding the quality of the magazine to herself. As for Richard, he proved harmless, if you kept his flirting in perspective.

In between interviews with various musicians participating in the Musical Sun Splash, Rhonda threw caution to the wind and spent most of her free time with Richard. They went to the beach, played tennis, danced all night, went running in the morning. For both of them, the end was coming too soon.

The picture of her as he had picked her up on the night of the Musical Sun Splash would remain with him for a long time. Richard had gasped as Rhonda opened the door to let him in. She was dressed in a black satin jumpsuit, with spaghetti straps that enhanced the breadth and smoothness of her shoulders and back. Its wide billowing legs tucked in at the ankles couldn't disguise her rounded buttocks. The short, sheer red silk jacket she wore out of modesty made the entire outfit even more seductive. Her long rhinestone earrings sparkled, giving her a regal look. As beautiful as she looked, he just wanted to undress her. The need to conquer, rule as lord over another soft pliant body was growing rapidly within him. *This is one woman I am not going to let slip away, Richard resolved.*

"Richard. Stop staring."

He blinked.

"I'm sorry, but you look good, real good."

"Thank you."

Unexpectedly, he reached and kissed her lightly on the lips. His lips, warm and tender, took her by surprise.

"I couldn't help it," he shrugged boyishly.

"Let's go before I knock you out," she said impishly.

The Musical Sun Splash was a success, though the many delays due to mechanical, and who knows what other kind of problems, made Rhonda suck her teeth in frustration. However, the bands with their colorful outfits and outrageously dirty lyrics made up for any lack with their choice of spouge, calypso, reggae and blues. And when the sweet ring of steel pans were added to the melodies, the whole stadium started to rock. Rastas in the crowd tossed their long dreadlocks from side to side and yelled, "Aye man. . . " as the spiritually uplifting music touched the souls of each member of the audience. Rhonda feared the stage would collapse from the jumping and makeshift dancing. She didn't need to take notes; the experience would be lasting.

Richard took her to dinner and a dance after the show. It was their last evening together as she was leaving the following night. On her doorstep, at six o'clock in the morning, heady from wine, food and, she didn't deny it, Richard's charm, Rhonda didn't resist when he drew her into his arms. His kiss stirred her. She relaxed against him, savoring the warmth of his lips. His ardor grew. She pulled away reluctantly, for it felt so good.

"You mean what you say, don't you?" he asked, his desire for her shining in his eyes, his arms holding her fast.

"Yes. I'm not into one-night stands. Besides, I'm leaving tomorrow."

"Your leaving means nothing and everything to me. I would follow you anywhere—anytime."

The declaration surprised Rhonda. She didn't think he'd care for her that deeply so soon, or maybe she had misinterpreted what he said.

"Wuh you mean?"

"I think I'm in love with you," he announced. He held his hand up as she opened her mouth to speak. "I know what yuh thinking. That's impossible. It's too soon. I've been saying the same thing myself. That's why I won't pressure you now. Maybe you'll see me again sooner than you think."

"I don't know what to say."

"Say nothing. It's good-bye for now. I'm sorry I can't see you off, but I have some business I have to take care of myself tomorrow.

He kissed her gently on the lips, turned and left.

After Richard left Rhonda, he drove over to Jennifer's apartment. The airline stewardess he had met two weeks ago would still be in bed. He knew from her schedule this week, that the alarm would be set for 7:00 am. He also knew she'd appreciate a wake up from him far more than the noisy clock. He let himself in quietly, the key she had cut for him days ago shone in the early morning sun. As he eased his naked body beneath the sheets next to the sleeping woman, he decided he would need more time to work on Rhonda. She was a tougher nut to crack, but he planned to enjoy applying every stroke of pressure. *New York was definitely in the cards.*

Rhonda plunked down on the nearest chair. *Oh God. What did I get myself into?* Too tired to think, she got up and dragged her weary body to bed.

Most of the next day was spent writing and typing her story. Shawn clamored for her attention. He knew from the packed suitcases she was leaving soon.

On the beach building sand castles with Shawn in the afternoon, she wondered if she was missing out on one of the most remarkable experiences in life. Shawn was adorable and she had gotten very attached to him. It must be pure joy to raise a child, even with all the natural child rearing drawbacks. But the pain of childbirth. . . she didn't think she could withstand it.

Even more frightening was the task of raising a black child in today's society, a task that requires the unconditional support of a partner in order to meet the odds at least half way. *Maybe having the right man makes it all bearable and workable.* Her traitorous mind jumped immediately to a picture of Alan Hussein. *He is strong, solid and dependable. He would take the business of childrearing very seriously,* she suspected. She snorted in disgust with herself: *Why were thoughts of Alan coming so easily and with such disturbing intensity?*

When Rhonda returned to Sandra's home, there was a message for her to call the office. She telephoned Alan.

"Alan, here," Alan answered, abruptly. *I miss that woman around here. Too many details to take care of and this damn phone won't stop ringing,*

"Hi, it's Rhonda. You called?"

"Yes. I'm glad I caught you before you left. Remember that conference for Caribbean youth that was postponed? Well it's scheduled for next Wednesday and it ends Friday. I know you wanted to cover it, so why don't you stay an extra week and take care of it, OK?" Alan said, his all-business tone disguising the gladness he felt at the sound of her voice.

I would prefer to have you back here, but. . . he thought.

"Alright. You know I wouldn't even have to think twice about that," Rhonda replied, laughing.

"Good. See you when you get back then," Alan responded, noting that Rhonda sounded like she was having a wonderful time.

Rhonda immediately went to her briefcase. *Some sixth sense must have made me pack that information on the conference. Good. I'll do some preliminary interviews on Monday and Tuesday. Sandra and Shawn sure will be happy. I may even give Richard a call. One more week! Yippee!*

CHAPTER ❧ FOUR

*R*honda, relaxed and lighthearted from her week in Barbados, returned to work in good spirits, refusing to let even the grayness of a wet cloudy New York dampen her mood. Everyone was glad to have her back and her carefree smile was infectious—everyone but Alan.

As she was settling down at her desk, her telephone rang. It was Alan.

"Could you come in here right away please." he asked abruptly.

Something was wrong. She heard it in his voice. Her stomach quivered in apprehension. After easing the straps of her white sandals back onto her heels, she got up and the white cotton skirt swished against her calves. She pulled down the sleeveless royal blue silk top and walked over to his office.

When Rhonda reached his desk, Alan threw a magazine across it toward her. His brows were knitted in anger, his nostrils flared and his lips were curled down in disgust.

"Turn to page four," he snapped.

She did, her fingers stumbling over the slick pages. Photographs of Richard and her—on the beach, laughing at the show, dancing, hugging—stared back at her. They were photographs of closeness. There was no denying that. One of Alan's friends had jokingly showed them to him, teasing him about hiding away his luscious assistant. The first sight of the photographs knocked the wind out of him, as if he had been cuffed in the stomach. His response to them surprised him as much as the photographs did.

Five of them had been liming at Eddie's house drinking beers and watching old movies. Wayne had just put in a videocassette of *The Harder They Come*, when Eddie, the realtor and comedian in the group, brought the current copy of *Top Class* over to Alan, who was sitting on the floor looking through another stack of tapes.

"So if you're not hiding her away, how come we've never met her?" Eddie had asked when he shoved the pictures of Rhonda at Alan's hand.

"Because she needs protection from animals like you," he had responded, producing a weak laugh while he gazed down at the intimate photographs of what appeared to be lovers enjoying a romantic vacation in the Caribbean.

Jerry had called Eddie over to ask something about some chick Eddie had introduced him to and Alan was thankful for the distraction. Hiding behind the guise of finding another tape, Alan had tried to put a hold on his rampant thoughts. *Who the hell is this man? She's not seeing anyone, as far as I know. She wouldn't just pick up someone just like that, would she? She was gone for only a short time, how could she. . . No. She's not the type to. . .*Visions of Rhonda's eager response to his kiss came back to him. *No. That was different. I know it. Alan, you just exchanged one kiss with the woman. What are you getting so bent out of shape for? She's not your woman. She can go out with whomever she wants to.*

Jealousy had gnawed at him and he changed from the relaxed buddy his partners were hanging out with, to a tense caged animal who just had to be unleashed.

"Hey, Eddie," he called. "I splitting, man."

"What! Wuh happen?"

"Nothing, man, nothing. Check you guys later," he had said as he hurriedly headed out the door. The others looked at each other, mystified, and turned their attention back to Jimmy Cliff on the television screen.

He had driven around Brooklyn for an hour, unable to explain his overaction—he had no right to feel betrayed.

Rhonda continued to stare at the magazine, too embarrassed to meet his gaze. She had no idea they were being followed around and splashed on the pages of *Top Class!* Well, the damage had already been done. Besides, her personal life was her affair, not the entire continent's. There was no husband to raise any objections, and she certainly was a very free agent at this point in her life. She raised defiant eyes, daring him to criticize her in any way.

"I hope your work holds up to the obvious amount of time you spent gallivanting around town." Alan sneered.

He was upset alright.

"Read the work before you prejudge it—that's the civilized thing to do."

They stared at each other, all hackles raised. Rhonda's nostrils were flared, and Alan couldn't contain himself any longer.

"Did you have to parade and carry on like a slut for the whole world to see?"

Shocked, Rhonda lost the ability to think; instead she acted: The sound of a slap pierced the tense silence permeating the room. Alan slowly raised his hand to his left cheek in disbelief, as anger threatened to burst from within him. Rhonda, standing above him, met his eyes levelly.

"I will not take that kind of insult from anyone. Do you understand me?"

Silence reign once more as they both struggled with surging emotions.

"You owe me an apology. The sooner I get it, the better things will be around here." With that, Rhonda left, closing the door quietly.

For long moments, Alan stood with one hand on the burning cheek, and the other clenched in a tight fist at the side of the desk. A vein at his left temple popped up, and along with the muscle on his jawline started throbbing madly. He got up and went to the window, his hands buried deep in the pockets of his black slacks. He was shocked. No woman had ever raised a hand to him. I *can't believe this! She really slapped me!*

But you deserved it, a small voice responded. *How dare you go around calling a woman a slut—that's definitely not your style. Idiot.*

"I'm losing it. Something is happening here and I have no control over it," he whispered aloud. He felt shaken and he examined the tremor of his hand. No, it wasn't his imagination.

"And she looked so good too," he added. The sun's kiss had darkened her skin to dark toast and the pink inner portion of her bottom lip stood out bolder in open invitation for sampling. *You can't blame another man for wanting to possess her, now can you?*

Alan returned to his desk and sat down. He spent the rest of the afternoon editing copy and trying to regain control of his emotions.

At her desk, delayed reaction took over. Rhonda's hands were shaking, as was her entire body. *How dare he?* she seethed. *How dare he call me a slut? But where did I got the nerve to slap him like that?* She was not a violent person, or so she thought. To be truthful, she was not only upset with Alan's behavior, but she was a little perturbed with herself for showing such a low threshold of restraint. *Oh Lord, why does he bring out the worse in me?*

The incident set the mood for the rest of the day. Other co-workers wondered at the sudden change in Rhonda's temperament. Alan and Rhonda avoided further contact for that day.

Alan left the office early, around 4:00 pm, hoping that some exercise would do the trick. Four hours later, after a jog through Prospect Park, a warm shower, a salad and three gins and tonic, he was no where nearer to the peace he sought. Bed was next.

He pounded his pillow for the umpteenth time and ended up throwing it across the room in frustration. Crossing his hands under his head, he stared up at the white ceiling until nature took over and his tired body drifted into sleep.

Lying in bed that night, Rhonda decided to look again at the notorious copy of *Top Class*, which she picked up on her way home.

The photographs were revealing because they were obviously private moments being shared between two adults who were attracted to each other, she admitted, but they were definitely *not* sluttish. "How dare he call me a slut!" she muttered. "Chauvinist!" She flung the magazine on the floor, flicked off the lamp and tried to sleep. It would be hours before she was successful.

❧ ❧ ❧ ❧

Struggling with two bags of groceries, her mail and keys, Rhonda tried to get in to answer the telephone before it stopped ringing. *It could only be Ma,* she thought. For a moment, it bothered her that she had few close friends, male or female. It seemed like the only person who called her was her mother. As she got to the telephone, it stopped ringing, but she knew it would start ringing again. It did.

"Hi Ma," she answered.

"It's about time you answer the phone. I was calling for the past half hour."

"I just got through the door."

"Wuh you doing two Saturdays from now?"

"Nothing, I don't think. Why?"

"How would you like to go to a wedding with me?"

"Who getting married?"

"I am."

"What? To who? Do I know him? How come you wait till now to tell me? And why you ain't tell me you was seeing somebody before now?"

"Whoa. Wait a minute. One question at a time. His name is Harold Bentley. He works at the gas company. He's widower with two grown-up children. Does that answer all your questions?"

"No. What's he like? You really love him? Are you sure he loves you? Does he drink? Remember you said my father drank too much. Where you meet him?"

"He's a quiet, soft-speaking man, but no mouse. He ain't no

drunkard, so you don't have to worry about that. I love him and I know he loves me too. Otherwise he wouldn't eat the coo-coo and steam fish I cook yesterday. He hates coo-coo."

"Not everybody like corn meal and okras you know Ma. Anyway, forget about the coo-coo. How long you know this Harold?"

"Well, I've been seeing him for about nine months. We're two old battle axes who don't need a lot of time to figure out what we want. He's a good man who went after what he wanted in life, and now just wants to settle down and enjoy it."

"Does that mean you won't have to work anymore?"

"Not if I don't want to. Besides, I getting too old to be straining my eyes at a sewing machine all day long. Maybe I'll still do something on the side. . . Well. . . You coming, right?"

"Can't I meet him first? I should, you know. You ain't got no right springing this on me like this."

"You always running me off the phone. You never home. You never come to see me. Wuh you expect?"

"I want to meet him first, alright? Can I come over to dinner Friday night? Invite him then," Rhonda insisted, knowing nothing she could say would stop her mother from marrying this Harold Bentley. Besides, she didn't have the right. She just prayed her mother wasn't making a terrible mistake in her judgement of a man for the second time in her life.

༡ ༡ ༡ ༡

After she hung up the phone, Deborah Baptiste emitted the long sigh she hadn't realized that she was holding. Sitting back in a high-backed chair at the dark mahogany dinning table that seated six, she stared off into space. With one arm resting on the lace covered table, she absently twisted the single black plait laying against her neck with the other. The hair's streaks of gray were a reminder that she wasn't getting any younger.

Although she wouldn't admit it to her daughter, Deborah Baptiste was nervous about this Friday night dinner. She wanted

Rhonda to approve of Harold. It had been just the two of them for so long, a man seemed like an intrusion, a violation of a sacred trust. She knew she was responsible for creating the situation, but she had done so to protect herself. She had nothing against men, but she had not made a good choice.

Rhonda's father, Frank Garfield, was a weak man who had hid himself in a rum bottle. Ah, but when she had first met him, the carefree attitude had attracted her to him. He could make her laugh and forget her worries and her inhibitions. As a young girl, loving Frank had made life so much easier to bear.

However, after she had thrown caution and her mother's disapproval to the wind to live with her love after she became pregnant, the responsibility of supporting a family with the chicken feed he got from the job at the foundry proved too much for Frank. He wanted the best for them but couldn't seem to get that big break he wanted. He started staying out with the boys, later and later, drinking in the rum shop. As time progressed, it was the women and not coming home for days on a stretch. Finally, they had a violent fight one day about the money he was to have brought home for the baby's food, and she had ordered him to get out. He did. . . .

Deborah stopped toying with the braid to pull her slightly pointed nose instead. The wide lush lips tightened harshly as the memories overpowered her.

She had cursed him until there were no swear words left to describe him. She had refused to shoulder any of the blame because she knew she had loved him with everything within her soul. Any need he had that she could fulfill, she had done it gladly. And if, at times, she pushed him too hard, it was for their own good. You could only succeed in life through hard work—there was nobody out there giving handouts.

That's why she pushed Rhonda so hard, refusing to back off even when she knew she had gone too far. She became obsessed with producing a daughter without a weak bone in her body. She knew to achieve this was unrealistic, impossible, but she tried anyway. She loved her daughter, but she considered that love something vulnerable that had to be controlled, held in abeyance. It shouldn't cloud the goals she had in mind for Rhonda. She knew her sister, Sheila, disapproved of the way she reared Rhonda.

"Rhonda is a child. She needs love and affection, somebody to hug she, somebody to kiss she. She ain't no a robot and she ain't no weakling like Frank Garfield either, so stop pushing she so hard," Sheila had stated angrily.

Deborah could remember listening to Rhonda's traumatic crying the night after winning another running trophy that she had given only a cursory glance. She was proud of Rhonda, but she didn't want it going to Rhonda's head. She wanted her daughter to be strong. She wanted the best for her and her education was more important than any race.

But now the tables were turned and Deborah needed her daughter's approval. She couldn't fail at a love relationship for the second time in life. She had to try. She had to. She was lonely— she needed someone to share old-age with, to laugh with, to shoulder the burden of life's struggle with. She just couldn't fail and right now she trusted her daughter's judgement more than her own.

Deborah lapped her arms across her middle and caressed her arms, as she looked over into the living room. She looked forward to leaving this apartment. The off-white walls, green carpet and living room set with its green foliage designs looked tired, shabby. Harold and she had been house hunting for three months. They had found a one-family, attached, brick house on East 57th Street that suited their needs. They didn't want anything too big, just comfortable, cozy, and not a whole lot of work to keep clean.

I didn't tell Rhonda about the house, she realized. *The wedding is enough for now.* Deborah slowly got up and went to the kitchen to make a grocery list. It was time to go the supermarket.

ﻬ ﻬ ﻬ ﻬ

Rhonda didn't have much time to worry about her mother's

upcoming marriage because Alan was on a rampage with his new ideas for the magazine. He had artists working on new designs; photographers experimenting with lighting, shadows, you name it; writers drilled for new angles, more indepth information. He was a man possessed and not a very easy one to work with.

He made no attempt to apologize for his insult and the matter remained unresolved. They met and talked for business purposes only. Rhonda's chaotic emotions threatened to overwhelm her many times. She felt cheapened and angered by his accusations, but the memory of his lips and touch still lingered in her thoughts. She didn't know which she hated the most: his fiery temper or his coldness. She knew that unless he broke the ice and apologized, she would have to do something about it. She couldn't stand much more.

Alan, too, was thinking about their quarrel and Rhonda's response to his accusation, and not for the first time either. He still couldn't believe that she had hit him—and hit him good too. *The woman has guts.* He knew he had overreacted and should apologize to her, but until he calmed down, he knew he would bungle the apology. Now mixed with the anger was a burning shame that he didn't know how to deal with. *She makes me feel like such a jerk sometimes, an immature boy. Why do I feel so helpless?* Somehow she had gotten under his skin and he couldn't get rid of the feel of her.

Sitting at her desk, Rhonda looked at the unchanged corrections that she had made twice before on the pages. *What is wrong with these people? Can't they follow simple instructions?* She threw the pages on the floor in exasperation and unexpectedly tears formed in her eyes and coursed down her cheeks. She was busily mopping her eyes and trying to regain control when there was a knock at the door, immediately followed by someone entering.

Alan had seen Rhonda enter her office ten minutes ago and wondered why she was still at work since it was already seven o'clock that Wednesday evening. He needed a copy of an article on St. Lucia's upcoming elections that Rhonda was working on and had no choice but to go to her office.

"What's the matter with you?" he grunted, catching a flicker of pain in her eyes before she had a chance to hide it.

"Nothing. Something got into my eye."

"I said one day you'd stop lying to me; how about now?"

Alan crossed the room and with both hands planted on the desk, he leaned toward Rhonda, so close his breath warmed her face. She inhaled the sweet smell of him acknowledging that he was more potent than any wine she had ever drank. His eyes searched for the hidden truth behind Rhonda's eyes, knowing that if he didn't find it there, he would find it on her lips. They trembled slightly under his avid inspection.

"Well?" He took her chin gently between his thumb and forefinger. "Why yuh crying?"

Rhonda would have paid any price to get away from his scrutiny at that moment when she was most vulnerable. She knew she could not lie her way out of this one. Getting angry and denying that anything was wrong would only alienate him further. Besides, she didn't have the strength to fight him anymore.

Tears filled her eyes quickly again and Rhonda looked down, away from his concerned eyes, at the blur that was his arm. She had noticed that after 6:00pm the sleeves were rolled back as if he couldn't stand being buttoned down one second more.

"Rhonda, honey. What's the matter?" he implored.

"Noth...." She stopped. Nothing. She couldn't really pinpoint what was bothering her, or was it that she was afraid to face the truth? I hate the *cold war with you*, she admitted finally. *Fighting was direct—open. While this silence is slow torture.*

"Nothing. Honestly. Nothing I can't take care of."

"I didn't ask if you could handle it, because you obviously can't. I asked what is it?"

"I'm feeling out of sorts," Rhonda forced a smile. "Put it down to PMS."

"No." Alan stopped her pseudo-smile midway with his thumb. "I wouldn't put it down to PMS."

"Is it work?" he added.

She nodded and shook her head 'no' simultaneously.

"Is it personal? Boyfriend troubles? Wuh happened? Wasn't the fun in the sun enough to keep him?"

Rhonda's temper started to rise. Trapped between his fingers, she could only frown at him. He, waylaying her anger, proceeded to caress her bottom lip with his thumb. His eyes watched the movement of his hand, fascinated.

Rhonda's abdomen tumbled. Heat started to spread all over her body.

He's so unpredictable—like a chameleon. She marvelled at his ability to anger and arouse her within seconds.

"No. I do not have boyfriend troubles. And stop that," she said, clasping his wrist.

Seconds passed. She became aware of the length of time she held his wrist, as if her fingers were glued there. She released his hand slowly, feeling the warmth that had once been there dissipate. She stood up and walked to the window, putting distance between them.

He raised himself from the desk and followed her, knowing it was he who had ruined his chance to get closer. He hadn't intended to anger her, but the thought that another caused her pain annoyed him considerably. This was the second time he had lost control with her. . . No, the third time. The first time he had lost himself in the power of her kiss. Now was the perfect opportunity to apologize to her. He had wanted to apologize in his own time and when he had prepared what he wanted to say.

"Rhonda. . ." he began tentatively. "Rhonda. I know this is long overdue, but I'm sorry for being an ass the other day. What you do with your personal life is your business and I'm sure you're a lady." he grinned, almost sheepishly.

"Don't give me that lady crap. I know you. You don't say things you don't mean."

"I refuse to get into a fight with you. I apologized. Take it or leave it." Alan blurted out with clenched fists.

They faced each other, tense, angry, overwrought. A stubborn Rhonda didn't want to give in, and Alan refused to beg or stoop to any woman, or man, for that matter. But they both knew that leaving the situation, unresolved and hostile made a comfortable working relationship impossible. It pained Rhonda to accept his apology, issued as it had been. She had wanted more humility than that. He aroused her darkest emotions to such a peak, she was beginning to wonder if she really knew herself or should even like herself.

"Where do you get off calling me names? You don't know one damn thing about me."

Slowly, Alan unclenched his fists. Some of the tension started to fade from his face. His brown eyes mellowed in their fierceness, and in its place, guilt and embarrassment ruled. He looked out the window, away from Rhonda's cold dark eyes and hard face, for they pained him.

"You're right. I really don't know you. I don't think I know me anymore, either. I am truly sorry. And believe me, it won't happen again."

Now that she got what she really wanted, a humble Alan, Rhonda should have been elated. But she wasn't. Those brown eyes and strong face, when softened by remorse, appeared so vulnerable. She simply felt like crying. *The way I'm feeling you'd think we are lovers patching up after our first fight.*

"I'm sorry, too. I shouldn't have hit you."

"Yuh right about that one. Don't think you can get away with that again."

"Why? Would you hit me back?"

"No. I don't hit women and I ain't have no respect for men who do. No," he shook his head slowly. "If it managed to connect before I could stop it, then that would be it." Alan moved away and walked over to her desk and sat, half leaning, against the front edge with his arms crossed on his chest.

"Wuh you mean?" Rhonda asked, turning toward him with full attention.

"Any time a man and a woman can't work out their differences without resorting to blows, then it's time for one of them to leave.

I would just walk away from the relationship," he said looking deeply into her eyes.

Some ground rules were being established and they both knew it. It was important for both of them to understand the other and the values and standards each one had. The unspoken understanding was recorded.

"Come here," Alan requested, the usual demanding tone muted. Rhonda walked over to him and took the extended hand. Alan raised Rhonda's palm to his lips, never taking his eyes from her face. She, mesmerized, could only stare. She was trapped by his hand and lips, and a sudden surge of feeling threatened to overpower her. *No*, her mind rebelled. *Don't let him kiss me. I can't take it.*

But her limbs wanted nothing more than to be weakened by his touch. Her lips craved the warm moistness of his mouth, and her skin hungered for the soothing caresses of his hands.

Alan pulled Rhonda to him, cradling her head in the nook between his neck and left shoulder. He could feel the tension and resistance as she withheld herself from him. But he had time. . . all the time in the world to hold her. He held her close, gently rocking and rubbing her back rhythmically, like one would a frightened child.

Gradually, Rhonda's body relaxed and molded itself naturally to the hardness and strength of his. He could make love to her now if he wanted to—and he did, badly—and she wouldn't resist him. At least, he was almost sure she wouldn't resist him. But that wasn't all he wanted from her. It didn't feel right, just wanting to take her. Besides what did she want of him. He prayed she wasn't like those women who just weren't happy with just one man.

Alan released Rhonda. He placed his fingers under her chin and raising her head said, "If you're hurting and want to talk to somebody, call me. I'm here for you, alright?" I don't care what it is or when, and I don't want you to worry about that either. Alright?"

He squeezed her chin, demanding a response. Right now

wasn't the time to decipher why he had offered himself to her like that. In the past, it had only led to unpleasant, unwanted relationships.

"Alright," she whispered. What else could she say? She was helpless when in held in close proximity to him, and the fact that she couldn't tell him that he was at the root of her turmoil compounded the problem. She turned her head away.

"Don't worry about me Alan. I can take care of myself. I didn't know you had it in you to care."

Now why did I say that? It's too la*te now*, she thought.

A flicker of pain crossed Alan's face, and the corners of his mouth tightened as he released her. Carefully, he stepped back, dropped his arms, and walked to the door.

"Goodnight, Rhonda," he said harshly, and left, slamming the door behind him.

In bed that night, Rhonda tried to figure out why she had tried to hurt him and couldn't come up with a definite answer. In his arms she had felt protected, warm, secure, and confident. He had held her with the gentle concern of a father, and the leashed passion of a lover, fearful of hurting his beloved.

Maybe tha*t's the way he holds all his women*, came the unbidden thought issued by an internal green-eyed devil. The thought discredited him, made him less of an admirable person in her eyes. But the image of another woman in Alan's arms unsettled her. She wouldn't admit to jealousy because that would make her possessive and insecure. Besides, he wasn't hers to possess about.

Unfortunately, as she tossed and turned, she couldn't help but wonder if he was seriously involved with, and possibly in love with, this girlfriend that she had heard whispered about in the office.

CHAPTER ❧ FIVE

*H*arold Bentley was not a weakling. Rhonda realized that soon after she met him. He didn't wear his feelings on his sleeve, but he wasn't cold either. He was reserved, but gentle. She appreciated the blend of hard and soft in him.

When her mother had opened the door, she had barely murmured, "Hello," her eyes looking past her mother, searching for the new man in Ma's life. He rose from the couch and extended a hand to her.

"Good evening. I'm Harold Bentley."

"Hello. I'm pleased to meet you." His handshake was warm, firm. Rhonda returned a strong handshake that hinted she wasn't a pushover. They followed Deborah to the table and sat down to dinner. Ma had gone overboard, and prepared what amounted to a Christmas feast: Baked ham, broiled pork, baked chicken with stuffing, green pigeon peas and rice, steamed beets and carrots, boiled yam, sweet potatoes, and fried ripe plantains.

For the first few minutes, Rhonda sat quietly, munching on the tossed salad, as Deborah and Harold talked about his work. Unnoticed, Rhonda sneaked peeks at him.

Physically, he was passable. Maybe by the time she reached her mother's age, things like paunches won't matter. Along with the slightly oversized gut on a five-foot-nine frame came a bald head. The hair had receded to the middle of the back of the head, leaving behind a smooth, shiny surface the color of a coconut's hard shell. Curled black hair, sprinkled with grey strands covered the sides and lower back portions of his head. When he smiled, the corners of his dark brown eyes crinkled into tiny lines. His eyebrows were very thick, adding menace to an otherwise gentle face. His nose was pointed, a sign of ancestral interbreeding, but his lips were truly African in their richness. Rhonda imagined her mother making love to this stocky man and was at once amused and embarrassed.

"So, Mr. Bentley, Ma tells me you work for the gas company, what do you do?" Rhonda asked when the couple became quiet.

"I'm Vice President of Public Affairs."

"And what does that mean, exactly?"

"It means, young lady, that you don't have to worry about your mother's well being. I can take care of her financially," Harold responded, a smile touching the corners of his mouth.

She was snubbed, gently, but his accent like Alan's made her feel a kinship to him.

"Ma says you have two children. How do they feel about you remarrying?" Rhonda asked, letting his response to her first question slide.

"They're too busy with their families to really care about what I do. But if they objected, it wouldn't matter too much. I have a life to live just like them," Harold replied, his fork suspended above the plate.

For long seconds, his eyes met Rhonda's dark regard. She was attractive, like her mother, and the floral short sleeve dress did justice to her shape and coloring. He admired the protective streak she had for her mother. And although she was drilling him, he saw she bore him no animosity—she was just checking to make sure he was good enough for her mother, and he respected that.

Rhonda knew that he was aware of her screening. But there was something enjoyable about the tug of war between them. Her mother offered little to the battle, but brought out all arms when Rhonda questioned Harold's attitude and feelings about sex and remarriage later in the evening. Harold had silenced Deborah gently and answered Rhonda calmly and honestly.

"Sex you should enjoy with the fullest consideration for your partner, for as long as you're physically able to do it. Remarriage: It should be better the second time provided you've learned from your mistakes. But like every marriage, first or second, it takes two people to make it work or ruin it altogether."

There was nothing more Rhonda could say after two nut-shell philosophical statements like those. She liked Harold Bentley. She had outgrown the need for a father in terms of building and molding her personality, but he would be the perfect choice as a stepfather. She knew their relationship would grow and they would learn eventually to respect and love each other.

Towards the end of the evening, they all relaxed totally, aware that the love match was accepted by the people who really mattered, themselves. They spent the time making plans for the wedding, giving their stuffed stomaches a chance to churn the delicious meal Deborah had prepared.

№ № № №

Alan stood over the tenor steel pan, attempting to pick Billy Ocean's *There'll Be Sad Songs (To Make You Cry)*. His hands just weren't working. He kept hitting the wrong notes. In minutes, he dropped the sticks in the pan, regretful that not even this would bring him any peace. Thoughts of Rhonda had been with him from the moment he got up. Twice he had picked up the piece of paper where he had written down her number the evening they had gone out to City Island. It was around 5:30 pm that Saturday evening and he wasn't in the mood for liming or anything really. But he was restless. He had spent the day cleaning and doing the laundry. Now there was nothing else to do. There were leftovers in the fridge if he got hungry. So he didn't have the excuse of cooking to keep him occupied.

The decision made, Alan walked over to the phone, dialed Rhonda's number, and sat down on the black leather couch in his den. Just as he was about to hang up on the fourth ring, she answered, breathless.

"Hello," she said.

"Hi," he responded.

"Hold on a minute, OK?"

He heard a heavy plunk, signalling that she had dropped the phone to go off somewhere. He waited patiently.

"Hi. Sorry 'bout that. I just got back from shopping." Rhonda recognized his voice immediately and was surprised to hear him.

"Did you get me anything?" he asked playfully.

"Nooo...I didn't think you needed anything." She felt a need to soften the statement in case he misunderstood, so she chuckled.

"Oh. There're lots of things I need."

"Oh yeah. Like what?"

Alan paused and then answered.

"You."

Dead silence greeted him. He didn't know what had come over him; the word just slipped out.

At his answer, Rhonda's abdomen lurched. She didn't know what to say. *What do you say to a direct proposition like that, issued by a man who doesn't kid around?*

Rhonda decided to ignore it. She'd handle it when and if he seriously pursued it and hoped by then she would have something sensible to say.

"I owe you an apology," she said instead.

"For what?"

"For that cruel remark I made on Wednesday. I'm sorry. I don't know why I said it."

"You're forgiven."

No one spoke for a few moments, uneasy with the personal turn in the relationship. They both had to adjust to this new intimacy at play outside of the office. His heavy voice was husky, almost hoarse, and its timber stroked her senses. For Alan, Rhonda's voice, low and soft, was raising havoc within him.

"How would you like to go out with me, this evening?"

"Where?"

"Oh, I don't know. . . A walk. . .To the movies. Anything."

"OK."

"I'll be there in half an hour."

"Can I at least have some time to grab something to eat and take a shower? I'm starving."

"I'll feed you. Just take a quick shower. I'll be right there."

Alan hung up the phone, jumped into the air with an extended triumphant fist and yelled, "Alright." He then ran to the bathroom and took the quickest shower in history. In eighteen minutes flat, he was in his black Honda Prelude and on the way to Rhonda's apartment.

When Rhonda opened her door to Alan a short time later, she was dressed in a red cotton shirt, white cotton pants and a white jacket. Alan had to resist the impulse to pull her into his arms immediately.

"I didn't know what to put on. Is this OK for where we're going?" she asked.

"Perfect. Look at what I'm wearing."

She did. He looked cool and comfortable in a peach shirt and white pants. He had cut his hair, low. The curls were tighter and he looked so much younger.

"Where are we going?"

"I don't know. I can't decide. Any ideas?" Alan asked as he waited for her to lock the door.

"Let's go for a walk through the park," he said when she didn't reply immediately.

"Alright. But I have to eat first," Rhonda announced.

"Oh. I forgot. OK. Where should we go? Hmmm,"Alan massaged his forehead.

"There's a nice quiet place on Seventh Avenue. Let's go there," Rhonda suggested.

Over a simple meal of shrimp parmigiana, with spaghetti and garlic bread, the couple talked about any and everything but the undercurrents they were both feeling. After eating, they took a walk through Prospect Park. It was still light out, and men were playing soccer, boys were playing baseball and people of all races and ages were just milling about enjoying the warm, gentle evening.

They didn't talk much, somehow realizing that being together was enough—they didn't feel the need to fill the air with constant chatter. As Rhonda bumped into him yet once more, this time in an effort to avoid jogger coming up behind them, Alan took her hand and laced his fingers through hers. Twice he brought her fingers to lips for a warm kiss. Only once was the rapport threatened, when he had allowed the desire to know the name of the man she had met in Barbados overwhelmed him.

"What's that guy's name you met on your trip?" he asked.

Rhonda's hand in his tightened. Alan felt a slight withdrawal. "Why?" she asked cautiously.

"I'm just curious, that's all," he replied quickly.

"Richard," she answered. But Alan felt the tense vibes being emitted through Rhonda's body language and steered the conversation back into safer straits.

"What do you think of the new TradeWinds production? Did you see it yet?" he asked to ease the rising tension.

After an hour in the park, they decided they had done enough walking and went back to Rhonda's apartment. She invited him in for a cold glass of mauby, which he accepted. He drank while she eased her shoes off her feet.

"That walk was great, but my feet are killing me."

"Let me," Alan said, getting up and sitting on the floor at her feet.

"What are you doing?" she asked incredulously.

"Just relax and enjoy it." Alan took Rhonda's feet one after the other and massaged them slowly and firmly for about ten minutes. Tingles shot up her legs, and she lounged back against the couch and groaned her relief. *God. This feels heavenly. His hands are like magic. If this feels so good, can you imagine what it would feel like if. . .* Rhonda stopped her errant thoughts abruptly. This setting was a little too dangerous.

"OK. That's good. Thanks a lot," Rhonda announced, sitting up suddenly.

"My pleasure," Alan said, rejoining her on the couch.

"I really enjoyed this evening," he continued, one elbow resting on the back of the couch, his head propped against his hand.

"Me, too."

"It was just what I needed to mellow me out. Now, I could just fall asleep right here."

He saw the flicker of panic that crossed her eyes at his innocent comment.

"Don't worry. I'm not hinting at spending the night."

"Thanks for a nice evening." Rhonda felt a sudden need for flight and got up from the couch.

"I'd better get going, anyway. Come lock up," he said, rising from the couch also.

At the door he turned to say good night and encountered the glow of her eyes and those maddening lips. He reached down to administer a brotherly peck and her breath held him captive. Placing one hand to the back of Rhonda's neck and the other on her waist, Alan drew Rhonda to him, helplessly. Her lips, pliant, warm, responded instantaneously. He felt a rush of blood immediately. *No. I didn't imagine it that first time. These kisses are lethal.*

After long moments, they broke the kiss reluctantly. Alan's face, softened by his need, was almost Rhonda's undoing. *He is becoming so hard to resist.*

"I should get out of here," he whispered. "Goodnight."

After Alan left, Rhonda turned on her TV to fill the void his departure had created. She didn't want to think about him. There were too many questions and she wasn't up to dealing with the yearning her body experienced whenever she thought of him. *Not tonight. We went out. We had a good time. Fini. You've been out with other men before. What's the big deal?*

But, in her mind's eye, the image of the open V of Alan's peach shirt emerged to entice fantasy: She would love to press her lips to the smooth, beckoning column, the color of fragrant spice, then lower to the skin darkened by tiny hairs. They would be slightly abrasive against her lips; they would tickle her chin. *OK, girl. I think you need a cold shower.*

Rhonda reached over and changed the channel, exchanging one set of garbage programming for the next. It was useless. She turned it off and settled beneath her pillow. *Now where was I? Yes.* . . . She would pull back and reaching up, unbutton the rest of the shirt. With her palms, she would run her hands upward over the ripples of his abdomen to the small buds on his chest, relishing that downy softness all the way to. . . .

ra ra ra ra

It was Saturday, the day of the wedding and Rhonda was as excited, if not more excited than her mother. Deborah had taken off her dress in despair three times within the hour, convinced that she looked terrible. Her stomach jutted out too much, she moaned. The dress showed this bulge or that bulge.

"I told you to cut out the bagels many times," Rhonda scolded.

Finally, Deborah was dressed. Rhonda stood back and looked at her mother, as if for the first time. This is where she had inherited her eyes and mouth. Deborah's nose was more pointed. Her thick, long black hair was braided in one cornrow down the middle of the head. The off-white, broad-rimmed, lace-covered hat sat jauntily to the left side of her head. Big, round, pearl earrings studded the ears. Her face, like Rhonda's, was naturally smooth and glowing, without the assistance of oil or perspiration. At fifty-five, she was beautiful. The long sleeved, off-white, lace

dress she wore fell elegantly without curves down her sides. The
girdle she wore and cursed continually didn't totally hide her
slightly bulging stomach, for Deborah gained ten pounds in the
past two months and swore she wasn't gaining any more weight—
one-hundred-fifty pounds was enough. *Nevertheless*, Rhonda
concluded a second time, *she looks beautiful*.

At the church, Rhonda watched with tears in her eyes and a
lump in her throat as her mother repeated the vows. Watching
Harold was equally as touching for he listened to those vows
intently, as if he wanted to pull them from Deborah's lips before
she said them.

Thirty people attended the small ceremony, but in true West
Indian style, many simply showed up for the reception. About
seventy-five guests arrived to eat, drink and party their hearts out.
Harold's cousin who owned a night club offered the space to the
groom for the reception as a wedding gift. The well-wishers
gathered there to dance to calypso, reggae and love ballads, and in
between sets they enjoyed the taste of roti with curried chicken or
curried goat, fried King fish and peas and rice. The children,
running and playing with balloons, stopped occasionally to demol-
ish the hors d'oeuvres of cheese or tuna puffs, tiny sausages with
pineapple and tiny meat pies. People were really having a good
time.

Halfway into the evening, Rhonda's eyes were drawn to a pair
of broad shoulders and a dark head that looked very familiar. The
person started toward the table where Rhonda sat with her mother
and Harold, and before she could stop the skipping beat of her
heart, Alan was upon them.

"Congratulations, Harold," he said to the groom, who didn't
hesitate to hug and slap him on the back when he rose from the
chair. "Didn't think you'd put that noose round the neck a second
time," he added laughingly. "Who is the unlucky lady?"

His eyes registered Rhonda for the first time. She looked
enticing in an olive-green and burnt-orange tie-dyed silk dress.
The low neckline and the row of tiny buttons running down the
middle drew attention to her neck and chest. A shock went

through his body at the possibility that Rhonda was Harold's wife. *Dear God, No.* Alan almost said aloud. *She can't be his wife. She can't be. She would have told me if she was getting married, wouldn't she? No. Brides wear white, not multi-colored dresses. What if she had changed dresses for the reception?* He paled visibly.

"This is my wife on my left and my newly acquired stepdaughter on my right."

Color flooded Alan's skin and his heart left his throat and resettled in his chest. He released the breath he was holding as slowly, and as inconspicuously as possible before extending his hand to the new Mrs. Bentley.

"Best wishes, Ma'am," he said, and turning to Rhonda he added, "I've already had the pleasure, and often, displeasure of knowing your daughter. We work together."

Throughout the entire exchange, Rhonda was quiet, fighting the rush of pleasure she felt at seeing him dressed so superbly. He was devastating in a dark blue jacket and white slacks, light blue shirt with a pleated front and a dark blue bow tie. Handsome was not the word to describe him. *He is gorgeous,* she nodded approvingly.

"You work together?" Harold said. "I don't envy you one bit. This is one mean lady. She doesn't let you get away with anything."

"Don't I know it. But she knows her job and does it very well. I'm proud of her."

Rhonda eyed Alan suspiciously, at once pleased with his praise and skeptical about its sincerity. The conversation was general after that and Alan joined the family as they greeted friends and relatives. Harold grew up with Alan's mother and as a close family friend, he was like an uncle to Alan. It was clear that they respected and loved each other. Like other close friends and family, Alan was shocked to hear Harold was getting married. No one close to the family had yet met the mystery lady.

Rhonda's thoughts drifted from one thing to another, as the relaxing murmur of the guests milled around and later floated away from her. Alan watched as Rhonda retreated into her private world. He marvelled at her ability to withdraw herself so completely from her surroundings. *As a child she must have daydreamed constantly in class*, he thought with amusement.

However, something about this personal quality irritated him. He felt left out, insignificant when she withdrew into that shell of hers. Varying emotions danced across her face, so fleeting that they disappeared before he got a chance to identify them. At least, they weren't the obvious resentment and anger he saw on the first day he started at *West Indian World*. Otherwise, he would have been worried about her possible disapproval of the love match between Harold and her mother. But he was sure her thoughts weren't unsettling, but her face never ceased to captivate him.

Rhonda, unaware of Alan's scrutiny was thinking about Richard. Or rather, about her unmarried state at twenty-six years old. *Old maid!* her mind taunted. Richard would probably be a wonderful husband. His kiss had pleased her. She had enjoyed his company. He was amusing, fun to be around. Richard had not faded into a distant vacation memory because he had attentively called and written since her return. In fact, he was coming to New York and requested that she pick him up Kennedy Airport. "I'll need somebody to take care of me in the Big Bad Apple," he had said, jokingly. Though he didn't mention his declaration of love and she repeatedly told him long distance relationships didn't last, she sensed his affection for her in the timbre of his voice.

"Rhonda. Rhonda?"

Snap! The sound of Alan's fingers broke her thoughts. She focused on Alan, alone at the table with her. *Where were the others?*

"Welcome back. You were gone a long time."

"I'm sorry. Where is Ma and Harold?"

"Dancing. Would you like to dance?"

"Sure."

She placed her hand in his and followed him to the dancing area. She hadn't hesitated when he had asked, and found herself marveling at this new complaisance. Maybe the joyfulness of the occasion had filtered into her. *Lord, I am feeling mellow. Why fight it tonight?* she asked herself. *I want to feel him close to me again.*

As John Holt sang the lyric, "If you let me make love to you, then why I can't I touch you?" Alan pulled Rhonda deeper into his arms. With her breasts pressed close to his chest, she couldn't stop the fire from racing to their tips, hardening them. She prayed the thickness of his jacket would conceal her arousal. She felt the warmth radiating from his body and the hardness of his thighs against her as their bodies flowed with the slow hypnotic beat. One of his hands was spread wide open across the small of her back, and he drew her even closer as the fingers of his other hand entwined with her to raise them closer to his cheek. His breath tickled her ear and the musky blend of his cologne and body scent made her senses reel. She felt she would become a trembling mass and collapse at his feet.

"Do you know what you do to me, woman. Huh?" he whispered.

He unwrapped her from around him so he could look at her face. He did nothing to hide the smouldering desire in his eyes. They raked her lips so vividly, she felt the fierceness of his kiss even though he was just looking at her.

"I want you," he said hoarsely. "I need to make love to you, now. Let's go."

Rhonda was weak, drowning. There was no one but them, and the heat of the moment. She wanted him. *Yes. Yes,* cried every nerve in her body. To have him touch every inch of her. To feel him close. Could she afford to do that? Give in to her desire, just like that? He hadn't mentioned love or even fondness—just "want."

"Alan. . ."

"No. Don't say anything." He stopped her words with his forefinger. "Don't deny me or the feeling between us. It exists. You know it and I know it. So no more fooling around. Alright?"

She didn't answer. She couldn't. He was right, but there was more to it than just that. She wanted more from him. Much more. She. . . .

He practically dragged her across the floor, without thinking about Harold and Deborah.

"Alan, we have to say good-bye to the others." Rhonda stopped in her tracks, refusing to be pulled like an animal.

He stopped, his face taut and harsh. By the time they reached the newlyweds, his expression was schooled, controlled.

"Rhonda and I going out for a while. We have some business to discuss. I'm sure you have lots of romantic plans for the evening. I just wish you both a world of happiness. Enjoy. . and so long. . ."

Rhonda hugged and kissed her mother good-bye. She hesitated, then hugged and kissed Harold, too. And as they walked out of the club, she turned and noticed Harold watching them with a speculative glint in his eyes. *Right now*, she realized in amazement, *I really don't care what he thinks about us going off together.*

Rhonda was almost surprised by her nonchalance. *Here I am leaving my mother's wedding reception with a man—a very sexy, desirable man. I guess I should be embarrassed that we're so transparent. But I'm not.*

In the car, Alan's fierce expression returned. He put the car in gear and drove off. Rhonda didn't know where they were going and didn't dare ask. She had never seen him like this before: angry and cold—yes. But never a glimmer of this intense brooding.

CHAPTER ✻ SIX

Soon, they were turning on Beverly Road, off Kings Highway, and as he pulled into a driveway of an attached, one family brick house, Rhonda surmised they must be at his home. Panic rose into her throat. Wh*at am I doing here?* Before she had an answer, Alan was out of the car and opening her door. He shepherded her to the door, into the house and through to the den. She didn't even have time to notice the color of the carpet in the living room.

"Would you like a glass of Harvey's? I remember you like your drinks sweet."

"Thanks," she responded, trying desperately to keep the tremor from her voice.

He went to the bar and poured the sherry for Rhonda and made himself a gin and tonic. After he prepared the drinks, he stood still for a few moments, his back toward her, his shoulders rigid. Rhonda hovered near him, unsure, ready for flight. He turned slowly and came to her.

"What you going to do about us?" he asked

"Wuh you mean, what am I going to do about us?"

"I already told you how I feel. Now the next move is yours."

"Is wanting me all you have to offer?" Rhonda asked, realizing too late that the words didn't come out right.

"What do you want? An estate along with it? You want my life's savings signed over to you before you even admit you want me?" If she thought she had seen him angry before, she was mistaken. He was enraged and the disgust he felt for her at that moment was almost tangible. *Now what the hell happened to that gentle man who took me walking in the park?*

"I don't have to stay here and accept your insults. Please take me home."

"No. We're going to resolve this right now."

"No. I'm. . . ."

Alan closed the space between them rapidly and silenced Rhonda's defiance with angry lips, allowing no argument. She struggled, denying the shivers and warmth invading her body. Pushing hard against his chest, she broke free, panting. He grabbed her wrists, entangled them behind his neck, and buried his face into her throat, inhaling her special, sweet scent.

After tugging at her earlobe with his teeth, he ran a restless tongue along her neck. Nibbling and kissing his way over her face and neck, he demonstrated that she was a slave to his caresses. He had made his point. She was beyond help. Her senses screamed, *yes*, to each burning, new trail established, and by the time he reached the soft mound of her breasts, Rhonda's knees had started to buckle beneath her.

As his lips plunged farther into the "V" of her dress, a moan escaped her lips, a sound so strange and wanton to her ears that she thought for a moment there was someone else in the room with them. Suddenly she was airborne because Alan had picked up her feverish body and lowering it onto the couch, impatiently chucking his jacket. Guided by Rhonda's passion-glazed eyes he eagerly returned to the arms she had opened for him.

Ahh! His weight feels so good on me, Rhonda thought while sucking in a sigh of bliss. His hands were everywhere. He explored each curve, the length of her legs, the smallness of her ears. He held her face, teased her mouth with his lips, outlining them with his tongue until she moaned his name. Now his hands were at the waist of her pantyhose, peeling the material away from her softness, rubbing her belly as soon as he had exposed the smooth flesh. Rhonda arched her back, wishing the barrier of clothing would disappear. Alan left her belly button and hips to snake his hands up to her breasts, alternately teasing the nipples, and then cupping the swollen throbbing mounds. Rhonda was moaning uncontrollably now.

"OK, baby, OK...We have all night," Alan soothed her, yet he didn't stop his onslaught of caresses. Her breasts were bare before his gaze now. She had felt his fumbling but didn't really think he had completely unbuttoned her dress and unclasped her bra.

"Gosh. You're beautiful, so beautiful. Look at me."

The slits that met his eyes signaled her need. She knew he'd seen the depth of passion he could arouse in her. She wanted him. She knew that. She also knew what she was feeling was more, much more than pure lust. It had to be. *Do I love him?*

What does it really mean to love someone? Rhonda wasn't sure, but didn't want to spend the time soul searching: She was about to make a fantasy a reality and that was overwhelming all rational thought. Her inexperience had never been a burden until now— she had never wanted or needed to know more, and the ability to understand the difference between sex and love was essential at this moment. *God, it had never been an issue with Peter.*

The sound of the doorbell penetrated Rhonda's dazed world; its jarring noise sponsoring a vulgar oath from Alan. He got up reluctantly, allowing her time to tidy her clothes and compose herself before answering the door. The interruption and the effect of her thoughts acted like a numbing anesthesia on heated passion.

Rhonda took the seconds he was away to clear her mind and rose from the couch to clinically examine the room. He's *really into black*, she thought. The couch and loveseat were covered in black leather. Wall-to-wall carpet with a bold design of black, white and grey geometrical shapes covered the floor. A large black and white photograph of African dancers hung against a white wall. A chrome-plated tenor steel pan on its stand shone from one corner of the room. She hadn't know that he played pan.

"Alan, baby," a female cooed in the distance. Rhonda stopped her musings to listen intently.

"Don't tell me you forgot I was coming over," the voice continued.

"Nadine. . .I. . . ."

"Come fix me a drink and we'll work on your memory."

A strong whiff of perfume reached Rhonda's nostrils before she saw the mysterious Nadine. When Nadine entered the den ahead of Alan, Rhonda's spirits sank. She looked beautiful.

". . . have someone. . . not . . ." Alan's attempts at stopping Nadine proved fruitless as she stood at the threshold sizing up her competition. Boldly, her eyes wandered up the length of Rhonda's body, committing every detail, every nuance to memory.

". . . now. . . Nadine, not now," Alan said as he almost moaned the end of his sentence. At first, the three remained frozen in silent expectation, each waiting for the other to forge ahead and establish the pattern for the tone of the scene.

The first thing Rhonda noticed on Nadine was her breasts. *She had to be at least a thirty-eight,* Rhonda thought in dismay. What man could resist those high full breasts? Her waist was small and her hips wide. She was shorter than Rhonda, but well built, no doubt about that. She was darker, too, almost the color of smooth ebony.

Rhonda's eyes travelled quickly back to Nadine's face. Her big brown eyes were expertly made up in subtle shades of purple and rose; her lips stained cherry wine. Black straightened and curled hair shaped her head in a stylish tapered cut. It was short on the sides and in the back, but a bundle of locks cascaded onto her forehead endearingly.

"Why didn't you tell me you had company, baby? I would have come back later, much later," she purred, not missing a pore on Rhonda's skin.

"That's all right," Rhonda found her voice surprisingly. "I was about to leave anyway."

"No you weren't. Excuse us." Alan drew a reluctant Nadine back into the hall, his fingers firm and digging into a slender arm. Soon the roar of an engine and the violent screech of tires told Rhonda that Nadine had left and was not very happy about doing so either. He hadn't introduced them and Rhonda wondered if she should be relieved or concerned by his omission: *Don't I merit an introduction?*

"Now. Where were we?" Alan said a little too lightheartedly on his return.

"You were about to take me home."

"That's not what I remember," he said softly. "If I remember correctly, you were driving me crazy with your loving."

The blood rushed to Rhonda's face and her skin felt hot, both from embarrassment and the intimacy of his tone and words. She turned away.

"I'd rather forget about that. It shouldn't have happened."

"Wuh you mean it shouldn't have happened? That's all we've been breathing for since the first day we saw each other. Look at me, damn it."

Rhonda hesitated and he turned her, not gently either. She couldn't let him see the turmoil and fear in her eyes. She didn't know how to deal with his type of anger.

"Look at me," he insisted.

Rhonda raised her eyes slowly, but only after she had masked her expression. *He must never know how much he affects me.*

"Why can't you accept the attraction between us. Why?"

"It means nothing. Thousands of people feel it every day, and for different people within days."

"That's crap and you know it. You wanted to make love as much as I did."

"So what? Humans must satisfy their desires like other animals."

"Oh yeah? Well since we didn't finish, maybe I should satisfy your animal desire now."

His lips bruised hers in a hard kiss. She tried to tear herself away, but he wouldn't let her. Then he released her so suddenly that she stumbled. Rubbing the back of her hand across her lips, as if to erase the taste and feel of him, she glared at him.

With clenched fists and fierce eyes he returned her angry stare. "You know something, you ain't nothing but a child and I'm not interested in playing games, especially with immature girls. When you grow up and you ready to handle this relationship, we'll talk. Until then, don't worry, I won't touch you."

He turned and left the room. Shaken, Rhonda sank to the couch which mysteriously seemed to still vibrate the heat of their former passion. What he had just said hurt, and hurt deeply. *Am I really being childish?* she wondered. *Was it wrong not to to want to be added to his string of women?* The thought of Nadine's body entwined with his nauseated her. *No. I refuse to be just another one of his women. And I am not a child either. I am a twenty-six-year-old woman, an adult capable of making my own decisions. And if the decision is, "No," then it's NO. And if he isn't man enough to understand, then tough!*

Rhonda decided that Alan Hussein was a rat and as far as she was concerned, he could take his good looks and gorgeous body and go to hell.

"Let's go."

The bellow at the doorway jerked her head up. He had changed into a white pair of jeans and red V-neck T-shirt that showed every muscle his torso possessed. Her insides did a somersault. *It's not fair,* she thought. *He had no right to look so good.*

Rhonda got up and walked past him, her eyes averted, knowing that if he should see the tears glistening in her eyes, it would be the last straw.

They drove to the apartment in silence. He walked her to the door and like he did the first time, he checked the entire apartment before he allowed her in.

"Goodnight," he said brusquely and returned to the door.

"Alan. . . ." Rhonda tried to stop him. She couldn't let him leave, not with this bad feeling between them.

"Grow up, Rhonda. For God's sake, grow up," he sneered and left.

That did it. Blinded by tears, Rhonda stumbled to her bedroom and threw herself across the bed. She couldn't remember when she had felt so devastated, so hurt, so lonely.

Oh yes, she could recall another time: It was the last time she had won a gold trophy for running the 400 meters at school. Her mother had barely given the golden statue a glance, for she was only interested in her school report. Rhonda had walked away with the trophy lowered because it was now tarnished in her eyes. She had wanted so badly for her mother to recognize her athletic prowess, to praise her, and most of all to hug her proudly. Now the only other person whose opinion of her counted was turning her away.

Rhonda's sobs bounced off the wall, echoing and re-echoing the anguish she felt. *No.* She cried. *I won't let you do this to me. No. No.* Her clenched fists pounded the bed beneath her, refusing to give in to the agony of Alan's rejection. Soon the tears subsided and Rhonda forced herself to function, deciding to prepare her clothes for next day's work. As she ironed her beige cotton skirt, she marvelled that a day that had began so beautifully could end in such misery.

᙮ ᙮ ᙮ ᙮

Work slowed for a couple of days and Rhonda took the opportunity to catch up on her personal writing. She wasn't ready to tackle that illegitimacy article yet. Writing poetry was her only salvation when she reached uncontrollable depths of depression. Even when she was a teenager, she turned to her writing as an outlet and a means of relieving life-inflicted wounds. She was working on an anthology of poetry, whose poems focused on life in the West Indies. As she sat reading one poem aloud in effort to capture the correct rhythm, Alan entered after a brief knock.

His face looked drawn, tight. He sat in front of her with hard, cold eyes, quietly observing her. Now what? her eyes questioned.

"Why you ain't come in to discuss the next issue with me? You know we're on a tight schedule and the sooner we get started, the better," he attacked.

"I didn't want to step on any mines," she muttered.

"What?" he barked.

"I didn't want to step on any mines," she repeated, louder. "I value my life." A smirk hovered at the corner of her lips, fighting for control.

He frowned, but couldn't ignore the twinkle in her eyes. He relaxed, and allowed the semblance of a smile to shine through.

"Don't worry. I disconnected the mines a long time ago."

Rhonda couldn't contain herself anymore and smiled openly at him.

"It's been World War II in your office for days and you'd have to be stupid or suicidal to go into such hostile territory. I'm neither."

"Yuh right. I've been unbearable. I'm sorry. But since when do you let personal differences interfere with business?"

Without fully realizing it, Alan admitted that their argument was the cause of his grumpiness. Rhonda allowed her foolish heart to hope a little. Maybe he wasn't angry with her anymore.

"What you working on?" he asked, noting the pencil poised in her hand and the steno pad on her desk.

Rhonda had forgotten about her poetry lying open in front of her, and a sudden shyness overcame her. She was tempted, as was the usual case with him, to avoid the truth when it revealed too much about her.

"A personal project," she answered, willing him to leave it at that.

He reached for the pad and she barely stopped her hands from holding on to it. He put his feet up on her desk and started to read her poems, oblivious to her presence. She watched the changing expressions on his face as he read for a moment, but she couldn't for long. She felt naked, helpless, vulnerable before him. She got up.

"Sit," he commanded, without lifting his eyes.

"No. I can't." Her embarrassment and discomfort penetrated her attempt at calm. He looked up and released her with his eyes.

Leaning against the file cabinet, she looked out the window at the Brooklyn landscape across from her. The graph-like buildings and gray skies receded and were replaced by coconut trees, small colorful houses, the rhythm and scent of Barbados: its people—her people, their feelings and eccentricities, her joys and disappointments. As Alan read, she pictured and relived every poem. Was it worth it to leave the essence of yourself and upbringing in pursuit of opportunity, success, and financial comfort?

The hairs at the back of her neck rose. She sensed his presence before she felt the warmth and pressure of his hands on her upper arms. He pulled her gently to lean against him. Lapping his hands across her middle, he rocked her softly.

"They're wonderful. . .need polish. . .but really good. I felt as if I was back home. Yuh know, yuh never realize how much you miss home until you hear a Trinidadian talk on the train or yuh hear a old time calypso. . . or read a poem like yours."

She remained silent. This moment was special, important to them. The wrong words, or any words at all could ruin the mood. She wanted nothing to interfere with this union of spirits and childhood experiences. If nothing else it was the one thing that held them together, made them the individuals they were today. He turned her around to face him; his arms stayed on her shoulders.

"Let's stop this fighting. I want to know every single thing about you."

"You can't know every single thing about me. It'd take a lifetime and more. Besides, most of it would bore you."

"No, it wouldn't. You fascinate me," he said, with a boyish grin, which didn't mask the intensity of his eyes upon her.

"Your life must be boring, if this fascinates you," Rhonda countered, making a sweeping movement from her head to her waist.

"Uh umm. No." He stopped her hand in mid-motion. "You

have a lot to be proud of and your body is the least of it. Have you eaten? Let's have lunch."

Lunch was a hilarious affair with Alan living up to his word. He delved into every facet of her childhood and years as a teenager, searching for things she hadn't told him about before. She learned things about him from pitching marbles to being a scuba diving guide for tourists. She called him a bully and a show-off intermittently as he told his tales of prowess. Alan had the capacity to laugh at his foolish mistakes and she admired that. He talked a lot about his grandmother. His mother he mentioned briefly. There was no mention of his father whatsoever. Rhonda was tempted to question him, but some instinct told her to leave it alone. He may be just as touchy as she was when it came to discussions about fathers. Their interlude was over too soon, as they both had to return to work. However, Alan insisted on taking her to dinner that night, despite her protests about it being midweek and not very practical. He countered by saying he had other plans for her on the weekend as well. She had laughed, eager to spend time with him.

She started dressing for dinner an hour before he was due. The calf-length dress she wore was rich cream, one her mother had crocheted for her. It hugged every curve on her body, simply, but seductively. A deep "V" plunged down her back, almost to the waist, but her chest was completely covered by the boat-like neckline. Low-hanging gold earrings were the only jewelry she wore. Her make-up was minimal, a blend of rose and bronze eye shadow highlighting her eyes, making them seem bigger.

At the sound of the doorbell, her heart jumped and she realized her hands were sweating, an unusual occurrence for her. This time she had requested that he come up for a drink before they left for dinner, and so she waited for him at the door soon after buzzing him in downstairs. Rhonda could not dampen the feeling of suppressed excitement—she was felt as if she were on the brink of some new, exciting adventure. She opened the door, after asking who was there, and he replied abruptly, "Alan."

The sight of her overwhelmed him. It was noticeable moments before he acknowledged her whispered greeting. Locking the door, he returned his hot gaze to her. She had told him to have a seat, while she got the gin and tonic, that he hadn't remember voicing a request for. As she turned, he whispered, "God," audible only to him. *That butt is gonna be the death of me.*

Her milk chocolate back was smooth and rounded buttocks enhanced by the design and cut of the dress held him breathless. He knew he'd have a hard time keeping his hands to himself tonight. Especially after he had promised himself he wouldn't touch her intimately. He was still standing when she returned. She handed him his drink, sank to the couch and patted the space next to her.

"Your drink alright?" she asked, at a lost for something significant to say.

"Uhumm. It's alright." His eyes never left her face; he had barely sipped his drink.

"Where we going for dinner?" she asked softly, immediately raising her drink to her lips nervously, unaware of the effect that simple act had on Alan.

"It's a surprise. I want it to be a surprise. I hope you haven't gone there before."

He had never seen her look so sexy: She had been pretty, beautiful, enticing, but tonight the sight of her went straight to his groin in a sharp stab. Rhonda was also having difficulty controlling her desire for him, but she wasn't surprised. She had reacted strongly to him the first time she saw him. If she thought he couldn't look better than he did at her mother's wedding, she was mistaken. The formal black dinner suit, offset by a white shirt showed his every attribute to the point of a poignant urge within her. She had no idea where the evening was heading, but she wasn't going to deter its natural course, for tonight she felt more confident, more at ease with her budding emotions.

"Let's go," he said abruptly, almost startling her.

The drive into lower Manhattan, where the South Street Sea Port was located, was done in partial silence. As they pulled closer to the restaurant where they would dine, each breathed in deeply of the raw smell of the ocean lingering on the cool night air.

Immense ships moored in the dock was the first thing that drew Rhonda's fascinated gaze. People milled around enjoying the fresh sea air as they strolled along walkways window shopping, while others romantically gazed into the lapping cadence of flickering waves.

But when she turned to comment on the ships, Rhonda noticed that a tenseness had descended on Alan's face. Quickly, she racked her brains to recall anything she might have said to upset him and came up with nothing. *I'd better leave well enough alone.*

There was no other word to describe the restaurant but sensuous. Candles glowed softly everywhere. Formally dressed waiters zipped between tables carrying trays high with the most exotic dishes. Alan watched the approval in Rhonda's eyes and was glad he was the one to bring her here for the first time.

Her eyes darted everywhere. She peered around bodies for a clearer view of new sights. She was lost in her private world, unaware of Alan; and for the first time, it didn't irritate him.

"Hello," he said. "You think you could find time to look at the menu?" She returned her eyes to him, smiling. Though sidetracked for a moment, he was the most fascinating thing in the room.

"Order for me."

Rhonda placed herself in his hands completely. It was a relief not to carry the burden of being in control, making decisions, no matter how small. Tonight, she was going to let down her shield and experience real living. She hadn't thrown caution to wind since the time with Richard in Barbados. But she had felt safer, more in control, with Richard. Alan was a different story. *What the heck?* Alan, deep in conversation with the wine steward, didn't see the trust in her eyes as she looked at him.

His conversation with the wine steward over, Alan returned his eyes to the woman who had crept beneath his defenses. He was still awed by the sensual picture she portrayed. He wondered how many men had looked at her with the hunger he was trying so hard to hide—Richard was one among many he was sure.

Yes, he avidly disliked the man in the photographs Eddie had shown him. He was curious about their relationship. . .What quality Richard had possessed to make Rhonda laugh and glow like she did on that semi-vacation. His jaw tightened automatically at the erotic pictures forming in his head. Luckily the waiter came for their orders and he was distracted.

"How on earth did you find this place?. . .No wait. . .I don't think I want to know," she said.

"As a matter of fact, this is my first time, too. A partner of mine recommended it. He said I'd have my chick eating out of my hands before we left."

"Is that what you want. . .me eating out of your hands?"

"No. Not really. I don't like my women too soft, but I do like them to listen to me."

"Hmmm," she said, not knowing what to add to that chauvinistic remark. Instead, she concentrated on running her forefinger around the rim of the wine glass.

"What's Richard to you?"

Rhonda's head jerked up, her eyes showing her instant shock and indignation at the suddenness and impertinence of his question. Alan was threading on dangerous ground.

He hadn't known the question was so close to his lips until he voiced it.

"Why?"

The tension that was so common between them was creeping in and he wanted nothing to spoil the night. He tried to lighten the atmosphere, but with half-hearted success.

"Didn't they teach you in school never to answer a question with a question?"

Suddenly he realized he was doing the same thing and started laughing. She recognized it and joined him. Soon they were laughing heartily at their own silliness.

"Alright. Let me put it this way. . .There's really no other way to ask the question. I want to know about your relationship with Richard. I don't want to be messing with anybody's woman and since I want to spend a lot of time with you . . . "he stopped mid-sentence.

"You do?"

"Yes and. . ."

"Wait. Wait a minute. What if I don't want to spend any time with you?"

"You don't?"

"That's not the point. But to answer your first question, Richard is a dear friend."

Alan accepted her answer for the time being, but it didn't satisfy him. But he knew pursuing it would only make Rhonda defensive. He was determined, however, to find out how she felt about going out with him.

"So how about going out with me next weekend?"

"We ain't even finished tonight's date yet. What's your hurry?"

"You know I impatient, especially when I want something. And I want you."

He reached over and took her fingers. The warmth of his hand travelled quickly up her arm. She was saved from responding by the arrival of their meal. Succulent duck smothered in a rich brown orange-flavored sauce, garnished with parsley and fresh yellow bell peppers sent a mouth-watering aroma to her salivary glands. Baby potatoes in a thick cheese sauce and crispy steamed broccoli completed the main course. Alan had ordered steak. Hunger pangs she wasn't aware of a moment ago poked her stomach walls.

"God, this looks sinful. Umm," she sniffed the air surrounding the table.

"Now I see where those hips come from."

She ignored him. But a smile at the corners of her lips showed him that although she refused to rise to bait, she was sorely tempted to.

"Let's eat," Rhonda announced, rubbing her hands in glee. They did. And if Alan didn't enjoy watching Rhonda tuck away her dinner, he would have been offended by her lack of conversation or attention. Any questions he asked were answered with monosyllables, grunts or nods. Still he finished before her and had the time to muse about the magic she seemed to weave around him. He had wanted answers to both his questions, but he didn't want to push her too hard, so he decided to let things ride for a while.

"I can't eat another thing," she announced after fifteen minutes.

"I hear they serve a bad coconut-filled chocolate cake for dessert."

"Coconut and chocolate. My favorites. You don't like me, do you? You just doing this to torture me."

He leered at her, a wicked gleam in his eyes.

"Cut it out," she laughed.

The mood was set. Once Alan got her laughing, he didn't stop. He told her jokes, obscene and otherwise, until she begged him, tears running down her cheeks, to stop.

"You're ruining my make-up," she accused him.

"You look better without it, " he said softly, looking into her eyes.

The atmosphere changed instantly. Panic and excitement welled up inside her, all the way up to her throat. She took out a tissue from her handbag to wipe under her eyes. It was hard to keep her hands steady with Alan acting as a second mirror.

"Let's go home," he said suddenly.

"I didn't have dessert yet."

Rhonda was afraid of the inevitable. Soon they would be making love and she was afraid of the depth of her response, of how much she would reveal to him.

"If you eat anything else, you're worse than Granny's fattest pig. And that's real bad," he teased.

"Alright. Alright. I wouldn't embarrass you with my eating habits."

The ride to her apartment was done in silence. The atmosphere was charged with leashed passion and Rhonda sat gnawing her bottom lip in apprehension. What if I can't go through *with it or worse—what if I disappoint him in bed?* She pressed her knuckles into trembling lips to stop the hysterical, "No," from leaving her mouth. She turned to look at Alan. He pulled the car to the side of the road.

"I'm not a rapist, so you don't have to look like that," he said harshly, once the car was still.

He turned and pulled her hand from her mouth. With eyes wide with fear, she continued to look at him.

"Why yuh so frightened? This isn't your first time, I'm sure, and you didn't act this way on the night yuh mother got married. What's the matter?"

Frustration gnawed her insides. She couldn't tell him she was afraid of displeasing him. She couldn't continue to lead him on either. She knew she should tell him to leave her alone and not have anything to do with her outside the office. But she needed him so much. Just seeing him lifted her spirits. She loved when he touched her, no matter how minor the touch. Being with him felt good, so right. Tears welled in her eyes.

"Wait. Stop. Don't do that. . . Rhonda, please don't cry. I'm sorry if I upset you. Just don't cry. . .You don't have to do anything you don't want to."

"But I want to. . . But it's just that. . . ."

"Shh. . . You have nothing to fear."

With that, he started the car and headed towards her apartment. Most of the ride was done in silence. Occasionally, he'd take his right hand off the steering wheel to grasp the hands laying in her lap. He caressed her fingers, soothing her. The time had come and there was no going back.

CHAPTER ❧ SEVEN

*I*nside the apartment, Alan held out his arms to her and she was engulfed in a warm comforting haven. He rocked her gently, his chin against her head.

"Don't you know I'd never hurt you intentionally . . . I'll do my best to always protect you."

Rhonda didn't answer. She just buried her face deeper into his chest— revelling in his warmth. Soon warmed by his body, she became aware that all her other senses were alert. The smell of him filtered into her brain and sent exciting messages to key zones in her body. Her stomach contracted, while her pulse and heart beat quickened. Like radar, Alan's body picked up her body's signals.

Grasping Rhonda's shoulders, Alan drew her away from the nest she had made near his neck. Gently, he took her face in his hands and lowering his head to sample her lips, tasted sparingly. Finding the taste pleasing, he plunged deeper, drawing a moan from her. Hungrily, they devoured each other's mouths. His tongue travelled over her teeth, tickled the corners of her mouth, and warred with her tongue. He sucked the breath from within her. He then released her face, only to wrap her tightly around him. Oh, the touch of her made his blood boil with need.

"Rhonda. You driving me crazy... God, I can't stop now. I don't want to stop."

Breaking the embrace for a moment, he gave her one last chance.

"If you don't want me, tell me now and I'll stop."

"No. Please don't stop. I want to make love to you."

"Oh, baby," he groaned, wrapping his arms around her once again.

His lips travelled along her cheek to her neck. He stopped, and laughing into her eyes, he said, "I wish you had worn this dress the other way around. But then again...I'd probably have had to beat up every man in the restaurant tonight."

She laughed shyly as he led her to the bedroom. He turned on the lamps, bathing the room with soft yellow light. When he reached for her, she went willingly, eagerly. He took his time kissing her brows, her cheeks, her ears, avoiding her warm lips. She endured the torture but for a moment and then, grasping his head between her hands, she pressed her lips to his, begging for mastery. He returned her kiss with equal fervor; she feared she'd satisfy the seemingly limitless depths of his passion.

"How do you get out of this thing? Where's the zip?" he asked urgently.

She raised her hands in the air, indicating that he had to pull the dress up over head.

"This is even better," he whispered, his smile a white gleam in the semidarkness.

Alan reached for the hem of Rhonda's dress, but the contact with her warm flesh made him pause for a moment. He slowly began to rub her thighs rhythmically. He raised the dress gradually, and as he reached her hips, he stopped and pulled her to him. As their bodies made contact, she felt the hard urgency of his desire. He tightened the grip on her hips, molding her pelvis to his hardened warmth. A shudder ran the length of his body.

Pushing her away reluctantly, he resumed the task of removing the dress. At the sight of her naked breasts, he gasped, his eyes following the agitated rise and fall of her chest. Dropping the dress to the floor, he cupped the twin globes in both hands and sank his head thirstily to them—first one, and then the other. Her raisin-sweet nipples pouted rudely from his assault. He couldn't seem to get enough of their flavor. Goose pimples covered her entire body, and her knees seemed to turn from jelly to water swiftly.

"Alan," she panted.

He lifted and placed her gently on the bed. In haste, he discarded his clothing. Then, just as hurriedly, he removed her underwear. The thought of their clothes strewn haphazardly all over her room simultaneously embarrassed and excited her. Having thrown the underwear into yet another pile on the floor, Alan returned impatiently to the warm body lying lying on the bed. His eyes devoured every inch of flesh, loving the fullness of her pert breasts, the smallness of her waist, her firm, smooth thighs.

He palmed the joining of her thighs. Its cottony softness and moist heat made him sink his fingers deeper into the welcoming flesh; he slipped in a middle finger and the fire raging in her core licked its tip. Rhonda trembled and moaned his name. She had to press her knuckles into her mouth to stop from screaming her pleasure. It was too soon. He wanted to explore every part of her and have her know him just as intimately. But Rhonda couldn't stand the suspense any longer. She clutched at his shoulders, imploring him to come closer. Straddling her body, he felt its warmth welcome him from top to bottom, and burying his face in her neck inhaled her light musk scent. He wanted to give in to her every demand, but the sweetness of her breasts beckoned him for another taste. He nibbled, kissed, and suckled them until Rhonda could stand no more.

"Alan. Please, no more. . .pleas. . . ." she begged.

"Stop?"

"No. . .No. . .I want you to. . . ."

She couldn't finish her breathless plea, but he understood only too well what she wanted.

He entered her body swiftly, for he had long lost control of his need for her. The fire that had teased his finger moments ago singed his manhood and he shuddered from the thrill. She was tight and he momentarily hesitated, afraid he was hurting her. She clung fiercely to him. Shivers of indescribable pleasure coursed through her body, replacing the slight initial pain she felt at his entry. When he moved inside her, she arched eagerly to meet his every thrust, instinct making up for what she lacked in experience.

No one had ever told her it would be like this. Yes, there were erotic books and films that had described the passion, the act itself; but nothing, nothing prepared her for the tremors that rocked her body right now. *It hadn't even been like this with Peter.*

Alan caressed her with hands, legs, feet, mouth. He rolled her from side to side heatedly. Eventually, she was on top of him, molded to his body from head to foot. His hands kneaded her buttocks erotically, bringing her body closer and deeper to his. Her body was aflame. Where their bodies joined was hot and wet, the central bank for all the pleasures that rode over them. Each tremor, each stroke rocked Rhonda farther and farther into oblivion.

Oh God! It felt so good. Oh Alan . . . Alan, she cried. But she couldn't contain herself any longer. "Oh, Alan, Alan," she groaned. "Ohh. . .Ohh."

"Let it go baby, let it go," he moaned.

He increased the tempo. His murmurings and sighs of ecstasy mingled with hers. Their breaths were one, misty, hot. Then a jolt of pleasure surpassing all the others hit her, forcing her to stiffen her body. It sent tingles to all her extremities. Joining in her release, Alan gripped Rhonda so tight that her ribs hurt. *Why didn't someone tell me it could be like this? This is more than sex . . . this is tenderness. . . this is loving.*

But her trembling limbs told her it wasn't always like this. It couldn't be. No man's smile weakened her like Alan's. No man's touch warmed her like Alan's. And now she knew without a doubt that no man's body could give her as much pleasure as Alan's did.

The couple laid quietly savoring the aftermath of their lovemaking. Alan smoothed Rhonda's back, and she rubbed her hand gently over his tummy, loving the feel of the tiny hairs that tickled her palm.

"When was the last time you made love?" he asked softly.

"A very long time ago."

"When. . .a month. . .two months. . .a year?"

"Six years."

"Six years," he asked incredulously. "Nobody goes without sex for six years. . .Didn't they tell you if you don't use it, it'll get cobwebs."

She laughed at his silliness.

Six years since she made love to Peter. Where did the time go? Was she really strange to have remained celibate all these years? No. She'd just been unwilling to settle for less—attraction was not enough, there just had to be more, there had to be this something special. She hadn't been interested in dating because it was too much work. Besides, after Peter she had a hard time believing men were interested in anything else but her bed.

"You're gone again," Alan said, bringing her back to the present.

"I'm right here," she answered.

"Did I hurt you?"

"A little."

"I'm sorry. Next time I promise I'll be more gentle."

"Is there going to be a next time?"

"Why. . .you plan to let it get cobwebs?"

She laughed and hugged him close. She waited for the next obvious question, but surprisingly he didn't ask. Knowing Alan, it would just be a matter of time before he asked about her lover of six years ago.

"As a matter of fact," he interrupted her thoughts. "Next time can start right now."

He pulled her to him and started kissing her neck and she reacted like putty in his wonderful hands. He chuckled triumphantly, and Rhonda couldn't help smiling at his obvious pleasure.

≈ ≈ ≈ ≈

Rhonda woke to a streak of sunlight warming the left side of her body. She snuggled deeper into her pillow, a smile on her face. She turned and caressed the spot where he had lain hours before, too drowsy to move a muscle. Disappointment replaced the contented glow of moments before—Alan had had to go home.

He'd promised his aunt he would come over to fix a leaking pipe in her basement and knew that if he didn't leave in the morning, he'd spend the rest of the day in bed with Rhonda. She smiled as she remembered the effort it took for him to get up.

"Rhonda, sweetheart, what time is it?" Alan mumbled his face buried in Rhonda's coffee-tipped breasts, his foot thrown carelessly over her firm thighs.

"Mmmm. . . I don't know. . . Ease up. Let me see," Rhonda murmured.

Rhonda raised weary limbs and resting on her elbows looked at the clock on the bedside table. It said 4:02.

"It's four o'clock," she said, turning to look at his face in the semi-darkness. His long lashes rested endearingly against the lower lids; his face was gentle, at peace. He reached for her, pulling her back close to him. Rhonda relaxed against the pillow and Alan threw his leg over her again.

Fifteen minutes passed before Alan stirred again.

"What time is it now?" he groaned.

Rhonda had drifted away and was barely conscious. She heard his question from far away.

"You look," she said. Rhonda was tired, delightfully so, and all she wanted to do was sleep. She turned and buried her face in the pillow.

Alan slowly sat up, leaned his back against the head board, watched the clock and then closed his eyes once again. Another five minutes passed.

"Rhonda, wake up. I think I'd better go while I still can," he said softly.

"Go away, Alan," she grumbled and turned to pump the pillow.

"No. Get up. It's not fair. I want to sleep, too." Alan started tickling her, making her weaker than she already was.

"OK. OK. Stop. I'll get up. I'll get up," she giggled, helplessly. Alan stopped.

"I promised my aunt I'd fix a pipe that's leaking in the basement today. I already put it off twice, so I have to go today. Help me get dressed," he said.

"Help you! Uh uh. You got your problems. I got mine," she laughed and got up.

Rhonda walked over to the closet and pulled out a robe. As she tied the belt, she watched him stumble into his underwear and pants—he was having trouble with his knees. She giggled and when he was steady he threw a pillow playfully at her.

Soon after he kissed her at the door, and promised to call her in the afternoon. Rhonda locked the door behind him and ambled back to bed. The tiredness held at bay for those brief moments, returned almost suddenly. She couldn't wait to snuggle under the sheets again, to smell his warm fragrance on her pillow.

Now this morning she was deliciously relaxed, at ease with herself and her body; like a fatted cat she felt contented—happy. The memory of Alan's loving warmed her with a languid satisfaction.

She wondered how Alan felt this morning: *Is he also reliving our night of passion right now? Is it possible that he loves me? He never once said he did, and I was too afraid to ask. Or does he think I'm really easy?* She could still hear her moans of pleasure. *There's nothing I can do about it now,* she thought. *It's done, and I wanted to love him.*

Suddenly, she sat up ramrod straight, fear written all over her face. She got off the bed and ran to the kitchen to check the calendar. *Whew! I'm due soon. It had better come soon,* she thought. *I can't afford to take chances like last night, safe period or no safe period. Oh no, what if it doesn't come? What will I do?*

Rhonda's heart skipped a beat and her stomach knotted nervously, *What if I become pregnant?* Panic began to set in. Her mother would kill her. *Rhonda. Rhonda, stop it. You're a grown woman. You don't live under your mother's roof anymore—whether you have a child or not has nothing to do with her. Who are you kidding? No matter how old you get, you're still a child in your mother's eyes.* She had sworn she'd never put herself in the same position Deborah Baptiste had survived: raising an illegitimate child alone.

The telephone rang suddenly and Rhonda jumped. Unwrapping her arms from around her tense middle, she answered the call. A stranger apologized for having dialed the wrong number, and hung up. But the call jogged her memory, for she was supposed to pick up a curiously helpless Richard at Kennedy airport at eleven o'clock. He was vacationing in New York for a month.

It'll be nice to see Richard again, Rhonda thought. *Maybe it'll be the best thing for me right now, despite the waning attraction. Too much Alan in my system. I'm taking risks I would never normally take, breaking childhood promises to myself—face it, that man steals away your mind with his smile, his kisses, his touch. Lord, I need some perspective here.*

She got up, dressed, and pushed thoughts of Alan and her anxiety away.

ᔕ ᔕ ᔕ ᔕ

The constant shrill of the telephone woke Alan from a deep sleep around 9:30 am. Groping for the phone on the night table, Alan felt as if his body was run over by a Mack truck.

"Uhhhh, hello," he croaked.

"Hi, baby. Sorry I woke you." It was Nadine.

"Uhumm."

"Wake up Alan. I want to make sure you hear me. . . Alan?"

"I'm up. . .I'm up. What's the matter?" Alan turned over on his back, tugging the sheet around his naked body and rubbing his grainy eyes.

"I lost my ride to the airport. Could you take me please? I could take a cab, but they charge too much. Can you come?" Nadine asked, her normal baby pitch even higher.

"Ahh. . .Yes. Wuh time?" Alan muttered.

"Pick me up in an hour, OK?" Nadine requested, relieved.

"OK." Alan hung up the phone and released a loud groan.

I getting too old for this marathon stuff. Jez. The memory of the previous night flowed over him, healing, soothing his weary body. *This is what you get for being so greedy. Damn. I couldn't help myself. The more I got the more I wanted. Oh, Rhonda. You're some lover, let me tell yuh. The man who marries you got it made, but he better have a strong back. Maybe I should get back on a rigid exercise program, because something tells me I'm going to need it.*

Alan pulled his body up, dragging the sheet with him. *I'll just take a shower and get going...Oh shucks! I'd better call Aunt Mable and tell her I'll be there this afternoon.*

🐦 🐦 🐦 🐦

When Rhonda arrived at the airport, she had to wait an hour because of the delay in Richard's flight. She had lots of time to kill, and so she wandered into the cafeteria to watch the chaos from a safe distance: people tripping over boxes and suitcases as they attempted to move from one line to the next; women travelling alone dragging heavy suitcases and children who were more of a hindrance than a help; and many running to their departing planes at the last minute.

Rhonda could feel the energy in the air—the sensation was similar to the vibrancy of Alan's magnetism. She mused at the powerful effect this possessive man had on her. He had the ability to weaken her with a smile or a simple touch. As she rose to leave, she saw a familiar face. *No, Oh...Lord, no....*

Turning, Rhonda watched as Nadine reached across the table, not far away, and kissed Alan on the lips. Suitcases sat down beside them.

Instant nausea rose like an erupting volcano within Rhonda. She gripped the chair to steady her trembling body and churning stomach. She couldn't afford to embarrass herself by vomiting all over the place. *Relax, Rhonda. Come on, breathe. You have to calm yourself down, or you'll be sick all over this nice pink dress of yours.*

You just left me...just a few a hours ago, she inwardly railed at the man whom she watched leisurely escort Nadine to a departure gate. *How could you?...What are you doing here with her? You said you had to fix a pipe in your aunt's basement. You lying bastard. Ma was right. You can't trust you men for nothing. You're nothing but a bunch of lying bastards.*

The anger flowed through Rhonda's veins, bringing new vigor to the previous limp body. She released the back of the chair, and walked away crisply. Rhonda looked as if she was ready to kill and people walking toward her noted the ominous expression characterizing her disposition and steered out of her way.

Standing in the Customs area, Rhonda tried to calm herself and think rationally. *Maybe there's an explanation. Alan didn't say anything about a trip, so maybe the suitcases are Nadine's. Maybe he is picking her up...or dropping her off.*

Reason was soon defeated, however, by anger and pain as her mind swirled with questions and recriminations directed at Alan. *But you could have said so; you didn't have to lie and give me that cock and bull story about fixing your's aunt pipes. I know you're seeing this Nadine person. Everybody in the office knows it. I even met her, even if you didn't have the decency to introduce me. So what's the big deal? All you had to do was tell the damn truth.*

But this is your fault, Rhonda, her mind accused. *If you weren't so eager to jump into bed with him, you wouldn't be feeling this way, now. Fool!*

With hands tightly lapped across her chest and a tapping right foot, Rhonda alternating cursed Alan and herself, or tried to find excuses for Alan and herself. She was a jumbled mass of confusion, anger and frustration when Richard walked up to her, and she made a supreme effort to mask the bubbling emotions.

When Richard saw Rhonda, a smile lit up his face. There was something special about her. No matter how many women he bedded, just the thought of what he wanted to do with her seemed to arouse him more. *Maybe it's because I haven't won her over yet, or should I say, under.* Hugging her, he smiled.

"Waiting impatiently for me, I hope," he greeted.

She was stiff, like a board. Something was wrong.

"I ain't had no choice. The plane was delayed," Rhonda laughed, but amusement barely softened her mouth and really didn't lighten the storm churning in her eyes.

"Are you alright? You look upset about something. Don't tell me you ain't glad to see me?" Richard asked, concerned about Rhonda's well being, but more concerned about how it would affect his plans.

"Of course, I'm glad to see you. Come, let's go. The car is in the parking lot."

Outside Richard breathed the humid summer air. *A little breeze would be better, but I ain't complaining.* His white pants and black shirt felt glued to his dark skin. He couldn't wait to take a shower. He was glad to be back in New York. The pace suited him fine. And the women. . .Yes. . . He had a whole lot to choose from. But for now, his mind was set on one woman: Rhonda Baptiste.

Once inside the car and on their way out of the airport, Richard decided to set things in motion.

"So what exciting thing you got planned for me today?"

"It's Sunday, Richard. Church?"

He grimaced.

"Heathen. I think you should go to your hotel, or wherever you're staying and settle in. We could go out later."

"I'm looking forward to staying with you," he said innocently, when they were settled in Rhonda's car.

"What?"

"I left home in a hurry, so I didn't have time to make arrangements to stay anywhere. Plus, none of my friends ain't expecting me. But since you were. . .I thought you wouldn't turn a fellow countryman out on the streets."

He turned his best sad-puppy look on Rhonda, who was torn between hitting him for his presumptuousness and hugging him because he looked so cute. She had forgotten how attractive those dark well-formed lips were. And how those almost black eyes could twinkle devilishly. He looked a little thinner, but still muscular and sexy. He had cut his tightly curled hair. It added to his impishness. Rhonda laughed and shook her head.

"I can't."

"Why not? You got another man staying there or what?"

"No. But if I did, it wouldn't be any of your business," she replied, a little short with him. *These blasted men. They really think they can do whatever they want with you.*

Shamefacedly, he turned and looked out the window. The possibility of another man didn't occur to him before, but he could deal with that. No problem. She'd never mentioned anyone, but he knew she lived alone. He simply had to play it cool. *Something is up. She ain't the same woman I met weeks ago,* he decided.

Rhonda turned Richard's request over in her head. Her immediate reaction was, no way. The place was small, one bedroom, and she really couldn't deal with someone else invading her space, especially not today. After her cousin's visit last winter she swore she wasn't letting another soul stay in her apartment because it took days to get everything back to the way she liked it. But a little devil poked inside her. *So you think I'm easy and you can do whatever you want with me, huh,* she said to Alan in her mind's eye. *You can do whatever you want and I have to live with it, right? You're not the only man on this earth, and I want you to know that.*

Unfortunately, her conscience refused to let the matter rest there and she found a little voice of practicality whispering, *Rhonda, what are you thinking? You really 'gon let a man stay in your apartment? What will your mother think?*

I don't care, she replied to herself. *It's innocent. Nothing is going to happen. I just have to keep Richard in line that's all. This isn't the middle ages.*

Yuh know you being stupid, came the final warning, *Yuh acting out of jealousy and anger. You shouldn't do it.*

"On one condition," Rhonda said, after a long pause.

"What's that?"

"You sleep on the couch. My bedroom and body are off limits."

"You didn't have to add your body to that list."

"Oh yeah? I know you. If I didn't add my body to that list, you would want to take all kinds of liberties with it. So let's lay down the rules right now."

"Alright. Alright, boss man."

Later that evening, they went to dinner. It was relaxing for both of them. For Rhonda, it meant no pressure, no tension, the battle of controlling her emotions, her physical urges, all the things she fought constantly to do around Alan. For Richard, the pace of slower than the one he kept up year round. Between working on the sites, spending time with his family and friends and seducing women, he had little time to unwind. Though he would like to explore the excitement Rhonda created within him, he wanted nothing more right now than the peaceful calm she wove around him.

After a long lull in the conversation, Richard looked up from his dessert. Rhonda was staring into nowhere, Richard obviously forgotten.

"I so glad you said you'd marry me. I can't wait. . ."

"Wuh you say?" she asked incredulously.

"I'm thrilled that you've agreed to marry me."

"What. Wait a minute. Where'd you get that idea?"

"It's not an idea. You said yes a few minutes ago."

She looked at him doubtfully. She was thinking about Alan and had probably answered his question, not thinking. *Did he really ask her to marry him? He has got to be teasing me,* Rhonda guessed. She looked at Richard closely, at last noticing the tell-tale signs of the effort he made to control a smirk.

"That was sneaky, Richard Manning."

"Well you deserve it. If you didn't make it so obvious that my company boring, I wouldn't have been tempted."

"Aww, Richard. It's not that. I just daydream a lot."

"You're too old for that."

"Thanks a lot."

They laughed and soon were talking quietly again. He talked about his plans to start another construction company, probably in St. Vincent or Grenada. She listened intently, offering advice where she could. It occurred to her while he talked, that not only would expansion be good for his business, but his personal life would get a boost, considering his many conquests. She decided to tease him a little about it.

"Are you sure strengthening your company is the only reason you want to expand to Grenada and St. Vincent?" Rhonda said slyly.

"Wuh you getting at?" Richard asked puzzled.

"Women, silly. Your favorite past time. And don't try to deny it. I have two eyes in my head, yuh know."

"It never occurred to me," he said in mock innocence.

"Yuh know with the kind of running around I'm sure you do, it's a wonder you don't have children all over the place. . .Or do you? Come to think of it, we never talked about that, did we?"

"No we didn't," he said, suddenly serious, a strange pained look on his face. Rhonda began to dread the worse. *Another man,* she scorned, *who is just like my father.*

"As a matter of fact, I don't have any children. I can't," he said gravely.

"Wuh you mean you can't. . .Yuh mean you infertile?" she asked incredulously.

"Yep. I can't have any children. . . God's way of protecting unsuspecting women from my wildness," he laughed humorlessly.

Rhonda felt sorry for him. It must be very difficult to accept and live with a realization like that. There she had been this morning worried sick about becoming pregnant. What if she couldn't at all? The thought boggled her mind. Aunt Sheila was infertile, but the family never talked about it. And becoming pregnant had never been a real fear until now.

"I'm sorry. It never occurred to me that you could be. . ." Rhonda said, embarrassed.

"Forget it. You couldn't have known. It's probably just as well anyway. I can have fun without a care or worry in the world." Richard laughed. His attempt at levity failed and Rhonda changed the subject, away from the sensitive topic.

"So, how soon do you think you'll be ready to start that new company in St. Vincent? Maybe I can do some type of story in the magazine," Rhonda said.

They chatted for a while, but soon it was time to go home. Richard wouldn't have lived up to his reputation if he didn't try to seduce Rhonda before he, dejected, went off to the cold comforts of the sofa.

As Rhonda stretched awake the following morning, thoughts of Alan shot through her mind immediately. How should she treat him? How would he treat her?

She trotted to the bathroom to start her ritual of preparing for work, but while brushing her teeth, she felt a familiar cramping sensation in her abdomen. *Yes. it's here. No doubt about it.* She checked anyway and experienced a welcomed flood of relief, for she had been right. Rhonda had been spared the agony of making a very big decision—this time around. "Lord, she said aloud, I promise to be more careful . . ." *The past few years of celibacy had had some benefits . . . .*

Glancing at the clock, she noted the time: 8:00. *Good, I have plenty of time to make the train and get in while the office is still quiet.* As she locked up before leaving, she glanced over to where Richard was still sleeping on the couch.

Well, I won't get to say goodbye, but I have been spared the burden of eluding his advances first thing in the morning. How did I get myself into such a stupid, idiotic position?

Rhonda, her conscience smugly provided a reply, *your anger can land you in the most stupid positions. And for what?*

🖎 🖎 🖎 🖎

At work, Alan was listening to the consistent ring of Rhonda's telephone. It was already ten o'clock, and she was rarely late. As he was about to hang up, someone, definitely male, grunted hello.

"Good morning. Is Rhonda there?" Alan asked brusquely.

After a long pause, the man asked what time it was and when Alan told him, he said, "Hold on."

"She's not here," the strange voice mumbled momentarily.

Alan muttered, "Thank you," and before replacing the phone, he heard a distant rustling, and then a definite click.

He had no idea that his face had turned to granite and the eyes that sparkled gayly that morning now resembled those of a tiger about to kill its prey. He sat, staring into space blankly. Then hot anger rushed to his brain and he clenched his fists. *Relax, Hussein, relax*, he soothed himself. *Since when do you let a woman affect you this way?* He tried Rhonda's extension once again, and finally she answered.

"Hello," she said, after getting no response to, "Rhonda."

"Rhonda, in the future, if entertaining guests early in the morning is going to make you late for work, let me know. I'm going for coffee. Be in my office when I get back."

Rhonda replaced the receiver, visibly shaking from head to toe. *The man was incredible. What the hell was he talking about?* Her anger jarred her from the daze she was in a moment ago. She couldn't deal with anything or anyone today, not after the experiences she had just had this morning. She just couldn't.

As he poured coffee from the urn, Alan tried in vain to control his anger. He knew he shouldn't have jumped on her like that, but somehow he couldn't control himself.

"Did you hear about that derailment on the No. 4 from Brooklyn this morning?"

Alan's head snapped around at the words of a woman standing next to the soda machine. She was talking to another woman.

"No," her friend replied, in disbelief.

"It happened about 8:30. It was an hour and a half before they got everyone off the train. A few people were hurt, but I don't know how badly."

Alan was openly listening to the conversation now. His face was even tighter than it was before. *Oh God*, he thought. *That's the train Rhonda takes. Maybe that's why she was late.* One small part of him wished it was; the rest was sickened at the thought that she might have been killed or seriously hurt. He returned to his office, carrying two cups of coffee instead of the usual one. There were two thick manila folders and a note from Rhonda on his desk. The note read: I'm not feeling well today. I'm taking the rest of the day off.

He'd just give her time to get home and call. How could they have been so close on Saturday night and miles apart on Monday? He'd called her on Sunday, after he'd taken Nadine to the airport, but there was no answer. Later in the evening when he returned from his aunt's home, after fixing the leaking pipe and having dinner, he called again, but there was still no answer. She probably was spending the day with her mother he had convinced himself. *She had felt so good in his arms. Perfect. Rhonda was born with me in mind. She had to be. Damn, it's going to be hard to concentrate today.*

Ultimately, he gave up trying.

CHAPTER ❧ EIGHT

She was crazy to take another train today. But, it was good therapy to jump back in again, wasn't it? Her swimming instructor had made her do that when she almost drowned in the pool. So she had forced herself to get back on that train. It had all been so sudden—the screeching and the jerk that had turned the train almost on one side. The screams of pain and terror had been piercing. Hands, feet and heads had jumbled together grotesquely, as people were lurched onto seats, the floor and fellow passengers. The movement had slammed her ribs into a pole. She knew they were bruised, but not broken.

Yet it wasn't as frightening as almost drowning. Now, the sensation of sitting in the train, rocking from side to side along with its motion, reminded her of the way her swimming instructor had wrapped her in a blanket and cradled her in order to calm her after the terrifying episode in the chlorinated water. The experiences were similar. Fear, just as it had been on that past episode, was like a metallic flavor in her mouth, and an acid chewing at her stomach. In fact, all of her senses seemed numbed with overstimulation.

As the A train travelled over Jamaica Bay on its way to Far Rockaway, Rhonda sat huddled in one corner: Beads of sweat coated her forehead, nose and upper lip; the hand that gripped the long silver pole was wet, slippery.

So much for my theory about overcoming fear, she thought ironically. *If I don't die in a derailment, I'll surely die of fright.*

Soon after the derailment, she had chided herself about not using her Capri to drive to work. But that car had a habit of stalling at the worse times, and twice in fifteen-degree weather, it had broken down in the midst of traffic. It was hours before she had gotten it moved. Thereafter, she had always opted for the train over the car as the safe bet.

Huh, Rhonda snorted in irony, *there is no such thing as playing it safe.*

Gradually Rhonda relaxed. Beach 44 was coming up in four stops, and she was finally optimistic that she would get there in one piece. She did.

On the beach, Rhonda stretched out, mindless of the sand littering her clothes with fine grains of tan, white and ground shell; she allowed her mind go blank. Idly, she watched children, home from school for the summer, as they played in the sand and water— they were far enough for her to still enjoy some seclusion.

Rhonda sighed, her brown eyes darkening at the memory of this morning's ordeal. At that moment, when her death seemed imminent, she experienced a strange exhilaration. Yes. That was what she had felt. The last person she had thought of as she prepared herself to accept Fate's judgement was Alan. Saturday night had been the happiest she had ever spent, and there had been no regrets for having experience the wonder of his embrace. She would have died happy.

But she had been given another chance. Alan was right: She owed it to herself to embrace as much of life as she could, for as long as she could. Which meant she couldn't wait around for anything or anyone. If her employers didn't think enough of her experience to promote her, then she'd go elsewhere for recognition of her capabilities. Yes, she had to start looking for a new job right away, or something. . .maybe start her own magazine like she had always dreamed of doing. After all, this morning made her realize that the time for dreaming was today. *Today.*

Another unsettled item on her personal agenda was her relationship with her mother. *I have to talk to Ma,* she decided. There were still too many things eating away at her heart that were connected to the past, and to old grievances. Her mother might not want to bring up the past and share her deepest, most intimate feelings, but Rhonda knew that she had to communicate her own feelings as well as to ask some difficult, disturbing questions. Questions about her father.

Rhonda spent the rest of the day on the beach working on her poetry and making plans for the future. The afternoon passed quickly and quietly into twilight. It was time to go home, but she really didn't want to. *It is so peaceful here.* Realizing that it was dangerous for anyone to be alone on a deserted beach, Rhonda forced herself to walk back to the subway station. The train ride home wasn't as scary as the one coming in. She'd survive the MTA yet.

When she reached home about nine o'clock, Richard was sitting in front of the TV, a beer in one hand, munching peanuts from the other. He looked comfortable. The sight of a man in her apartment pleased her. *It's time for me to settle down,* she thought.

"Hi," he said.

"Hello," she greeted in return.

"You home. Wuh to eat?"

Typical Bajan man—woman, where's my food? On second thought, how ready am I to come home to this? she thought humorously.

"Don't you know how to cook?"

"Never learned. There was always someone to do it."

"Well, like they say, it's never too late to learn."

She grabbed his wrists, dragging him from his seat. He rose reluctantly. Needless to say, that first cooking lesson was a disaster. Rhonda spent her time humoring his impatience, answering his numerous questions and waylaying clumsy attempts to do things his way. But she salvaged the meal of steak, baked potatoes, mixed vegetables and a tossed salad. Over dinner, he told her that some man had called a million times for her.

"Who was it?"

"Somebody named Alan. He sounded like he didn't believe me when I said you weren't here."

"Did he leave a message?"

"No. Just said he'd try again later."

But the phone didn't ring again that night. Rhonda went to bed at 11:30, despite Richard's attempts to get her to go to a movie or do anything to relieve his boredom. He'd gone walking earlier in the afternoon after sleeping until 1:00 pm. But it wasn't enough. Already he was thinking about being with a woman, any attractive woman who would have him, and to hell with Rhonda. Face it: He was a miserable person without a warm body next to him, wrapped around him.

Rhonda arrived at the office at 7:45 the next morning. She was already deep in her work when Alan knocked at her door and entered. She looked up in time to see a look of hesitancy on his face.

"How are you?" he asked.

"Fine," she answered.

"I called to see how you were yesterday."

"I know. I didn't know you'd called until very late."

He entered the room slowly and sat down. His eyes never left her face. There was something different about her. A hardness coated her eyes, making her face seem thinner.

"Were you in that derailment yesterday?"

"Yes."

He lowered his gaze to her desk, hiding his reaction to her answer.

"Were you hurt in any way?"

"My ribs and a few other places are sore. Nothing serious."

"Did you go to the doctor?"

"No."

"I think you should."

Rhonda didn't answer. She had no intention of going to the doctor because there was nothing wrong with her that some warm water, Epsom salts and Bengay couldn't cure. She wondered at his obvious concern. He sure hadn't shown it yesterday when he barked at her. But she forgave him. It was becoming too easy to forgive him.

However, the royal inquisition wasn't over. She knew she'd have to wait for his apology. She then remembered her resolution yesterday; he shouldn't be allowed to get off too easily. She raised her hands as he opened his mouth to railroad her into going to the doctor.

"I'm fine. Please leave me alone. I have work to catch up on." Her voice was cold, brittle. He flinched.

"It seems I'm always saying sorry to you for one thing or another. I'm really sorry about my attitude yesterday morning. As you know I called to make amends."

She didn't respond. He rose from the chair and headed toward the door.

"Now isn't a good time to talk to you. You're still upset."

That did it. The anger seemed to spread throughout her body infecting her with its fever.

"Does it salvage your pride to put the blame on me whenever you're wrong?"

She knew she had touched a nerve, when his shoulders hunched over suddenly. Secretly, Rhonda congratulated herself.

"Why do you persist in trying to make me grovel?" he asked, walking toward her. He planted his hands on the desk, in the same position she was in. Up this close, she caught the full radiation of his anger, and he felt hers.

"Know what I'd like to do right now? Shake some sense into that hard head of yours."

Rhonda continued to stare at him, unflinchingly.

"You're supposed to be an adult, not a silly child who throws a tantrum every time she doesn't get what she wants."

Rhonda just stood, staring. She goaded him beyond control

with her disregard. He reached out, gripped her shoulders and shook her so hard the dancing of her head on her shoulders started to put a strain on her neck. Tears of anger and humiliation sprung quickly to her eyes. She tried desperately to stop them from falling. She succeeded, but not before he saw their glitter.

"Get out," she snarled through gritted teeth when he had stopped.

He released her so suddenly, she tripped against her chair, almost falling.

Alan left, slamming the door behind him. He'd lost his cool this time—boy did he lose his cool. He had to get out of the building in order to walk off his frustration and to settle his rattled nerves.

That woman! I'll be damned if I can understand her. I definitely can't control her. Sure, I told myself I could, I thought that I would want the control, but in the end I really didn't. There it was again, that haunting theme: the thrill of the chase, the joy of the challenge. I am far from finished with Ms. Baptiste.

With Alan gone, Rhonda's blood pressure returned to normal. *We must have made quite a picture of professionalism,* she laughed humorlessly. She hated fighting with him, and would have preferred to make peace as soon as possible. It wasn't realistic to expect him to grovel—she wouldn't be attracted to the grovelling type anyway. But she made no attempt to see him that day and neither did he, for they both needed time to lick reopened wounds.

A strained working relationship between the two continued for the next three weeks. Occasionally, they'd forget their differences and would laugh over something silly. At times, in meetings, Alan would catch Rhonda staring at him, an indecipherable look in her eyes. Other times, Rhonda intercepted his gaze upon her. As time rolled on, they handled each other with kid gloves. It was a period of awareness, and of concern for each other's feelings.

🐤 🐤 🐤 🐤

This is one Saturday I'll let this apartment go to the dogs: I refuse to lift a broom or a mop. Forget it. I'm goofing off today. Those were Rhonda's thoughts as she got up that morning around 9:00 am, and for once she lived up to her promise. It was almost 3:00 pm and she had spent the day chatting on the phone with friends she hardly called, reading, and working on her anthology. She was still in her mini black robe and had had nothing in her stomach but a cup of herb tea. She was thinking about raiding the fridge when the phone rang.

"Hello,"

The silkiness of Rhonda's voice never ceased to please him.

"Hi," Alan said. "Have you written me off completely or can I still talk to you?"

"I don't think I could write you off even if I tried."

"No? Why is that?"

As always, a combination of fear and excitement washed over Rhonda at the intimate turn of their conversations. She was afraid to voice feelings she wasn't even sure of, and the idea of how he would respond if she dared voice some of her thoughts thrilled her.

"Sounds like I put you on the spot." Alan said when Rhonda didn't respond to him.

"I guess you did."

"How would you like dinner at my place tonight? I could treat you to some real food. All yuh women don't really know how to cook, yuh know."

"Yuh asking for trouble with a remark like that, yuh know that."

"I'm willing to take my chances. I dare you to try me."

The double meaning of his statement didn't escape either of them and the ensuing silence was revealing.

"I'm game," Rhonda replied. "But I'm walking with some antacid just in case."

"Let me give you the directions, you fool," he chuckled.

When Rhonda arrived at his house three hours later, Alan was dressed in black slacks, a black silk shirt, and a greasy, messy apron. She laughed outright as he let her in and closed the door.

He smiled sheepishly, noting that as always, she looked beautiful. She was wearing one of his favorites: the tie-dye outfit she wore to her mother's wedding.

"I hope you're hungry, because I went a little overboard," he declared.

He sat her down and took off the apron. She gulped at the sight his slightly opened shirt presented. *One of these days, I won't be able to help myself. I'm going to go right up and kiss that neck.*

As Alan went into the kitchen, Rhonda looked around the spacious dining room. Like the long oval dinning table, the china cabinet was done in black lacquer. In one corner an unusual Z-shaped four-level table carved out of some kind of thick, dark wood displayed African earthenware. Four small pictures of tropical foliage and flowers enlivened the brilliant white walls.

When Alan returned, he dimmed the lights and lit the two red candles standing in slender crystal holders on the table. Then he took a rose from a vase of lush, red roses and baby's breath, specially cut and trimmed it with a knife, and stuck it in her hair, above the left ear.

Rhonda raised her eyebrows in surprise and smiled. "To what do I owe the honor?"

"For being you, that's all," he said, with lowered eyes, and started to uncover the dishes laid out on the white tablecloth.

Rhonda's salivary glands stung as she inhaled the delicious aroma of the callaloo with crab, stewed red beans, sauteed carrots and brocoli, rice, and baked chicken. She was hungry; a cup of tea is nothing to exist on. *I'm going to destroy this*, she thought.

It's a wonder she's not as big as a house the way she puts away food, Alan thought in amusement as he watched Rhonda cut down a plate piled high with a sample of everything.

After the meal they retired to the living room. Alan put on a tape of Luther Vandross and sat sideways beside Rhonda on the loveseat. He watched her face quietly as she took in the room.

Surprisingly, there wasn't a stitch of black anywhere in the living room. Bamboo wood, and woven cane were the motif. The rims of the sofa and loveseat were made from them. The chairs' cushions were made from a bumpy, but soft off-white cotton material. A large round straw mat displaying various stitches sat in the center of the room.

"Do you like it?" he asked.

"Like what?"

"The room. That's all you've been looking at."

"Yes. We have similar tastes."

"I wonder what else we have in common?" Alan asked seductively.

"Oh I don't know. . .We spend more time arguing than trying to find out."

"Do you want to find out?" he asked softly.

Rhonda didn't answer right away. With a bowed head she looked down at the hands sitting idly in her lap. Alan got up and sat closer. Then he took a hand and placed his lips against it.

"Look at me, " he said.

Rhonda raised her head slowly. Her eyes, darken in turmoil caused his stomach to flip.

"For once, can you just look at me, without trying to find an excuse or a reason, and just tell me what you feel?" Alan implored.

"Yes. I'd like to find out what else we have in common," she said so softly that he hardly heard her.

"Good. We will. You can count on it." Alan stroked Rhonda's cheek with a forefinger.

"There's something I've been meaning to talk to you about," he continued. "Could you tell me about that man in your life six years ago?"

Rhonda burst out laughing at Alan's question, and he looked at her with a slight smile, but a puzzled frown creased his eyebrows.

"It took you long enough," Rhonda said still laughing.

"Am I that predictable?"

"Not always. What do you want to know?"

"Everything."

"Well. It's pretty simple really. He was my fiance and he died in a car accident soon after the engagement."

Alan's eyebrows shot up. He had no idea he was concerned about a ghost. "He was your first lover, wasn't he?"

"Yes. We were pretty young," Rhonda said, shaking her head, her eyes focused on the past.

"Did you love him very much?"

"Oh yes."

"Are you completely over his death now?"

"Yes, I suppose I am—for the most part," she sighed sadly. "Sometimes, the memories are overwhelming, but that's all that's left now. Memories."

Now that he knew about the mysterious lover, he felt a little foolish. There was really only Richard he had to worry about.

Rhonda watched as Alan drifted away deep in thought. A stillness settled over him. He was fast becoming an important part of her life, and this emotion was new to her. She really didn't know what it entailed or how to proceed, and she found herself wondering just what it was that he felt for her—there was a curiosity, she knew. He was attracted. Yes. Together they were fireworks. But he wasn't relentless about bedding her, not like Richard, and that was unusual. This fact contradicted every theory and premise she maintained about men wanting nothing but a woman's physical offerings. This evening was a perfect example: By now Richard would be on Strategy C: Any And All Moves—Just Get The Bra Off.

"You're daydreaming again. Are you ready to call it a night, or would you like some Ovaltine?" he asked, bringing her out of reverie.

Rhonda giggled, "How did you know I was an Ovaltine girl?"

"You and that sweet tooth of yours are good clues. Wanna help?"

"Can I have marshmallows?"

"Yes, you can have marshmallows," Alan replied with exaggerated patience.

"Alright!" Rhonda yelled, leaping up to follow him into the kitchen.

The kitchen was spacious and spotless. It was done in white, with red accessories. Rhonda was impressed. *I would enjoy cooking in here.*

"You like it here, too, hmmm?" Alan ran some water into the kettle and turned on the burner under it after he put it on the stove.

"Yes. I suppose this is close to the kitchen of my dreams," Rhonda said, her back leaning against the counter.

"How about the owner, do you like the owner too?" Alan came to stand directly in front of Rhonda, up close. He didn't want to miss a flicker of emotion.

Rhonda's eyes, at level with his chest, remained lowered for long moments. She was afraid to look at him, but looking at his exposed chest wasn't much better. This time she'd give in to impulse to kiss that strong, tan column.

The warm lips against his flesh stunned Alan. Rhonda had just leaned forward and touched his neck softly. It was the first time, she had initiated any loving. Taking Rhonda's face in his hands, he took her lips and kissed her soundly, sweetly.

"Does that mean you like the owner?" he asked gently.

"Yes. Very much," she whispered.

Just then the kettle started screaming. Alan turned off the stove and proceeded to make the Ovaltine. Rhonda poured the water into the mugs, while Alan replaced the ingredients he had just used; together they returned to the living room to gingerly sip the steaming beverage.

The quiet, charged atmosphere was unnerving him. He wanted to touch her; yet something was making him hold back. Everything was right: the place, the time, the mood. But he didn't want her to think he was taking advantage of the situation. He also knew that if he got started now, there was no way she was going home tonight. *You're getting senile in your old age, Alan ole pal,* he thought. *You're going to pass this up? . . . Shut up, you devil.*

"Alan, that woman I saw at your place, who is she?" Rhonda asked suddenly, startling him.

"Nadine, why?" Puzzlement creased his brow. He got up and put down the empty cup on a side table.

"Is she the Nadine everybody in the office talks about?" Rhonda asked, looking up intently at him.

"The people in the office know about her?" Alan asked in disbelief, his hands stuck deep in his pant's side pockets.

"You'd be surprised at what they don't know." Rhonda chuckled ironically.

"When did you know that you were taking her to the airport that Sunday?" Rhonda continued, no longer smiling.

"What? Airport? Wuh you talking 'bout?" He was genuinely confused and it showed. Alan sat back down on the couch, giving Rhonda his full attention.

"The Sunday morning after we made love. Did you know when we were together that you were going to the airport the next day?" There was a slight tremor to her voice, but she was determined to find out the truth tonight.

"No. She called me that morning when I was trying to get some sleep at my place and woke me up as a matter of fact. She'd lost her ride, asked me to take her. Why?" he paused, his mind rushing to put the pieces together. "Wait a minute. How do you know all this?" he asked, concerned that something important was happening and he was missing it.

Rhonda took a deep, stilling breath in order to gather her courage. She had to clear the air, she had to know. "Because I saw you together while I was picking Richard up—New York is smaller than everyone thinks it is, isn't it? I thought you were supposed to be fixing your aunt's pipe." Some of the hardness and anger she still felt crept into her voice.

"I was. I did in the afternoon after I dropped Nadine off at Kennedy." Something was going on, but Alan wasn't sure what.

"So you didn't know before hand you were taking her to the airport?" Rhonda persisted, a need to know, absolutely, goading her.

"No. . . What is this? Wait. I get it. You thought I lied to you. The morning after we make wonderful love, I'm off somewhere with another woman and really not at my aunt's house like I said

I would be, that's what you thought, isn't it?" Alan stood up once again, no longer relaxed.

So that's why she was so cold afterwards. And I thought it was because of the way I had mishandled the whole derailment thing, and my jealousy. Now I understand, he thought.

Rhonda didn't answer. She really didn't have to. She simply sat with a bowed head.

"Rhonda, come here," Alan said, with a hand extended toward her.

Rhonda rose and put her right hand in his. He took her other hand as well, but her head remained lowered.

"Look at me," Alan said firmly.

Rhonda raised her head and let her dark eyes meet Alan's serious brown gaze. A tightness had formed around his mouth.

"Let's get something straight, right now. I'm not a liar. You should know that by now. I keep my mouth shut before I tell lies. You're just going to have to learn to trust me if we're going to have anything together." Alan squeezed her hands, tightly, communicating his insistence. "Is that clear?"

"Yes," Rhonda whispered, lowering her eyes once again.

"No. Look at me. I ain't vex with you, just a little disappointed. I can understand your doubts, especially after what we had just shared. It's new to you. It's new to me. We'll just have to take it one day at a time, but you've got to learn to trust me, OK?" Alan stated, clutching both of her hands with the gravity of his request.

"Yes sir," Rhonda replied a little shamefacedly, wishing to lighten the atmosphere.

"Now that we got out of the way, I think you should head home before it gets too late. I don't like the idea of you driving at this time of night."

"Don't worry. I'll be fine. But you're right, I should go home."

Alan took the mugs to the kitchen and returned to escort Rhonda to the door.

"I enjoyed having you over. Thanks for coming." He bent his head and kissed Rhonda on her forehead, then the tip of her nose.

He wasn't touching those luscious lips with a ten-foot pole, or all noble notions would be lost forever.

"Thanks for inviting me. The food was great. You're a good cook, I must admit."

Rhonda looked up at him, the yearning she felt clearly written in her eyes. *It's really not that late,* they seemed to imply.

Alan bite down on his lip, hard. "Good night," he whispered. "And drive safely." He unlocked the door.

Rhonda lowered her gaze. "Goodnight," she replied and left.

You're a fool Alan Hussein, a stupid fool, Alan thought as he leaned up against the door. *Now what are you going to do? Take a cold shower? No, I'm going to do dishes.*

ᔕ ᔕ ᔕ ᔕ

One Friday, Richard called Rhonda while she and Alan sat working in her office. Alan made no effort to hide the fact that he was openly listening to the conversation. Consequently, Rhonda felt uncomfortable and answered Richard in monosyllables. They made plans for a bus ride on Saturday, and Richard wanted an "OK" from her since he was spending the night at a friend's house. She wasn't surprised. He'd only slept on her couch four times since his arrival. Obviously, some woman was offering him a warm comfortable bed, which held no comparison to a cold couch.

Surprisingly, it didn't bother her that he was sleeping out. In fact, it made her life a whole lot easier. She didn't have to fight off tentacles at every turn. Once when she had been kidding around with him, he grabbed her and started kissing her. She didn't fight him; she had simply gone limp in his arms, refusing to respond physically. Finally, he had released her with a sigh of resignation. Some of Richard's previous charm had definitely worn off since his arrival. It was just a kiss, but his persistence, which had warmed her in the beginning, was rapidly grating on her nerves. There were even times when he got angry, and last week his frustration had sparked the first major fight of their relationship . . .

She had been at the kitchen counter preparing dinner when Richard walked up behind her and wrapped his hands around her middle. He had started nibbling her neck.

"Cut it out, Richard," Rhonda said, moving her head to the side. Richard ignored her and went on to attempt to lick her ear.

Turning around Rhonda pushed him away. "I said to stop. What is it with you?"

"No, the question is: What is it with you? You've been giving me the brush off ever since I got here. You wasn't that way in Barbados."

"Well. Barbados was vacation fun. But that's over now."

"Wuh you mean it over? You led me on."

"Lead you on? We shared one, maybe two kisses. Richard, two kisses don't make a relationship . There's a lot more to this business than fun and games."

"I can prove to you how good it can be Rhonda," he said.

"I'm not interested. I laid down the rules when I picked you up at the airport."

"Rules, my ass. You just playing hard to get. I don't have to put up with that crap."

"I know. So, go. Go where yuh sleeping since yuh come."

He sneered and then slammed out of the apartment. Four hours later, he called. She was already asleep and the ringing phone woke her up.

"I'm sorry," he said. "I was out of line."

"Yes. You were."

"I'm really sorry." Richard paused. "Can I still stay with you?" he asked timidly.

Rhonda sighed, "We're friends, Richard—just don't abuse the friendship."

"Alright!" he exclaimed excitedly, only to catch himself and murmur, "No, I won't," humbly into her ear. "Thanks."

Richard kept his word. Unfortunately, the fights didn't stop there; lately, their major area of disagreement was about his sloppiness. She was sick of his clothes and garbage all over the apartment.

"You know, you're becoming a real pain in the rear," he had complained angrily as he sat in the couch, guzzling a beer.

"I'm not your maid. You don't like it, you get out and find somewhere else to stay."

Richard hadn't pursue it. His vacation wasn't going at all the way he had planned it. He had come with one goal in mind: To bed that short hair, light-skinned beauty. Something had changed and he wasn't turning her on. He had got up and left, saying. "Don't worry. I'll be out of your hair in a few days."

❧ ❧ ❧ ❧

"Rhonda, who was that?" Alan asked as she hung up the telephone and returned to earth.

She hesitated, tempted to give him a fight, but she knew it would be useless. Richard's presence stood between them like the Rock of Gibraltar.

"Richard," she answered, finally.

"The same 'Richard' that is staying in your apartment?" He couldn't hide the disapproval in his tone.

"Yes." The temptation to fight him grew stronger. He stoked her temper.

"Once before you said you and he were friends. Is that still true?"

"Yes."

"You sleeping with him?"

She hesitated, but only to gain control of blazing anger, but the control was beyond her. Alan didn't realize that he was leaning forward, holding his breath and dreading her answer.

"That's none of your damn business."

"I making it my business. Are you?"

Should she answer him? She didn't know. Stalling and evading the question was childish. Answering it honestly would reveal more than she wanted. Lying to him was deceitful, and she no longer wanted to hide behind her lies. Besides, he always knew when she was lying.

"No."

Alan relaxed. He settled back into the chair.

Well. So much for that, Rhonda thought. *You'd think we were talking about the weather.*

They worked together for the remainder of the morning. Normally, he would return to his office to work more comfortably; but today, he put his feet up on her desk and edited the material for upcoming issues. It took Rhonda a few minutes to relax, but once she did, he became nonexistent. At one point, Alan glanced up to see her sitting sideways, her legs hanging over one arm of the chair. He smiled. It was a comforting picture. A long time later, a loud growl broke the silence.

"What the hell was that?" Alan asked.

"My stomach. The worms are hungry."

"Jez. Better feed them before they decide to attack me."

They went out to a nearby coffee shop for lunch. They ate silently for the most part, periodically touching on general topics or discussing the magazine. Rhonda was drinking the last of her pineapple juice, when out of the blue, Alan attacked.

"Why he staying in your apartment?"

She moved too quickly, and her juice spilled onto her blouse. A few drops dribbled down her chin. He calmly handed her a napkin to mop up the mess, while waiting patiently for her answer. She wasn't angry anymore. She just felt numb, cold inside. He demanded so much from her and offered nothing in return. She was tired of it. Dead tired.

Alan noticed the change in her face immediately. It reminded him of the expression on her face the morning after the derailment. Something about that made him very uneasy, but he didn't know what to make of it.

"I'm sick and tired of you prying into my life. I don't ask you the kind of questions you always asking me. Leave me alone."

"No. . .I can't," he said bluntly.

"Then stop demanding to know every single thing I do."

Am I really demanding? Was it wrong to want to know everything about her? What she did, who she saw. What she did at night. My God, I am becoming obsessed with the woman, he realized.

The more he tried to get to her, the farther away she backed off, putting up hurdles all the way. He knew he had backed her against a wall. She had nowhere else to go and would destroy him if he got any closer. But he was stronger. *I could make her give in—I'd done it before*, Alan shook his head in denial, *No, the thought doesn't appeal to me. I want her to come willingly to me. So I'll leave her alone for the moment. Yes, something wasn't right. I have to find out what it is. Richard?* a grimace crossed his distinctive features because the mere thought or mention of the man incensed him. *I'm afraid to ask her flat out if she loves the man. I can't deal with the answer, yet. And although I don't quite know where I fit in, I know that I don't want any other man in her life. Ever.*

They ended their lunch silently after her last comment. Back at the office, Alan settled into the chair that he had vacated earlier. He worked quietly, not disturbing her. At the end of the day he insisted on riding home with her.

Something has changed in our relationship, Rhonda admitted to herself. *That one conversation established the stakes, somehow.* She could feel its rippling effects, but as is the case with an earthquake, she couldn't quite calculate the end of the aftershocks.

CHAPTER ✣ NINE

*T*he bus ride was a blast. What Rhonda thought would just be a few close friends of Richard turned out to be a group of thirty following a steelband's bus ride. Seven car loads made their way to Island Beach State Park in New Jersey. The park was huge: Acres of trees and soft grass provided the perfect getaway for those who had worked hard all week. They put five picnic tables close together, stacked them with goodies, lit the three grills and soon had chicken, ribs and burgers puffing fragrant barbecued smoke into the air.

They were a noisy bunch, talking loudly over the blast of calypso and reggae coming from a huge radio/cassette recorder. Richard was busy trying to arrange card games, cricket and volley ball, making sure that everyone was having a good time. Rhonda enjoyed the laughter and fun for a while, then sought some peace and quiet. It was always like that. In the midst of festivities, she would suddenly feel depressed.

After a while the need to be alone with her private thoughts surfaced and she found herself walking away from the fun-lovers towards the beach. The soothing roll of the waves called to her and the rocks beckoned. She crossed them cautiously, going farthest away from anyone seeking the same solitude. She sat down and cupped her chin, letting the sound and smell of the sea serve as a welcome balm.

Occasionally, a wave would break on the rocks and its spray would sprinkle her face and arms. Even so, she regretted forgetting her notebook and pen. As always the sea inspired her, for it gently exposed emotions, impressions, and memories that she had kept buried within. But she didn't fret about it for long, and allowed the sea to work its magic.

After an hour, a pain in her buttocks from the hardness of the rock and a gnawing in her stomach told her it was time to go back. She rubbed toasted arms and became aware of the sun's burn for the first time. She walked slowly back to the group, only to find that almost everyone was playing one game or another. Some new people had arrived while she had been gone, and her steps faltered as she recognized a familiar voice. Alan was among the newcomers. *Small world*, she thought, *a very, very small world.*

She tried desperately to avoid a detailed examination of his appearance, but found it impossible.

Her eyes were drawn immediately to his hairy muscular legs, outstanding in the white, wide-leg shorts that fell a little above the knees. Today, he opted for dark brown Loafers, no socks; his feet looked vulnerable in their nakedness. It was hard to believe those same legs and feet had swept hers with gentle caresses. He was wearing a loose-fitting salmon-colored shirt, but it didn't hide the wide breadth of his shoulders. His hair had started to grow back and the riot of curls reminded Rhonda of the first time she saw him, that boyishness softening those masculine features. The summer sun had darkened his spice-colored skin and the warmth and sensuality it radiated increased two-fold. There was no getting away from it. She got a thrill just looking at him. She found the natural flare to his nostrils, sexy, as strange as that may seem. She had difficulty looking into those light brown eyes for any length of time. Whether searing or soothing, the effect of those eyes was the same: devastating. But those lips were her downfall: Full, wide, lightly pink and oh so heavenly to kiss. *You'd better cool it, Rhonda; you're starting something you can't finish.*

Nadine is probably here with him, Rhonda concluded, deliberately dousing the sensual musings. Her guess was proved correct when said femme fatale giggled a high-pitched squeal while one of Richard's friends apparently flirted. Alan seemed unconcerned, his eyes wandering the crowd for any familiar faces as he piled a paper plate up with goodies from the barbecue grill.

Rhonda, how are you going to get out of this one? she asked herself. *It is only a matter of time before. . . .*

Once his eyes found hers, they didn't leave her until she came right up to him with a plate in her hand. By this time, he was already standing there with a plate already filled—he had patiently waited by the food, knowing that it was only a matter of time before her stomach would force her to stroll over. He watched intently as she placed two pieces of barbecue chicken on her plate, next to beef pelau and potato salad.

"Come sit with me," he said.

Nadine had moved away from the potential conquest and was now sitting with a group of friends—her mind quivering with the need for gossip, and was disinterested in filling her body with food. Rhonda observed the quick glance she threw at them as they made their way to an empty table farther away. She had forgotten to ask him why he hadn't introduced them before. She had been too busy trying to find out if he had lied to her . . . They sat down quietly, and each proceeded to satisfy the void in their respective stomachs. Alan hadn't eaten breakfast that morning and practically attacked his food. Rhonda wasn't far behind. Before they got around to finally talking to each other, Richard was approaching their table.

"You disappeared on me. Where were you?" he addressed Rhonda, ignoring Alan.

"Richard, this is my boss Alan Hussein. Alan, Richard Manning," Rhonda introduced the men. They shook hands civilly. Richard returned his attention to Rhonda.

"So where were you?" he asked, sliding onto the bench opposite the couple; his eyes squinting as the sun shone into his face.

Alan disliked the proprietary tone of his question. He was tempted to tell him it was none of his business where Rhonda spent her time.

"Relaxing on the jetty. Why?" Rhonda asked looking into Richard's dark eyes, and for the first time, she noticed their change to a black tone when he became serious. She had never seen such a grave look on his face before.

"Just wondered, that's all. Come play volleyball with us. We need another person," Richard said with a smile that didn't quite reach those dark eyes.

"I'm not in the mood." Rhonda replied, slightly annoyed and not really knowing why.

He shrugged, sensing tension in the air. He looked from one to the other, noticing that they sat close together. The body language of both—they were turned to face each other, their backs angled as if to shut out the rest of the world—indicated that they obviously wanted to be alone.

Well, Richard, my boy, how do you feel about that? he wondered. Rhonda was special to him. He cared deeply about her. When he was ready, she'd be the kind of wife he would choose. But he wasn't ready for that kind of commitment yet, or was he? For the past few weeks he had partied and loved women to his heart's content; but he wasn't satisfied. Right now there were three women bidding for the night with him, but he didn't really care about any of them. In fact, he had planned to spend the evening with Rhonda. He had often wondered why she never seemed to mind his sleeping out with other women. He was leaving tomorrow and had to find out where their relationship stood. He had a strange premonition he wouldn't have much say about her final judgement—he had run out of time.

"I'm saving a seat next to me for you later. Alright? So don't disappear on me." Richard said, smiling at Rhonda.

Throughout the entire exchange, Alan sat quietly, looking at the plate of chicken bones in front of him. A muscle started to throb along the rigid line of his jaw.

Richard got up and extended his hand to Alan, who returned the challenge with a handshake that was firmer, more determined. After Richard's departure, neither Alan or Rhonda attempted a conversation immediately. Rhonda was busy trying to control her body's reaction to Alan's nearness.

Alan was suppressing a desire to run after Richard and punch him in the face. A good old-fashion duel would suit him fine right now. *Richard is a handsome man*, he admitted, grudgingly, and would probably give him a good workout. He hadn't overlooked the man's muscular, powerful frame. *Damn it. I have competition, real competition.* The man cared about Rhonda, he could see that, but no way as deeply as he did. He knew that too, but could she see that? He wasn't the type to back down from a challenge. In fact, the scent of the race excited him. Besides, his future was at stake here, and there was no way in hell he was giving her up without a fight. *Are you listening to yourself Hussein? What are you saying? I love her. I can't hide from myself anymore. I'm in love with this woman.*

"So that's the famous Richard, huh?" Alan's voice was hard, cold, as he looked Rhonda full in the face.

As usual, he irritated her with his line of questioning.

"Yes. That's Richard." She returned his stare. Her answer was totally devoid of any emotion.

"Attractive man. Seems decent, too. He doesn't love you enough." Alan lowered his eyes to the plate in front of him. He couldn't look at her. The emotions were too raw, and he was afraid they would show in his face.

Now where did that come from? How am I supposed to respond to that? she wondered. Already, Rhonda was getting warm, very warm. *Boy, does he make me mad.*

"Run that by me again?" she asked.

"Richard doesn't love you the way you deserve to be loved, the way you should be loved," Alan said with his eyes still downcast.

"And what would you know about that?" Rhonda asked with her eyes straight ahead, unaware of the difficulty Alan was experiencing with his feelings.

This was it. The perfect opening to tell her that he loved her the way she was meant to be loved. Totally. But the words stuck in his throat. The revelation was too new. He hadn't had time to sort it out yet. For the first time in his adult life, he acknowledged that he was a coward, at least where Rhonda was concerned. *Why are men so afraid of rejection?* he silently asked himself.

"I could see that he cares about you. But it's not deep enough to sustain a long-lasting, strong relationship," Alan responded.

"You just met the man, for God's sake." Rhonda turned on him, her annoyance quite clear.

"Trust me, alright, trust me," Alan turned his sombre eyes on Rhonda, with the hint of a plea in his voice.

Rhonda was shocked by the intensity of his gaze. His light brown eyes begged for her understanding. Her stomach did a somersault at their softness, the slight vulnerability she saw there. She did trust his judgement, but what good did it do her?

"I didn't expect to see you here," she said, steering the conversation into safer channels.

"I hadn't planned on it. Nadine talked me into it. I guess she and Richard have mutual friends. I thought it might help me take my mind off
. . .things."

She didn't ask him what things since he obviously didn't want to talk about them.

"How come you didn't introduce me to her that day we met?"

"No particular reason. At the time, if you remember, I had other things on my mind."

"Would you like to meet her now?" Alan asked, innocently.

"No," Rhonda replied hurriedly. Inwardly she scolded herself for being a coward. They were silent. This new tension between them was extremely uncomfortable, but neither could come up with light conversation to clear the air.

"When is he leaving?" he asked bluntly.

"Excuse me," Rhonda said rising from the bench, ignoring his question.

Alan reached out, put a firm grip on her wrist and stalled her exit.

"You ain't going nowhere. Not before you answer me."

She pulled her wrist from his grip. It cost her because it hurt like hell.

Her strength surprised him. He'd forgotten she was in such good shape, well-conditioned. Rubbing her burning wrist, she turned on him, the flame of wild fury in her eyes.

He met her angry eyes, flame for flame.

"Listen *you*," she said rudely. "I'm not a child or any possession of yours that you can treat however you want. If you ever lay a hand on me again, I'll give you my knee where it hurts. So. . . " she said as she punctuated every word with an index finger jabbing his chest boldly, "don't. . . push. . . me."

What the hell is this? he thought. *This shrimp is threatening me. If I wasn't so angry I'd laugh.* And he did. He couldn't help it. It was ludicrous sitting here watching a whipper snapper of a woman threatening him with a knee, no less.

Does she really think she can get away with hitting me a second time? His shoulders shook with mirth.

With his head thrown back, white teeth gleaming, he was devastating. The man was too attractive for his own good. She was also so angry she could punch those same gleaming teeth right down his throat. She stood, impotent. Before he could stop her, she skirted the bench and moved away from him.

Maneuvering her way briskly and skillfully between running bodies and toddling children, Rhonda headed for the jetty once again. She should have never left her haven. The tide had risen. Now splashes of water spotted her thin white cotton blouse and navy blue shorts and trickled down her arms and legs. *Why does he affect me this way? I should really have nothing to do with him outside of work. He drives me crazy.*

But Alan, after waiting a scant five minutes for the sake of escaping the scrutiny of Nadine and the others, followed her angry departure at a more leisurely stroll. Turmoil had been painfully written all over Rhonda's face, and Alan had identified it plainly. He didn't want her to go off alone in that state, and it upset him that he was probably responsible for her misery. After catching up with her angry strides, he had hung back and silently watched her for several moments as she walked on the beach.

It was close to sunset and the golden rays of a dying day was expressed in a joyous proliferation of color: pastels of purple, red, and yellow, complimented the vivid orange of the setting sun. Water lovingly lapped at her bare feet as she discarded her sandals, her white shirt and blue shorts were kissed occasionally with the vibrant sprays of water as it leaped up from sharp rocks. Her face was turned towards the open sea, longing painting a wistful picture of homesickness on her face. She paid no heed to anyone else on the beach, and moved fluidly and silently toward the most secluded section of sand. She reached up and hastily brushed away what he imagined was a tear from her cheek as she sat down on a large boulder. The warm breeze moved off the water to softly finger her hair and face.

Alan approached cautiously, quietly attempting to gain her attention without startling her. Finally, he reached down and laid his hand on her shoulder. She flinched. It went right through him. But she didn't shrug him off, and that was a good sign. He sat directly behind her, his legs stretched out alongside the sides of her. Cupping the rounded curves of her shoulders with firm hands, he drew her back against his chest. His chin rested on her right shoulder. His face was warm, caressing her cheek.

"I'm sorry," he said.

Rhonda didn't know what to say. Minutes before, she had a world of angry epithets to throw at him. Now she was totally confused. His closeness was affecting her lower abdomen. He started to rub his cheek against hers. The rough, smooth texture made her skin tingle. Then he started kissing her: behind the ear, on the neck, on the cheek, tiny little kisses. He kissed the corner of her mouth.

I should stop allowing this, she thought. I should stop this teasing seduction. But it felt like it had been ages since he had touched her intimately like this. *Just one more gentle touch of the lips and I'll put a stop to this madness,* she promised.

Again, he teased the corner of her mouth. She turned, not sure whether her lips opened to scold him or give him easier access to her mouth. He took the initiative and captured her lips in a hungry kiss. With head thrown completely back against his shoulder, her throat exposed to the sun's warmth, Rhonda gave herself up to his plunder. Hot and wet, lips and tongues slithered against each other erotically. She raised both hands and pulled his head closer, much closer.

Although they were lost in the thrill of their kiss, the awkwardness of their sitting position forced them to stop. Alan released her mouth and she his head. He then ran his lips and tongue across the sun-kissed column of her throat. He wanted this woman, badly. One night of passionate loving had just whetted his appetite for her.

"Rhonda," he whispered. He didn't know what he wanted to say to her. There were no words to describe the tension in his arms that wanted to press her painfully close to his body, or that nagging ache in his groin. Now his heart had a song it wanted to sing to her and stage fright held him paralyzed.

She stood up to face him, placing her right hand on his shoulder for balance. She looked down at him; a sad smile outlining her lips.

"Let's stop this before we regret it, " she said to him. "Let's go home."

"No, Alan. This isn't working. I don't know what you want from me. And even if I did, I don't know if I can give it to you."

"I need you. . .in my arms, in my bed."

She shook her head, no, and moved away from him.

"Where you going?" he asked as she made her way across the rocks.

"To find Richard."

He never thought that three simple words could knock the wind from him like those words did. He'd be damned if he ran after any woman. Let her go to Richard. She was a fool if she thought he'd be a faithful lover. A man like him would run rings around an innocent like her; and she'd be so dizzy from the circles that a straight jacket wouldn't help her.

Alan watched as she made her way cautiously across the rocks, a grimace on his face. He decided to stay put for a while and calm down.

Rhonda met Richard sitting under a tree, guzzling a Guinness. Without moving the bottle from his lips, he patted the grass next to him, indicating she should sit. She sat, watching the gulping movement of his Adam's apple.

"Having a good time?" he asked after putting down the empty bottle next to him.

"Yes. It's fun. The food is great. . .Richard, we need to talk about us."

Panic set in. Now that he was being cornered about his feelings, he was afraid.

"What about us?" he asked.

"Well. I know we haven't been doing anything but fighting these last few days. And I think I'm to blame for the most part. When we met back in Barbados, I was out for a good time, just fun, not sex. I thought you understood. I'm sorry if I misled you. I'm not a tease."

Richard sighed, acceptance and resignation coloring his tone, "I know that now. I was so bent on getting you in bed I didn't listen. I'm sorry. I just didn't want to accept it. I hate to be corny, and I never, never thought I'd really mean it after having said this to many, many women, but, 'Can we still be friends?'"

"Of course. I don't hate you. You just have to learn to keep your hands to yourself when a woman says no."

"It's not always that easy," he moaned. "And for some reason it was extra hard with you. When I told you back then I was falling for you, it was a ploy to soften you up, but I think I almost got trapped in my own net. You're special to me." His brown eyes, earnest, sought the depths of her own to solemnly explain, "I want you to know that."

"You're special to me too. I hope one day you'll find someone who will make you stop all this running around."

"You're the only one who came close. So she'll have to be some woman." Richard looked up, a smile turning up the corners of his lush, full lips, "Nah. I'm not ready to settle down yet... One kiss, for old time's sake?"

She smiled at his carefree attitude towards life and nodded. Softly, he pressed his lips to hers. She allowed further probing as the soft warmth made him seek a deeper contact. It was a sweet good-bye kiss. In his mind, Richard had a moment's doubt that he'd made a mistake. But, for Rhonda, though the kiss was expertly administered, it lacked the fire of Alan's. She was only fooling herself if she pretended otherwise.

The kiss ended and Richard cupped her cheek lovingly, "I still have that seat next to me waiting for you, even though it's your car."

She laughed. "No. You go on. Spend your last night in style. . .but please, go easy on yuh back. . .don't overdo it."

They would always be good friends, and if time and place were different, they might have fallen in love. *It just wasn't meant to be*, Rhonda admitted sadly.

Richard helped her up and they made their way back to the center of activity. Thirsty, hungry players were raiding the coolers and grills. Alan was standing with one arm around Nadine, a Guinness stout in the other hand. He'd seen the kiss, she felt sure of it, for he was looking at her with anger and contempt. It hurt that he would condemn her, applying a different code of standard to her behavior as opposed to his own, but he would never know just how much his consistent double-standard bothered her. Rhonda decided to say good-bye to Richard and his friends and make her way to the parking lot.

As Alan watched her departure, the glow of the day seemed to dull. He had seen them kiss, and the jealousy was driving him crazy. Now as he turned to where Richard was playing one woman against the other while Rhonda left, he wanted to vomit. *The bastard had no right to treat Rhonda like this!* he fumed. He decided that he had had enough, and walked over to Nadine to tell her that he wanted to leave.

Rhonda was roaming the parking lot, attempting to locate her car when she saw them. The two were engrossed in conservation while they walked toward the far end of the huge lot, where many of the latecomers were parked. Nadine's hands were locked around Alan back and middle, while his right arm was thrown carelessly across her shoulders. She was smiling and whispering to him. Whatever she said amused him considerably for he threw his head back and laughed heartily.

Alright, Rhonda, cool it, she cautioned herself at the tightening of tense stomach muscles into a sharp knot. She didn't realize that she had clenched her fists into painful balls until she felt the sharpness of her nails biting into her palms. *Alright. I'm calm*, she thought.

No. I'm not calm, she moaned a minute later. *Seeing them together bothers me. It bothers me a lot.*

What are you saying? Are you jealous? inquired an inner voice.

Yes. Very, she answered honestly as she swallowed the bitterness quickly rising in her throat. She prayed they wouldn't see her. They didn't as they located Alan's car and opened the door to allow the trapped heat inside to cool down. Rhonda gave them five minutes before moving from behind a large, old Cadillac.

Damn. The car was still too hot for them to leave. She decided to chance it and ambled around some adjacent cars to reach her red Capri. Out of the corner of her eye, she saw him look her way with a start. He had seen her. Feeling foolish, but nonetheless justified, Rhonda crouched down, and ducked behind a brand new Mazda.

Alan kept his eyes focused to where he'd seen Rhonda. A few people passed by; she wasn't there. Maybe he hadn't really seen her. *If that is the case Alan ole' pal, then you have it bad—real bad*, he thought as he and Nadine gingerly got into the car, cranked down all the windows, and drove away.

At home, Rhonda finished Richard's packing for him. She felt restless and guilt made her feel as if she owed him that much. But she knew she didn't. *Maybe I'll go to a movie or something,* she thought. *Ah ha!* She had a discount voucher for the play *Fences*. She had been promising herself she'd go for a month now—tonight was the perfect night to go. Maybe it would distract her, and maybe force her mind off from thinking about men for a while.

But then, wasn't Billy Dee Williams in that play? Billy Dee Williams in the flesh. What a man!

                 ເ⩾ ⩾ ⩾ ⩾

En route to Nadine's apartment in the Bronx, Alan drove oblivious to the woman's warm hand running lightly over his thighs. He was thinking about Rhonda and the conversation they had at the picnic.

There is something about me that makes her close up and erect barriers. Yet when I touch her she opens up like flower. OK. So I am not the most tactful man around. And I have a nasty temper. But you can talk to me. I listen. She knows that. Why can't she be up-front with me? Tell me what's bothering her.

"Baby, you're extra quiet today. What's up?" Nadine asked, pausing in her caress.

Nadine's voice, fine, babyish, went well with her small frame. In the past, he had found it cute. Now for some reason, it grated on his nerves. *Maybe it's because I'm on edge.*

"Nothing," he answered, firmly.

"Are you sure? You haven't been yourself since the picnic—you were distracted," she added.

"I'm OK." Alan was abrupt. His voice stated quite clearly that the topic was closed.

There you go again. No tact. And she hasn't done you anything. She deserves better treatment than that.

"Don't worry Nadine. I'm just doing some heavy duty thinking, that's all." Alan turned to look at her, a slight smile gentling his face. She looked small and vulnerable in her yellow shorts and white shirt. But he knew that she was all woman and nowhere as soft as she looked or came off.

"Anything you want to talk about or I could help you with?" Nadine inquired as she resumed her caress of Alan's thigh.

"No, but thanks anyway." Alan took one hand from the steering wheel and patted the small, well-manicured hand.

As Alan's hand made contact with Nadine's skin, he remembered what he intended to do when he dropped her off and didn't relish the idea. Throughout the ride home, he would rehearse the words in his mind, but knew they probably wouldn't come out that way when the time came. His conviction was strong, because all he could think of was his love for Rhonda, her rejection of him for Richard, and Richard's sickening performance from woman to woman.

Inside Nadine's apartment Alan stood at the door, hesitant to really go any further. He wanted to get it over with and bolt.

"Aren't you coming in?" Nadine asked, heading into the apartment, and stopping when she realized that he wasn't following.

"No. I don't think I will." he said slowly.

Nadine came back, concern on her face.

"I want to break off our relationship," Alan announced bluntly.

"What? What are you talking about?" Nadine's brows drew together in shock at the suddenness of his statement.

"I want to end it, at least the sleeping together bit. We can be friends, still, if you want. But..." Alan stopped, unsure of how else to phrase his intent. He dug his hands farther into the pockets of his white shorts. His shoulders slumped dejectedly.

Surprisingly, tears sprang to Nadine's eyes and gripping her arms she turned her back to Alan.

Alan reached out and turned her to face him, gently. The shine of tears glimmered softly in her eyes.

"I'm sorry. I know this is kinda sudden, but...." He was having a hard time finishing his sentences.

"Why? Haven't I kept you happy?" Nadine asked sadly.

"Yes. You've been great, but. . . ."Alan didn't think he'd have such a hard time.

"It's that bitch, isn't it? The one I saw at your place and the picnic?" Anger replaced sorrow swiftly and Nadine faced Alan with clenched fists and fierce eyes.

"You use me and now you want to dump me like garbage." Nadine raised her hand to strike Alan, but he stopped the blow before it connected to his face.

"Listen. I'm sorry, but we both went into this with our eyes open. And if you remember, it was you who came on to me." He released her hand.

"But you sure didn't turn me away," Nadine sneered, hands on hips.

"Nadine, this doesn't have to end this way. I know you're upset and I may have even hurt you, but it was not intentional. It's not as if I'm the love of your life. You made it perfectly clear, you're married to no one."

There was a long silence as both inspected each other's face. Nadine's nostrils flared and she inhaled long, calming breaths.

"Fine," she announced rigidly, "To hell with you." She stifled a sob by covering her lipstick-smeared mouth, and while lowering her eyes, she moved slick fingers to stroke away a tear that had fallen, "Get out. There are plenty more where you came from. I don't need you."

Alan looked regretfully at Nadine and didn't say anything else. He turned and opened the door.

"To hell with you," Nadine shouted behind him and slammed the door.

Laying in bed that night, Alan told himself he had done the right thing. It wasn't fair to him or Nadine to continue with the charade. He was in love with someone else. The months they had spent together were good, but now it was over. He hadn't even slept with her since he made love with Rhonda. It was best. Even if it didn't work out with Rhonda it was the best thing to do.

CHAPTER ✤ TEN

*T*he following Monday was hectic because Murphy's Law was in prime form: Stories were too long or too short; deadlines were missed. In total, the day was a disaster. At seven o'clock, Rhonda gave in to her tired body. She put her feet up on her desk, heedless of her red skirt falling back to reveal her tan, satin thighs. She clasped her hands behind her head, closed her eyes and leaned back in her chair. It felt good to relax for a minute.

But the quiet was soon shattered, for Alan was in the room, seconds after a brief knock. *I should have known this moment of peace would be fragile.*

"Something is wrong with this story. It doesn't make sense," he bellowed.

She ignored his exasperation. At the sound of his voice, the headache that had been threatening all day came on full force.

Her posture stopped his tirade. He rarely accomplished anything when he tried to bully her, and he definitely couldn't fight her when she looked like that. So Alan took a queue from Rhonda; he sat down with his feet propped up on her desk.

"Have dinner with me, " he asked after a moment of silence.

"I know yuh hungry," he added when she didn't respond.

"I'm too tired to eat," she replied eventually.

"C'mon, then. I'll take you home. We'll deal with this mess in the morning."

She was reluctant to leave. Her head was pounding and she just didn't have the energy.

"In a minute," she said.

Alan left. When he returned, carrying a brown paper bag, she was dozing in the chair in the same position he had left her. He watched the outline of her breasts as they moved in a breathing motion underneath her black silk blouse. Clearing a space on the desk, Alan removed the boxes of Chinese food from the bag. He had even purchased a bottle of plum wine because he had felt festive for no particular reason. Maybe it had something to do with finding out over the weekend that Richard had returned to Barbados. Wickedly, he decided to place her favorite beneath her nose—shrimp in garlic sauce. The aroma was driving him crazy, but she didn't budge. As he was turning away, the low growl of her stomach stopped him. *Well I'll be damned*, he thought, *even when she's asleep her stomach has radar.*

"Rhonda, honey, wake up." Alan shook Rhonda gently.

Rhonda opened her eyes, commanding them to focus, twitching her nose and murmuring, "Chinese food."

"One track mind," he muttered.

Taking her feet down she settled down to the royal meal he laid out before her. When they were full, they put their feet back up on the desk and sat back. *Now I can handle him,* she groaned in satisfaction.

"Thanks for the food. It was good."

"No problem," he replied.

"I've been thinking," he continued. "Let's work on getting your poetry published. I'd like a break from this cut-and-dry stuff for a while. It would be the ideal thing for you, too."

His timing was uncanny. She'd been working on her poems like a maniac since their last blowup. She was wrapping up the final draft and was ready to attempt publishing the work. It would be her first if she got a publisher to take the risk. After all, poetry wasn't best seller material.

She smiled, her eyes still closed. This wasn't the first time their thoughts moved in union.

"How should we handle this?" she asked.

"How soon can you finish?"

"I'm doing the final draft now."

"Good. I know an agent who might be able to swing a really good deal for us. Give it to me when you're done. This time, the editor in me alone will read them."

She made a face at him, not moving from her original position. It was too much of an effort to move. She felt drugged from the food and wine. Without too much encouragement, she'd spend the night where she was.

Neither knew at what particular moment the atmosphere in the room changed; the quiet was now charged with electricity. Her heart and pulse beats quickened. Behind her closed eyes, a vivid impression of Alan's body on the night of their lovemaking loomed and the muscles in her belly tightened in response.

In reflection all the tiny details overlooked in the fervid activity came to the fore. Against hers, Alan's skin had been feverish, the hairy portions lightly grazing her softness; the lamp's dim yellow light had cast a glow on the cinnamon hue, making it even more tempting to touch and taste. The slightly salty tang wasn't unpleasant, quite savory in fact, as was his musky blend of perspiration and cologne. Fine stubble from the previously clean shaven cheeks and chin had scratched her face, breasts, belly, wherever he had coursed a path. Poised over her, Alan's face, solemn, devoid of all niceties, was an animalistic grimace of raw bliss. The spattering of dark moles stood out, dark, distinctive. His lips, swollen and reddened from her ravishing were opened slightly to expel an occasional hiss. Those sexy nostrils were widened still more by harsh, quickened breaths, the heavy blowing heightening her excitement. Creased thick eyebrows hung

over eyes darkened and made more striking by the man's arousal;
the black pupils, dilated, vanquished the irises and sucked Rhonda
into their bottomless depths. His black silken coils, tousled and
mussed by her agitated hands complemented the wild portrait of
Alan consumed by lust.

"Rhonda, " he called softly.

He had a sudden need to see her eyes, to see beyond the shell
she was encrusting around herself.

After the bus ride he had decided to cool it for while. He needed
time to adjust to the idea of loving her. He wasn't sure how she
really felt about him. They were good in bed. Wonderful, in fact.
But he wanted more than that from her. With Richard gone, there
was some room to maneuver. He had asked around about Richard
and what he heard confirmed his suspicions: The man was a
womanizer. He hoped that Rhonda knew that and wasn't setting
herself up for a fall. He was more concerned now with where he
stood with her, where he fit in her life. And he didn't know how
to approach her about this sensitive issue.

He suspected, at that moment, that she was sexually aware of
him, and of the urgency he was experiencing. Alan glanced down
at her throat where a pulse was beating in time with the throbbing
of his body.

"Rhonda," he repeated when she didn't respond to his request.

His voice scared and thrilled her at the same time. It was
vibrantly hoarse with the need that she had surrendered to once
before. She had very little resistance when it came to his touch,
and she would find it difficult to continually resist this man. Now,
she felt her body reaching out to him and she was powerless. Her
eyes, which were laden before, blinked open and locked with his.
What is it you want? they begged him.

I need you, his replied. She closed her eyes again. It was too
much, this intensity, too much.

The shock of his touch on her thigh jerked sleepy eyes wide
open. She hadn't heard him rise out of the chair. Now he was
kneeling, looking across at her, his eyes fiery with arousal. His

hand was burning a hole in her flesh. Never taking his eyes from hers, Alan attacked the encasement of her heart like he'd never done before. He passed a hand along her thigh, pushing her skirt farther upwards and out of the way. Then he palmed the core of her womanhood, firmly, sweetly; and she could feel liquid fire rushing to meet his hand.

Rhonda closed her eyes against his assault, her hands gripping the arms of the chair. He moved, but his hand didn't. Within moments, she could smell his warm wine-laced breath as he opened his mouth to gather a sensitive earlobe within its depths. Her fingers sank deeper into the leather of the chair's arm, for his magic was working its way into her bones. *Stop this craziness*, her mind screamed. But Alan's other hand gripped the back of her head and his mouth claimed moist, open lips before she could obey her mind's command.

Moving in circles, his mouth licked and stroked her lips and tongue alternately, willing her to respond in kind. He rubbed his hand against her forcing her to open her legs wider to give him easier access. His kiss deepened at her acquiescence and her hands left the leather to caress far more pleasurable territory: his shoulders, his neck, his soft curly hair were all thrills to sensitive fingertips. They were lost in the heat of the moment consuming them.

Gradually, she became aware of the beginning of his withdrawal. Her body cried out in disappointment.

"Close yuh legs, hussy," he whispered hoarsely. "Yuh want the cleaning woman to find us like this?"

Only then did the close whirr of a vacuum cleaner penetrate her foggy mind. He was busy straightening her skirt while she tried to compose herself. She was afraid to look at him. He kissed her briefly on the lips and stood. The turbulence was momentarily at bay, and so she rose also.

"I think I'd better go home," she commented, her restless eyes carefully avoiding his own.

Placing his hand under her chin, Alan raised her head to look deep into her soul. She shivered inwardly at his penetration. His eyes probed and searched. *Don't fight me*, they warned. *Why are you so afraid?* If he had spoken aloud, the question couldn't have been any clearer.

"Yes, you should go home," he said, as he released her.

He drove her home. And when the ritual of checking her apartment was over, he kissed her good-bye, with the parting words, "You have nothing to fear from me."

"That's what you think," she murmured to the dark as she settled down under the sheets. Sleep was elusive, her body frustrated from lack of fulfillment. In an effort to recapture those heated moments she had spent with Alan, she reached down and timidly placed a hand on the area he had fondled, wondering at the chemistry of a simple touch, the chemistry of sexual attraction. Forcing her thoughts away from Alan, she conjured up a picture of pounding sea waves in an attempt to relax her knotted body. It worked eventually and she drifted off into a fitful sleep.

ૐ ૐ ૐ ૐ

For the next few weeks, outside of regular work, they concentrated on whipping her poetry into shape. The editor in Alan, slashed, reworded, and reorganized. Many times it felt like he was brutally destroying her very soul. Arguments raged long and hard between them. With her new found strength and confidence she defended every word, every image. Sometimes she won; sometimes she lost. But the damage from losing went way beyond her writer's ego.

The fight over one particular piece would always be prominent in her memory. *Slingbacks,* was a short prose piece which told of a 14-year-old girl's eagerness for adulthood being squelched by a domineering mother one Sunday evening. The young girl is severely reprimanded when she botches a meal her mother expects to be perfect. Daydreams of slingback shoes and lipstick are quickly replaced by hurt and humiliation.

"This is nonsense," Alan stated suddenly, standing up from his position beside Rhonda on the couch in his living room.

"You fooling yourself with this garbage," he added, hitting the sheet of paper in disdain. "She wanted to throw that pot of rice in her mother's face, didn't she?" he continued.

"No. She wanted to please her mother, make her happy, not hurt her." Rhonda defended, standing up also.

"Damn it. Tell the truth. She hated her mother at that moment. Didn't you? Didn't you want to hurt her like she hurt you?"

Rhonda hugged her body tightly and shook her head fiercely.

"Who said anything about me? This is a story for pete's sake."

"Com' on Rhonda," he said eating up the space between then in hungry, impatient strides.

"No," she cried out, unwilling to meet his piercing brown examination.

"Yes," Alan shouted, gripping her shoulders. "Let's stop the crap—this book is so personal, it's about you, your family, your hopes, your dreams, your pain, and your fear... Don't try to brush this off as just another project." Rhonda stood still, disbelief and fear freezing her body and face in a rigid stance, her arms locked in front of her in self-protection.

"Didn't you want to hurt her?" he continued, shaking Rhonda's taut body.

"Why do we have to get so personal? Can't we just. . ."

"No. . . " Alan insisted, "I need to get at the root of the work, the real meaning behind the words. What did you mean to say?"

"Alan, I don't want to . . ."

"What did you mean to say, Rhonda?" he probed. "Tell me. . ."

"Yes," came the first agonized whisper.

"I can't hear you," he said softly, lowering his ear to her face.

"Yes," she shouted, tears rolling down her cheeks.

"I can't hear you."

"Yes," she screamed. "Yes. Yes. I hated her sometimes. I hated her."

The tears and sobs were uncontrollable now. Her entire body

was crumbling in its pain. Alan's arms enveloped her. He rocked her, crooning soft words of comfort. He had removed the fragile scab from infested wounds and the pain flowed freely now. Alan drew Rhonda back to the couch so that they both could sit more comfortably. She cried helplessly against his shoulder, and he held her even closer.

"Shh, baby, it's alright."

"No."

"Yes. Yes. It's alright."

It was a long time before the hiccuping and heaving subsided. Rhonda sat snuggled close to Alan, her fingers releasing their death grip of his shirt collar. Embarrassment settled in as she became aware of his sodden shirt. On queue, he handled her his handkerchief to wipe her face and blow a runny nose.

"I'm sorry," she said softly when she could breathe almost regularly again.

"You have nothing to be sorry for."

"But I love her very much."

"I know. But a part of you hates her too. She can't be blamed for the type of life you had to live. I'm sure she had her reasons for raising you the way she did. Now that you're grown up and understand life a little better you should talk to her. Get these feelings out into the open. It ain't healthy to keep things bottled up inside," he advised, gazing down at her vulnerable, reddened eyes.

"She won't want to talk to me," Rhonda was quick to offer.

"You won't know that until you try. Your mother ain't the same person she was ten years ago."

"I'm sorry I forced that out of you that way. I could see something was missing; the true feeling and meaning was covered up. I didn't mean to hurt you this way." Alan said caressing her arm.

"You didn't know I'd react that way," she replied in a forgiving tone.

"C'mon. Let's get you home," Alan announced.

Rhonda buried herself farther into his warmth and comfort.

"No," she protested.

"Rhonda. . .Yuh asking for trouble. Let's go," he begged.

She disentangled herself reluctantly. Raising her eyes to his to communicate her gratitude, Rhonda discovered that Alan was fighting a desire to hold her longer—fighting the desire to make love to her. It was there in his eyes. But he knew now wasn't the time. She was too vulnerable right now, her entire psyche unbalanced by impressions of the past. If they made love now it would cause them to return to the confused, angry, uncommunicative days that marked the beginning of their relationship.

"You're very welcome," he said aloud.

She smiled, appreciating the quiet moments like these when they didn't need words to communicate a thought or feeling. It was amazing that after so much fighting that they had evolved to a point where they could be so in tune with one another.

Alan took Rhonda home and she went to bed. It was about ten o'clock. Six hours later she awoke with a start. She had been dreaming a particular recurring nightmare: She was in a school walking down the corridor looking for a bathroom, but each stall was filthy, and dirty water soiled the floor. She went from stall to stall looking in helplessly.

Lying there in the dark, she wondered at the significance of the dream. She had had it so many times over the years. Insecurity? A lack of self esteem? What was she constantly searching for? Her father? That's farfetched and you're no psychologist, she teased herself.

Once the thought of her father occurred to her, there was no getting away from it. And with thoughts of him came thoughts of the article on illegitimacy that she still hadn't completed.

"Are your parents married?" Alan had asked.

"No," she answered, now.

"Don't know your father, do you?" had been his second question.

No, her brain screamed in reply. *No, I do not know my father. All*

I have is a name and snatches of accusations—Oh, he ain't no good. . . He got women all over the place. . . God knows how many children he got... A woman don't need a man like that.

"*Papa was a rolling stone. Wherever he laid his head was his home..*" The words and melody of the Temptations' song played in her head. *Rhonda, girl, you cracking up,* she thought.

"Who are you?" she whispered to a faceless entity in the dark. Other questions poured into her mind, questions that throughout the years she had kept at bay.

Where are you? Where were you when I graduated from Queens College and UWI? Not even a letter, a postcard, a hello, a question. Do you know if I'm alive? Do you care?

That kind of thinking ain't gonna get that article written, girl, whispered an inner voice of practicality.

"I can't do this," she said aloud to the stillness of the room. The green light from the clock/radio that read 4:43 cast an eerie glow about the bed. In the crackling silence, her thoughts amplified, making her feel as if she was going mad.

You have to. Try not to think about the personal attachment. Think about all those other children raised by a mother alone or a grandmother or an aunt. Think about them. It isn't just you...Alright. Alright. I know it isn't just me, but why. . .why?

Rhonda got up and went to her typewriter. For fifteen minutes nothing came and she sat looking at the stark whiteness of the paper hanging over the roller. Then, placing her hands on the home keys she took a long deep breath and started typing. The words and the tears flowed together.

"Daddy, if you're out there come to me. I want to see you. I want to talk to you. I want to get to know you. . . ."

Rhonda stopped typing after those first words. Placing both palms over her eyes, she tried to control the emotions ripping through her. Inside, she felt like one jumbled mass and she shook her head in denial. But she knew she had to continue.

"Daddy, I wished you had known what a good girl I was, that I came first in English many times. Daddy I won lots of cups for running. . . Daddy, you would been so proud of me, but you were not there."

Rhonda stopped once again and reaching down pulled the neck of her night shirt up to wipe the tears from her cheeks and the liquid running from her nose. *Will I ever be over this need for my father? Will I ever stop wondering if having one really makes a difference?* She started typing again.

"These are the agonized thoughts of a young woman who, like many other young men and women, have grown up without a father. A large percentage of these youths are illegitimate and they live with either a mother or another family member—often a grandmother or an aunt. One can never answer all the questions attached to illegitimacy, but an examination of its many facets can only lead to a clearer understanding of why the condition is so rampant and what effect it has on its victims."

Once Rhonda got those opening paragraphs down, the rest followed like blood pouring from a wound. Eventually, the tears stopped and the writer's craft took over. She wrote and rewrote, and when she sat back blurry-eyed hours later, the sun was shining through the bedroom windows.

As she stumbled up from her chair, the crackling of balled-up paper under her feet testified to the many sheets she had discarded in frustration. *Thank God it's Saturday*, she thought as she made her way back to bed.

Rhonda slept most of the day. When she awoke it was twilight and almost time to return to bed, but although she was still tired, she wasn't sleepy. She decided she would heat up some leftovers for dinner and take a long, hot bath afterward.

In the tub, she wondered why Alan hadn't called. He had gotten into the habit of calling her every weekend. In the beginning they talked just about the magazine, but lately their conversations were more personal, more intimate. Maybe he was giving her time to heal after the *Slingbacks* episode. If only he knew how much more she'd gone through since then. Writing that article had been rough—emotionally she felt stripped and raw.

An hour later, as Rhonda sat under the covers leafing through the latest issue of *Essence*, the phone rang. It was not Alan. It was her mother calling to invite her to dinner on Sunday.

After yesterday's episode with Alan, I'm not so sure I am ready to face Ma just yet.

≈ ≈ ≈ ≈

When Alan reached home from dropping Rhonda off, he went straight to the den, made himself a gin and tonic, and sat down on the couch. Taking a big gulp from the glass, he relived the ordeal he'd just undergone.

He had no idea that Rhonda was carrying such pain around. He had suspected from the hurdles she put down every time he got too close, that she misgivings about being intimately involved. Oh, he wasn't talking about physical intimacy, rather he was thinking about emotional, personal intimacy. She would let a man get so close and no more.

When he had got on her case about the poem, he didn't think she would react so strongly. But she obviously had problems with her childhood and her mother. And he suspected there was a lot more, for he vividly recalled the shock and fear that had briefly crossed her face when he had asked her about her parents. It hadn't escaped his notice that she hadn't completed the rewrite on the illegitimacy article. He just hoped she would take him up on his offer and call him if she needed someone to talk to.

God, I feel so helpless. It pained him to see her wretched and torn like that, for she was a warm, caring person. *She deserves to be happy and at peace. If only she would realize that and let go the past.*

≈ ≈ ≈ ≈

Now that she was Mrs. Bentley, Deborah called Rhonda occasionally instead of three or four times a week. She was contented and that explained a great deal. But there was something nagging her that she could not quite put her finger on. All she could conclude was that it was linked to Sheila's letter.

Sheila had adopted an eleven-year-old girl "to ease the burden of old age" as she put it jokingly. She had also said, quite seriously, that Sonia reminded her of Rhonda at ten years old—all legs and just as nosy. She missed Rhonda over the years and felt a need to love and be loved by someone as affectionate and as lively as Rhonda was at that age. She didn't want a permanent relationship with any man. Men caused more problems than she was willing and able to deal with.

Deborah was happy for her sister. She had often teased her about being a lonely spinster, but she knew deep down Sheila would never allow herself to get lonely and her unmarried state was from choice, not lack of proposals. They were times she was jealous of Sheila's and Rhonda's relationship and had often berated Sheila for spoiling Rhonda, and for being too soft with her.

The old jealousy returned. Sheila was visiting with her adopted daughter. Although Deborah was eager to see her sister after not seeing her for nine months, a part of her wished she had stayed away. Sheila stirred up too many memories of the past.

Rhonda was ecstatic about the news of Sheila's visit as Deborah knew she would be. But Deborah was uneasy about this visit, for the feeling that she had reached a pivotal point in life and was hovering unsteadily at the edge, could not be shaken. And before she could prepare herself Sheila arrived. *My sista timing don' change,* Deborah sighed. *It always bad.*

Rhonda and Sheila hugged and squeezed each other beyond the pain of crushed ribs. With glistening eyes of joy, they pulled back to survey each other.

"Yuh lost weight," Sheila accused.

"You too."

"I can afford it. You can't. What's the matter?"

"Nothing...Who's this?" Rhonda asked, seeing the young girl standing, timidly, in the back of Sheila.

"Don't think yuh get away. Yuh still gotta tell me why yuh losing weight...This is Sonia, my daughter," Sheila said.

"Your what?" Rhonda stared, incredulously.

"Deborah ain't tell you. I adopted Sonia six months ago."

"I wanted to surprise you," Deborah said defensively before Rhonda could turn accusing eyes on her.

"Hi," Rhonda greeted, holding out her hand to the young girl. Sonia shyly placed her hands in Rhonda's. Dark brown eyes shone from a dark chocolate-colored round face. Her nose was wide, proud, and her lips full, with the soft innocence of an African child. Her hair was parted down the middle and two long plaits with white ribbons tied at the ends stuck out from the sides of her head. The pink and white cotton dress with short puffed sleeves, form-fitting blouse and wide billowy skirt was pretty, but did nothing for her lankiness.

Rhonda drew Sonia to the couch. They sat appraising each other. Although Sonia was bashful, curiosity put boldness in her stare.

" I heard a lot 'bout you," Sonia announced.

The drawl of her heavy Barbadian accent stirred Rhonda nostalgically. It was hard to believe she sounded like that, or use to sound just like that. Now everyone said she didn't have much of an accent, but when she got excited or was in the company of other West Indians she knew the tell-tale drawl was there.

"Oh yeah, like what?"

"Like the cups yuh win from running. Mummy got them all over de house. I like de big, big one the best. Mummy does shine it almost every day. Yuh think yuh could teach me to run like dat?" Sonia asked in a rush.

So, this is what it feels like to be a star—such adoration, Rhonda marveled as she gazed into the adoration radiating back her from coffee pupils. She allowed it to go to her head for a silly minute. God knows, the way I'm feeling lately, anything would make me feel good.

"You coming to live with us in New York?"

"Yes," the little girl replied eagerly.

"Auntie Sheila?" Rhonda spun around to inquire.

"I don't know. This place too fast. I don't wanna lose she in this mess," Sheila offered hesitantly.

"Please, Mummy," Sonia begged.

"We gon talk 'bout it later, Sonia," Sheila said firmly.

Rhonda saw the light die in her cousin's eyes; she felt her disappointment deeply. She had been there.

"Sonia. This is what we gon' do. We gon' go running every day that yuh here, alright?"

"Goodie," she said, perking up again.

Soon they all went in to dinner and the evening passed pleasantly. Harold spent the time trying to draw Sonia out of her bashfulness. But to no avail; the only people she openly talked to were her mother and Rhonda.

As time passed, Rhonda spent more time at her mother's home while Sheila and Sonia were visiting than she had in years. Deborah regretted that it took her sister to draw out Rhonda's warm, loving nature. She found that now that she had Harold, the desire for a close loving family unit was strong. Rhonda was her immediate family and she wanted to be close to her. As Deborah and Rhonda worked on dinner together in the kitchen one evening, Deborah spouted her jealousy.

"How come you only come over here when Sheila here?"

"Because she does make me feel comfortable," Rhonda replied after a long pause.

"And you don't feel comfortable 'round me?"

Rhonda's silence confirmed the worse. She continued to cut up the onions and tomatos for the salt fish.

"All my life I do my best to feed and clothe you, and you ain't comfortable 'round me," Deborah shook her head angrily. Sweat trickled down her face as she stirred the pot of hot puffing coo-coo on the stove.

"You spent so much time feeding and clothing me, you didn't have time to love me."

"Wuh you mean I didn't love you? You are my child, my only child. Who else I gon love?" Deborah's voice rose painfully; she stopped stirring the coo-coo. Rhonda's eyes filled with unshed tears.

"You don't understand Ma. Food and clothes important, yes, but so is a hug, a kiss. You never hugged me, not even once that I could remember, not even when I won a cup. I ran for you, too. But Auntie Sheila was the only one who loved me. She have all my cups. They ain't mean nothing to you, so you give them to her... You ain't know nothing 'bout loving nobody. If you treat my father the same way you treat me no wonder he left."

Deborah was furious. She couldn't believe what she was hearing. All those years she worked from dawn to dusk, and for what? Deborah put down the coo-coo stick and before Rhonda knew what was happening, Deborah had singed the right side of her face with a backhand slap.

"You don't talk to me like that. I couldn't talk to my mother so and I ain't tolerating it from you."

Rhonda raised an onion-coated hand to her cheek. The tears rolled down, unchecked now. She felt like she was going to burst from anger, humiliation and pain. With her face contorted and wet from crying, Rhonda faced her mother in disbelief.

Deborah had to get out. She needed some fresh air. She needed some oranges and bananas, too. A walk to the vegetable store would do.

Sheila found Rhonda huddled over the kitchen sink, trying hard to control her sobs and tears. She folded her to her ample bosom and rocked her gently like she had done so many times in the past. She didn't question Rhonda until the last shudder subsided.

"Now, now child, what's the matter?"

Rhonda groaned, her nose stuffed. "Ma and I had a quarrel."

"I never see you in this state before."

"I know. This was a bad one. She slapped me."

"What! Wuh you say to she?"

"I tell she ain't know nothing 'bout loving nobody and if that is the way she treat my father no wonder he left."

"That was a cruel thing to say. You don't really know yuh mother. When yuh father left she was the most miserable person to be 'round. She worked day and night nonstop and was always in a nasty mood. The only body she thought she had or needed was you and nobody was going to hurt you. She raise you to be strong, independent. She always use to say nobody ain't making a fool outta she daughter, not like Frank Garfield make a fool outta she."

"I guess between between the two of you, I came out all right, didn't I?" Rhonda squeezed her aunt tightly.

She had been blessed with two wonderful mothers and hadn't really acknowledged that blessing. Growing up with both her mother and father would have been ideal if they could've made it together, but they couldn't and didn't, and that was just a fact of life. Her mother could have found another man, someone to be her father, but she didn't want to take the chance of screwing up. Her daughter was too precious for that. Deborah knew who she was, her capabilities and limitations, and she hadn't wanted to take on the responsibility of someone else's shortcomings.

And although it was a bitter pill to swallow, Rhonda knew that if Frank Garfield really wanted to know his daughter he would have found a way. You can't force someone to love you. He just did not care enough. If he did, nothing would have stopped him from seeing her, caring for her, providing for her. Her mother never stopped doing any of these things. She could have abandoned her, given her to Sheila to raise. God knows, she wouldn't have had any argument there. But she cared enough, loved enough.

Ma just wasn't physical about expressing her love, Rhonda thought. Maybe after all this time they could learn to touch each other lovingly, without embarrassment, without tension. Rhonda hoped so. She was willing to give it try. She loved her mother very much; she just didn't know how to show it, how to share it with her because she had never been taught how.

But now I have to do it, and I have to do it well because I love another. I have to learn to trust in love.

🐸 🐸 🐸 🐸

When Deborah got off the bus in front of Harold's office, she stumbled momentarily. She hadn't planned on coming here. Even as she opened the door with the sign, "Harold Bentley, Vice President, Public Affairs," she wasn't quite sure how or why she was there.

"Hi, honey," Harold greeted his wife, kissing her briefly on the lips. "What strange wind blew you in here?"

When Deborah didn't respond immediately, Harold was sure that something was seriously wrong. He was so surprised and happy to see her that he hadn't paid any attention to the tightness surrounding her bare lips.

When Harold pulled back to look at his wife, he saw a face twisted with pain, eyes flooded with tears. But within seconds the eyes were dry with just a glimmer to indicate their recent turmoil. She swallowed her hurt once more. Her face relaxed and for the first time in years, she set out to share her pain with someone.

Miraculously, no emergencies needed his attention, so Harold drew his wife down to the couch with him and she told him the story. He listened quietly, patiently.

"There was nothing wrong with what you did. It was what you didn't do. Children need lots of attention and affection; it's important to their security and confidence. Rhonda had no concept of the big, bad world at that age and you forced her to be a grown up before she even knew what being a child meant. The reason why it's such a big deal now is because she's in love. And since she has had such a negative view of love from the only person she had ever wanted to love her, she's in a tizzy. She's not sure what it entails, whether to trust it or herself. She's afraid to love a man because you've taught her men can't be trusted." Harold said, patting his wife's shoulders.

"She's in love with who?" Deborah asked, the shock clearly written in her dark eyes.

"Alan Hussein."

"How you know that?" Deborah sat forward, out of the circle of Harold's arms.

"Ahh, my secret," he said tapping her on the nose.

Deborah smiled. She took her lecture well and surprised herself. She knew he was right, but had covered it up so well over the years; she had convinced herself that her way was the only way. Old rules are hard to unlearn. Her mother had never hugged her as a child.

Well, they say you're never too old to learn, girl, she thought. She prayed that it wasn't too late to mend all the painful feelings between Rhonda and herself. In many ways it was, but they still had a lot of tomorrows to work on it. And one of the first things she wanted to work on was Rhonda's feelings towards Alan Hussein.

ðǝ ðǝ ðǝ ðǝ

Rhonda left her mother's apartment soon after her talk with Sheila. She drove home and parked the red Capri, and then headed across the street to Prospect Park. A walk was the next best comfort to sitting on the beach and she'd have to settle for that. As she retraced the steps she had shared with Alan weeks before, she allowed the revelation to take form: *I'm in love with Alan Hussein.*

Once she had accepted the fact that although she loved she didn't really knew how to show it, it was easier to understand why she went numb whenever Alan tried to probe. It also may have been why making love with Peter wasn't as wonderful as it should have been. She had loved Peter, but she had not been in love with Peter. It had been easy to accept Peter's love because it didn't threaten to overwhelm her with its power. She had been in control and had felt comfortable and independent.

However, Alan was a different story. Rhonda Baptiste had to fight for every ounce of her personal identity with him—he, and the emotions he inspired, threatened to seize control. Part of the problem was also not wanting to acknowledge that love for Alan. *You can't trust men; they ain't no good,* whispered the age-old, knowing voice.

It was a hard lesson to unlearn. All around her, she had seen men at their worst for most of her life. And loving a man meant some lack of control and she didn't like that. Always, she had to be in control.

I may as well admit it now: I'm fighting a losing battle, she thought as she continued to walk. *I have no control when it comes to Alan. One kiss and I'm a goner. . .I really do love him.*

Visions of him, holding her tenderly, comforting her without taking advantage in her weakest moments rose in her head. *I wish he was here with me. He's the only one who can help me through this. Since Peter, he's the only man who has taken the time to get to know me, even cared enough. But I can't burden him with this. I have to work it out for myself.*

When Rhonda returned home she decided to take the week's vacation she had left for the year. She needed to put her life and future into perspective. She left word of her intention on Alan's answering machine, telling him that if she hadn't heard from him by twelve o'clock, Saturday afternoon, she would assume it was alright and spend the afternoon putting her work in order. Sunday she planned to be sitting on a beach somewhere—anywhere.

CHAPTER ❧ ELEVEN

*O*n the third day into her vacation, Rhonda finally felt capable of planning her future. For two days, Rhonda had laid in Puerto Rico's sun, walked its beaches, and roamed the charming cobbled streets of old San Juan; oblivious to time and to the world. Luckily, no one bothered her; in fact, the people were gentle and warm. She swam and played in the sea by herself until her fingers were like shrivelled prunes, relishing the water's similarity to Barbados' but noting the difference in the color of the sand.

For the first time, Rhonda had even broken her personal safety rule of supplying travel information to the office or to someone at home; she had told no one where she was headed. Granted, it was a foolish thing to do since no one knew how to reach her if anything went wrong either at home or here in Puerto Rico. But for once she refused to worry about maybes. And it was absolute heaven. ESL Towers in San Juan wasn't a luxurious hotel, but it was affordable on such short notice and suited her fine.

"I'm going to quit my job." Rhonda said the words aloud to reduce the frightening impact. She wanted to start a magazine in Barbados, for it was time to return to her true home. New York was not for her, at least not in a permanent sense. She had dreamed of creating a magazine of her very own for years; yes, it was time for *Caribbean Woman*. She recognized that she and the concept for the magazine were both ready.

The idea of the magazine was timely she was sure, there was a market in the Caribbean and in the United States, but the drawback was money—her savings just wasn't enough. *Where can I get the money to get started?* she wondered.

When I get back, she resolved, *I'll talk to Harold, maybe he can help me.* She already had a few contacts for advertising in Barbados who were very interested in her idea.

What the hell am I going to do about a staff? God, what makes me think I can do this?... Think small...You're thinking too big. Start small and build. So what if you're the only one doing everything at first? That's the breaks for entrepreneurs. She laughed at the word entrepreneur tripping off her tongue. *Me. I can do it; I know I can.*

ख ख ख ख

Back in New York, Alan was sitting at home looking unseeingly at the television, a Guinness stout in one hand. He thought she would be back to work today, but she wasn't. A week was up and during that week, he avoided thinking about her because it enraged him: *How dare she take off without telling me where she was going? How dare she make me worry about whether she was alright?*

After some badgering, Harold had told him about the fight between Rhonda and her mother. He had forced her to face the truth and now she was somewhere hiding, nursing her pain. He could understand that, but what he had trouble understanding was his exclusion; he wanted to be with her, to hold her, comfort her.

"Damn it. How dare you?" he muttered to the empty room.

The next morning Alan was in the office at 7:30 sharp. He was sure she would be back and wanted to be there to greet her before everyone else arrived. If she didn't show up, he didn't what he would do.

He found her already at his desk, rifling through folders. She was so engrossed that she didn't hear him enter. When he barked, "What you doing at my desk?' she jumped, knocking a folder to the floor.

Alan laughed. Anger had fled at the first sight of her. Relief had washed over him like a cold glass of water on a searing fire—he could almost hear the sizzle of his anger as it cooled.

His laugh sounded so good, Rhonda thought as she savored the sound of the sweet rumble of mirth. Their eyes locked. *God. I missed him so much.* For days, she had to force thoughts of him away so that she could plan her venture carefully.

For long moments they stared at each other, the papers on Rhonda's lap lay on the floor forgotten. Alan felt rooted to the spot where he stood. It occurred to him, right then, that she had become so much a part of his life that he would have difficulty identifying the boundaries of their lives—he couldn't envision a future without her. The days he hadn't seen her rolled away, nonexistent. She looked so good, he wanted to run across the room, gather her into his arms, and rain kisses all over her face, neck and chest. But he wasn't sure how she'd respond to his impulse. He felt like he had to wait for her move before he made any of his own.

"I thought you had skipped the country," Alan said, grinning widely.

"I should have. This stuff is a mess." She smiled, almost timidly. A sudden shyness overtook her when he looked at her like that, so tenderly. The love she felt for him swelled inside her and she was afraid it would spill over into her eyes.

When she bent down to retrieve the papers, the intimacy was broken; a veil shrouding her eyes.

"Certain details are important to me. Others. . ." he shrugged. "That's your department. . .Let's have breakfast. I'll bring you up to date."

At breakfast, Alan curbed the desire—with difficulty—to question Rhonda about her trip and the reason for it. He had learned that badgering her and trying to overpower her independent nature drove her away. Rhonda didn't provide any openings either; she didn't bring up the trip.

Instead, they talked about *West Indian World*. No major disasters had occurred while she was gone. She was glad, for she wasn't quite ready to deal with any additional tension, and she needed the monotony of the job to help build her fortitude. He filled her in on one possible publisher who really liked her anthology and was quite sure it could be used in schools here and in the Caribbean. At the news, she cheered up considerably. At least something was going right. Maybe that was a sign.

The slight animation of her face at the news was the closest thing to happiness he had seen on her face since her reappearance. Alan had a premonition that all would not be right in his world in the near future. The hardness that he had glimpsed in her after the train derailment had increased twofold.

What the hell is going on in that head of yours? his brown eyes frequently questioned, but Rhonda seemed impervious to the momentary flashes of curiosity.

"Have dinner with me," he blurted out in his usual fashion.

"I'm sorry. I can't. I promised Ma and Harold I would come to dinner tonight."

"Tomorrow, then."

She shook her head. "I have other plans."

Alan felt a foreboding sense of anxiety flow over him, and tried to counsel himself to be patient. *What other plans could she possibly have? She's avoiding me for some reason. I can feel it.*

He wanted to push her, as always, but decided against it. He had to learn not to expect her to give in to his every demand. He would give her time to readjust to the routine, then they would talk. And they had to—very soon. There were too many things unsaid between them.

ता ता ता ता

Dinner at the Bentleys was strained for the first fifteen minutes. When Harold had called inviting Rhonda over on Tuesday night she had tried to get out of it, saying she had to catch up on some work at the office. But Harold had insisted, pointing out that she could not avoid her mother forever. They had to work things out.

Dinner got off to a bad start when Deborah, unable to contain herself, lashed into Rhonda for taking off and not telling anyone where she was going. Rhonda listened with buttoned lips, eyes downcast.

"How could you be so stupid... What if something did happen to you? Huh? How were we going to find you?" Deborah had yelled.

Harold, the peacemaker, had added softly, "Your mother is right. She was worried sick. But you're here now, so let's forget about it."

"No. We shouldn't forget about it. We deserve some kind of explanation. Just because she's a big woman now, don't mean she can get away with murder."

Still Rhonda was silent. She sat toying with a piece of baked chicken, with no appetite for either that or the pigeon peas and rice in front of her. She was in no mood for a war, but if her mother wanted to go at it, fine.

"Look, Ma. I'm sorry you were worried, but if I had to do it again, I'd probably do it the same way. I am a grown woman and I have to be allowed to make mistakes. You can't protect me all my life."

Rhonda faced her mother with a fire she hadn't dared show in the past. It would be some time before all the barriers were broken down.

"This ain't got nothing to do with overprotecting you. It's pure common sense and common courtesy. I raise you better than that. And I ain't gonna tolerate no disrespect from you."

"I am not being disrespectful. If you would stop thinking 'bout you for a change, you would see this had nothing to do with you. It was 'bout me. It was something I had to do, my way."

"OK. That's it. Stop this nonsense," Harold banged a closed fist on the table. The dinner ware rattled. Rhonda jumped, for her nerves were already stretched taut. They had forgotten about him. Both women turned to look at the new man in their lives. He was a force to be reckoned with, clenched fists and angry eyes.

Boy, he would have been some father, Rhonda thought. *My behind would have been in flames for some of the things I did.* For Deborah, the sight of her husband—angry, strong—was an unusual thrill. *A real man. I married a real man,* she thought proudly.

"I want the two of you to reach across the table, take each other's hands and squeeze tight. I want you to look into each other's eyes and let the love wash away all that resentment and pain. Go on," Harold said, crossing his hands against his chest.

It was long seconds before the two women moved simultaneously and reached out. The hands touched, embraced, and held, warm, firm. It took a little longer for the eyes to meet and hold, because the years of ill-feeling surfaced.

For the first time in her life, Rhonda faced her mother with the depth of her dislike unveiled, the disappointment, bitterness, and pain throughout the years shining clearly in her eyes. It shocked Deborah, a sick feeling thrusting itself into her body so sharply that she felt close to vomiting. But Deborah, after a hastily drawn breath, still held on and fought back. Underneath all the anger and bitterness, Rhonda felt ashamed of these malignant emotions that were appendages to the love and respect she did feel for the woman she called Ma. It was this thought that triggered the essence of her love for her mother. It rose from the depths of her spirit and shone from her eyes. The force of that love was even more overwhelming than the animosity.

Deborah felt doubly sick. *My baby, my beautiful baby girl. . . and I threw away the best years of watching her grow up.* She tried, but couldn't really remember Rhonda at seven, eleven, thirteen, sixteen. It seemed like all the memories were of dirty diapers, of slaving for money to buy food, school uniforms, text books.

What had happened to the time in between that? Deborah thought remorsefully. *Sheila could tell me. Lord, for me to have to depend on my sister for information about my daughter is ridiculous. But there is still time to show Rhonda the depth of a mother's love. And I will. Yes, I will— starting right now.*

"I lo. . ." Deborah's voiced cracked on the words, for never, never had it been expressed out loud. She cleared her throat on the second attempt, and her head and back reared up in pride, "I love. . . love you my beautiful daughter," Deborah whispered softly, her eyes shifting slightly to the side of Rhonda's head at the last moment. She closed her eyes, shook her head as if to clear it, and repeated the words, looking deep into Rhonda's eyes. "I love you." She then raised Rhonda's hands to her lips and kissed them, gently.

"I love you, too, Ma, " Rhonda replied, repeating the words they had never once said to each other.

And the tears fell. Rhonda saw her mother cry for the first time and it was her undoing. Soon they were both crying and laughing at the same time; their squeezing hands unable to convey the depth of their love. Unshed tears shone in Harold's eyes. He had been given the chance for a second family and he had no intention of letting that family fall apart.

"Come here, you two big babies," he said rising.

He gathered them to him, one at each side.

"Now stop this nonsense. It's enough to make a grown man cry."

ᴥ ᴥ ᴥ ᴥ

Rhonda handed Alan her article on illegitimacy that Friday after her return. She didn't wait around for any comments. She gave it to him, said goodnight and practically ran out the door. He was on the phone and couldn't waylay her.

He started reading even before he got off the phone. It was a great improvement. He had been waiting patiently for the rewrite, forcing himself not to push because the prodding would have influenced the outcome. It had to be her story. In the beginning he had wanted to see just how honest she could be with herself. He had no tolerance for dishonesty, no matter how minor. This personal bias accounted for his low tolerance for Rhonda's elusive quality—it got on his nerves every time Rhonda hid behind fibs or prevarications just to keep him from getting too close. Although that was still true, he was now more concerned about Rhonda's emotional state. The article, he knew, would give him some insight.

He also had a personal interest in the controversial issue because, like Rhonda, he was born out of wedlock. Alan Hussein was what Trinidadians called a carnival baby, a baby conceived during carnival time when rhythm, song, revelry and rum went to the head and groin of many.

His father, of Hindu descent, was a seaman on shore for two weeks. He had sat next to Eleanor Barker in a calypso tent and conversation and partying had led to steamy lovemaking within days. It was Eleanor's first love and she had given into the wild abandon she had been raised to curb. Hassan Hussein was a smooth, skilled lover whose love of the sea overpowered even his infatuation with Eleanor. He returned to sea and never once fulfilled his promise to write to her.

A month later Eleanor had discovered she was pregnant. She didn't know where or how to find Hassan so she decided to face the music alone. And boy, did it play. Granny had told him that the only thing Grandpa didn't do was skin his mother alive. He had wanted to, threatened to, but was forced to settle for cussing and carrying on instead.

Granny's disappointment in Eleanor had gone deep. She had told Eleanor that she'd better learn to control that hot blood of hers if she wanted to make anything of her life. And when Eleanor had continually dropped the baby off for one reason or another, Granny decided to take over. Alan was her grandson and she had no intention of letting Eleanor's instability affect his upbringing. At first, Eleanor resisted. She wanted to raise her child. And she would do it herself, despite the gossip and snickers behind her back.

But it had been hard. Eleanor couldn't work and take care of the baby at the same time. She asked her mother to keep him for six months until she had a steady job and could save up some money. "Doing what?" Granny had said. "I didn't send you to school so you could make fast money ironing nobody's clothes or baking bread in no bakery. You suppose to be studying to be a teacher, not chasing after men and a fast dollar, and with a child to mind."

Quarrelling and cussing had been a natural part of Alan's childhood and sometimes the only relief he got was from visits to Uncle Kenny down the street. Uncle Kenny, a close friend of the family, had been a retired school teacher who had never married and didn't have any children. He was a thin man, almost the color of tar, with white, cottony hair.

As a young boy, when he wasn't under the house or off somewhere playing with his friends, Alan lost himself in the rows and stacks of books in Uncle Kenny's home. There had been books of all shapes, sizes, for all ages, and in every condition from yellow with age and dust to stark white with the strong chemical smell of fresh ink. Driven by a hunger to know all, especially about the history of his people, Alan read everything from poetry to sociology to geography.

Next to reading, his greatest love was writing, and he had written voluminously. Often, until late in the evening, he would sit at Uncle Kenny's feet reading his stories. Uncle Kenny had sat in the shabby armchair and the occasional puck, puck, of his lips pulling on his pipe would be the only sign that he hadn't fallen asleep. On some evenings, they had worked at the kitchen table reorganizing and rewriting. Uncle Kenny was a hard task master. Although Alan had talent, Kenny was bent on making him the best he could be. And if at times, he was a little hard on Alan and forgot that he was just a boy, it was for his own good.

Many nights, Granny came to bring him home. She would watch from outside the window, as the muted orange light of the kerosine lamps cast eerie dark shadows on the ceiling and walls. It had warmed her heart to see her grandson there, out of harm's way, learning. She couldn't offer him much in the way of a formal education but she taught him all she knew about life and the soil. She had been a woman of the land and knew that if you took the time, you could find an answer to almost anything right there.

For Kenny, Alan was the son he never had and he poured all his love and knowledge into the boy. Alan brought happiness to his last, lonely years. There was no question that whatever he had would go to Alan when the good Lord was ready for him.

Kenny died a year after Granny died. When Granny died and he had moved to Port-of-Spain, his visits to Uncle Kenny became fewer, as he had joined a steelband. He had some regret that he had not spent more time with the old man during the last year of his life; but Kenny had understood. He had told him so when he had guiltily voiced his regrets for not coming more often.

"You're a young man now. I know you have other interests outside an old man like me. Now, tell me, them darkies still as nice as they use to be in my days?" Uncle Kenny had laughed slyly.

"Yes, Uncle Kenny. They even better than they were in your day," Alan returned and they had hugged each other like two old buddies.

At Kenny's funeral, when Alan helped lower the casket into the earth, snatches of Uncle Kenny's teachings had played in his head. "Son, don't ever think a hill is too high to climb. . . And never let anybody make you feel they better than you. . . Seek the truth always and tell the truth always. . . Know yuh history. Pass it on to yuh children and teach them to pass it on to their children."

At the time, although Alan was saddened and knew he would miss Uncle Kenny badly, he had so much of the old man within and around him, that he felt as if Uncle Kenny would never leave him.

With the inheritance he had received from Uncle Kenny, Alan went to college in England for six years and returned to Trinidad to start *The People's Voice* with an old friend, Sebastian Morgan. The weekly newspaper was popular with the people but not so popular with the government. Some politicians couldn't handle the truth and Alan had to fight attacks and attempts to close down the newspaper. But he had persisted because there was no way he was going to let dishonesty hurt his people. . .

Alan slowly drifted back to the present. Memories and spirits of the past floated around the room and goose pimples rose along his arms. The editor within him resurfaced and he refocused his attention on Rhonda's article. She had done her research well, exploring the sociological and economic aspects of the issue. She had even interviewed some parents and children. She had raised more questions than she had answered, but with a topic like this it was unavoidable. He too had questions of his own: *Why are there so many children born out of wedlock? Does the institution of marriage go against some natural inclination to make love without thought of the consequences?*

Realization sunk in and a pained groan shattered the silence of the room, *I did it with Rhonda, didn't I? No thought of the consequences, just the beauty of the moment. My mother and father did it. And people will continue to do it. Unless the people involved are responsible, it's just nature's way, I guess. Then why the stigma? Why, since it is so common among people, are the children made to feel and bear the shame? It doesn't make sense.*

But Alan knew there were no real answers to his questions. Life was made up of shades of gray, not black and white. The one thing he knew for certain was that people had to have a strong sense of responsibility to be any kind of decent human being. And although his heart ruled his head when it came to Rhonda, most of the time, nothing or no one would keep him from living up to his responsibilities if she should become pregnant. He wanted to marry her. There wasn't a question of that. Would she have him? That was the question.

Until I know for sure, I'd better play it safe. It's one thing to live up to your responsibilities, but when you're forced to do it on somebody else's time, that's another. No. I want to be able to put my child to sleep every night, kiss him awake in the morning, and spank his butt when he needs it.

And I want to share all of this with a wife—I'm not settling for anything else. And if that's being an idealist, then so be it, but I've experienced one of the alternatives, and I don't want any child of mine wondering about me. I want to claim my child.

Alan stopped his private musings and returned to the article. He could feel Rhonda's presence in the room. From the article he picked up the underlying yearning for her father and knew that it must have been hell to write the piece. Unlike her, he didn't have the same yearning, the same need to know. Grandpa and Uncle Kenny were all he had or ever needed. Those two strong men had fulfilled the role of father quite adequately. Sure, he was curious about the man whose physical traits he possessed, but it was a fleeting wonder, nothing more. He was sorry that Rhonda did not have an Uncle Kenny or a Grandpa in her life. It might have made all the difference.

How can I make her see that I understand? I understand so much now.

੨੪ ੨੪ ੨੪ ੨੪

Rhonda was hanging the kitchen towel when the phone rang. With the dishes out of the way she was about to take a shower and settle down for the evening.

"Hello," she answered.

"What are you doing?" Alan asked.

Rhonda hesitated before she replied. She'd had a feeling he would call tonight, but she wasn't ready to talk to him. And if he wanted another rewrite, he could do it himself because she had no intention of going through that again.

"Nothing," she replied lazily.

"Were you really doing nothing, or just giving me your usual pat answer?"

"Honestly. I just finish washing the dishes and was on my way to take a shower when the phone rang. Satisfied?"

"Yes. I liked your article," he blurted out. Silence reigned as he waited for her to respond.

"Oh. . ." she finally chimed, "And?"

"And I need to talk to you about some things. Can I come over?"

Rhonda breathed a heavy sigh, "I am *not* doing a rewrite. So if that's what you have in mind, forget it."

"Don't be so defensive. Don't you have any confidence in your abilities? You know you can do great work when you put your mind to it. The article is very good. "

"So what do you want to talk to me about?"

"You'll find out when I get there. Can I come over?"

"You're asking permission?" Rhonda asked in surprise.

"Yes, my dear. I'm a pretty fast learner. Well. . .Can I?"

Of course, you can come over. But I'm not sure if I can keep my hands off of you, she thought.

"OK. I should be out of the shower by the time you get here."

When Rhonda opened the door to Alan thirty minutes later, she was clothed in an ankle-length dashiki, colored in rust, gold, black and white. A towel was thrown around her shoulders to absorb the water still dripping from her hair.

"Hi. Come in." Rhonda smiled in greeting as feelings of warmth toward Alan bubbled up inside her.

Rhonda's scrubbed appearance and sweet soapy smell filled Alan's senses. He watched as a drop of water trickled down from Rhonda's hairline to her nose. As she reached up to wipe it away with the towel, he held her hand and stopped her. Reaching over, he licked away the water with the tip of his tongue. Rhonda watched mesmerized as he lowered his head again to remove yet another drop. Soon he gathered her to him and was licking away every glistening trickle before it made its way down Rhonda's face. The soft licks turned into gentle kisses to the cheek, the forehead, an ear, pliant lips, and before he knew what had hit him, Rhonda had pressed herself to him, returning his fervent probing with a zeal of her own.

When they separated minutes later, they were breathless from the attempt to consume the other.

"Hi," he whispered, against her lips. "Can I go out and come back in again?"

"No, silly," she laughed. "Let's go inside."

They walked hand in hand to living room. He refused her offer of a drink and instead requested a cushion for her to sit on while he dried her hair.

She started to object to the intimacy of his idea, but a certain rigid look in his eyes warned her not to make a big deal or deny him that small pleasure.

Rhonda sat on the floor between Alan's legs and gave herself up to the soothing massage of his fingers. He towel-dried and combed her hair with caring hands and no words were exchanged. Sexual currents laid quietly at rest and in their place a warm camaraderie ruled.

"Do you trust me?" Alan asked suddenly.

"Yes." Rhonda was surprised at her quick response. In the past, it was always easier to hedge and dodge the truth when he became personal.

"Enough to share your deepest feelings with me?"

"Yes," she replied, simply.

Rhonda was telling him the truth. He had no doubt about that and it meant a great deal to him. That was one major hurdle out of the way. If only he could get her to release the fear that he would suddenly become a man similar to her father; if only she would not wait for him to betray and abandon her. It was true he had never shared his feelings for her openly, but he had shown her in so many ways that he cared. And if she didn't know that the sight of her drove him crazy, then she was beyond hope.

"Why did you run away?"

Rhonda took a long time to add form to the myriad of emotions she experienced when she left for Puerto Rico. Somehow discarding the excess baggage she had carried around for years had left her bereft. It hadn't mattered that it was all crippling and she was better off without it. It had been a part of her for as long as she could remember and when it went, a part of her went with it. Puerto Rico was all about rebuilding, refurbishing her self esteem, her self worth. It was all about making herself whole again, in a more positive way.

"I was hurting, Alan. . . real bad. I had to get away from

everyone." She turned sideways to look up at him. "I felt unloved, humiliated. . . I wanted desperately to be held and loved by a man I'd never even seen."

Rhonda lowered her head. Her throat was one big ache. Unshed tears gathered behind her lowered lids. Alan placed fingers under her chin and raised her head once more.

"Don't look for love from ghosts. There are people here all around you who love you. And you're as worthy of that love as much as you think you're worth."

"I know." Rhonda sighed.

"Come up here," Alan said, helping Rhonda to his side on the couch.

Alan placed his arms around her and settled her in the comfort of his chest.

"I was so angry with you... Then I was so worried about you... to the point where I wasn't sleeping at night... Please don't ever do anything like that again."

Rhonda didn't know what to say. She felt like a naughty child being reprimanded, but gently.

"And remember what I told you. Anytime you need to talk to someone, anytime you're hurting like that again, call me. I'm here for you, always," Alan added.

Rhonda nodded. It was good to know she could depend on him, but she doubted she would turn to him in that way any time soon. She was still very much afraid of herself and her reaction to him. To admit a dependence on him for anything, anything at all left her wide open. And she wasn't ready to accept that, not yet. She still wanted to do things her way. She had to have that control.

"What was it you wanted to talk to me about?"

"We've been talking about it." Alan replied, stroking her arm.

"But this has nothing to do with the article," Rhonda returned.

"Yes it does. . .Have you ever tried to find your father?" Alan asked.

"No." she replied softly. He picked up the slight guilt in her voice.

"Why not?"

"Oh I don't know. Too many conflicting emotions I guess. Most of the time I was mad with him, hated him. I felt he didn't love me. Then I was afraid that if I did find him, he wouldn't want me and I didn't think I could deal with that rejection." Rhonda's hand around Alan's middle tensed.

"How do you feel now? Do you still want to see him?"

"I'll always want to just see him, at least once. But I don't really need him to be a part of my life anymore. I've come to terms with it."

They were silent after that, each deep in thought.

He was glad he had come over instead of just calling. He felt better being there, holding her. It gave him more assurance that she was alright. He would be able to see and feel if she wasn't. She had come a long way with him. It was the first time she had really opened up to him, and he suspected it had been very difficult to do. He was perhaps the only person she had ever shared these feelings with. He felt honored. There wasn't anything he could do to help her through this but to be there to listen and comfort if necessary.

And I don't plan on going anywhere, he realized. *You know, this is bloody nonsense. If we were married I could be right here all the time. None of this, make one move, watch and see, make another move. . . And God knows I hate leaving her to go home to an empty house. Wonder if she has any strong feelings about marriage?*

"Rhonda. . .Sweetie?"

Rhonda didn't respond. It was then Alan noticed that her breathing had become heavier, regular. She had fallen asleep and he didn't have the heart to wake her, but he guessed he had to.

"Rhonda, honey, wake up." He called her softly, still leery about disturbing her.

"Uhmm," Rhonda moaned sleepily, trying to make her body more comfortable. "Alan. . . Alan I love you," she slurred and settled further into his warmth.

Alan's heart leapt into his throat. Disbelief and joy battled for supremacy. *She didn't say that. I'm imagining things. No. She was dreaming, you idiot.*

"Rhonda," he said a little louder, shaking her. "Wake up."

She bolted up, disoriented, blinking her eyes.

"Wuh happen?" she asked, her voice scratchy with sleep.

"You fell asleep," Alan said, looking closely for any sign that she was lucid when she blurted out her love for him.

"I did? What time is it?" she asked looking around.

"Time for you to go to bed," he sighed in disappointment. "Come on, let me out and go to sleep."

"Oh. I'm sorry. I didn't mean to fall asleep on you like that. We were talking and then. . ."

"Don't worry about it. . .OK? I'm going. Goodnight," he said, getting up and helping her to her feet.

At the door, he kissed her gently on the forehead and left.

On the way home, he relived her declaration of love. He knew he shouldn't accept it; she was obviously dreaming. But he couldn't help but let his foolish heart hope a little, yearn a little.

Alan felt that it was time for a little conversation with God, after all, a little prayer never hurt anything, did it? *Oh God I love that woman dearly. Do you think she really loves me, just a little? Give me the courage to tell her soon. I pray that when I do she doesn't throw it back in my face.*

CHAPTER ❧ TWELVE

*R*honda got back into the routine of her job easily enough, but she lost patience quickly. The slightest drawback or mistake caused her to flare up. She lost her temper with the copyeditor once and with Alan twice over meaningless things in the two weeks since her return. He was puzzled at her behavior, but because he sensed that something outside of work was bothering her, he didn't react very strongly. In fact, he brushed off her tirades jokingly. But he came very close to losing his temper with her just before he left for home that Friday.

Rhonda stormed into Alan's office with an article in her hand on Dominica's efforts to improve farming in its mountainous terrain.

"Where's the section for the Dominica article you said you'd have ready days ago?"

"I'm still working on it," Alan responded, his head down, the top of the pencil in his mouth. He was editing another article.

"You know, this is really ridiculous. You should have finished it a long time ago," Rhonda announced nastily.

Alan lifted his head, eyebrows raised, eyes grave.

"I ran in to some problems with it. You'll have it soon. There is still time to work on it," he said slowly, carefully.

"Time for who? When you give it to me I still have to work on it. Then I'm the one stuck with getting it ready in time, " Rhonda shot back, the backs of her hands on her hips.

"Whoa. . . Wait a minute here. What's the matter with you? You've been very short-tempered lately." Alan got up and came around his desk to stand near Rhonda.

"I'm sick and tired of people not pulling their weight," Rhonda responded, hands still on hips.

"Listen, young lady, whatever tick you have up your behind you'd better get rid of it. I will not have you harassing my staff with your nasty attitude." Leaning on the desk with arms crossed against his chest, Alan faced Rhonda with flared nostrils and the tell-tale throb along the jawline.

"Now if something is bothering you and you want to talk about it, fine. Talk to me. But there's no need for this attitude," Alan continued.

Rhonda dropped her hands from her hips. As hot as she felt then, she was no match for Alan Hussein, incensed. She knew that. And although she would stand up to him or anyone when she had cause, she realized he was right. She had been very unreasonable the last few days. For some reason she couldn't control the irritability she felt with everyone and everything. Perhaps it had something to do with her decision to start her magazine and the fact that she loved Alan and didn't know what to do with it. She felt very disoriented and didn't quite know in which direction to turn.

"No. There's nothing I want to talk about. . .I think I'd better call it a day and deal with all this on Monday. Goodnight." Rhonda turned and headed out the adjoining door.

Alan, one hand in mid-air, intended to stop her, but thought better of it and said goodnight to her lovely retreating figure.

By Monday Rhonda was her old self again and Alan couldn't help but wonder what took place over the weekend. If Richard was still in town, that might have explained it, but he wasn't. Unless she had a new man in her life? He didn't think so.

If you don't do something soon, you're going to lose her. He hadn't called her during the weekend because he had felt that she needed space to work out whatever was bothering her. Besides that, he, Eddie and Wayne had to move Eddie's brother to New Jersey. So when he got home Sunday morning around four o'clock he was dead beat and slept most of Sunday.

That Monday afternoon, as soon as Alan hung up the phone from talking with Michael Ramdeen, the phone rang again. It was Harold Bentley.

"I know I'm the last person you expect to hear from at your office," Harold said laughingly when Alan realized who it was.

"You're right. Everything OK?"

"Yeah. No problems. I just called to talk to you about Rhonda's project."

"Rhonda's project?" Alan asked, eyebrows drawn together, puzzled.

"Yeah. You know. The magazine she wants to start back home in Barbados."

Alan want numb. A myriad of thoughts raced through his head at the same time. *A magazine. . . In Barbados. When did she decide this? How come she ain't tell me 'bout it?. . . When is she doing this?*

"Alan. . .Are you there?" Harold asked, concerned that he may have been disconnected.

"Yeah. I'm here. Just in shock, that's all."

"You mean you don't know anything about it?" Harold asked, in surprise.

"Nope. Not a damn thing." The feeling returned to his numb body and brain. Anger and disappointment formed like hard crystals in his chest.

"Well. I guess it's too late now. I already let the cat out. I'm sorry I was the one to tell you. . I thought she had told you."

"It's alright, Harold. . .What did you want to talk to me about?"

"I'm not so sure I should now. But what the heck? Rhonda approached me for a loan, but I don't have the full amount and I thought if you had it you might be interested in backing her as well. I know I'm the first person she's approached. And I thought she might not have approached you for money because of your working relationship, conflict of interest, you know," Harold explained.

"Sure. Money is not a problem. Rhonda can have anything I have if she wants it. In fact, I can probably finance the entire amount. Let's do it that way. Let her believe you're supplying the money until I can settle things," Alan decided.

"You sure you want to do that? The money is not a problem with me, you know, and when she finds out, she's going to be as mad as hell," Harold pointed out.

"No. Don't worry about it. I'll take care of it," Alan said.

Before they ended their conversation, they made arrangements on handling the loan and promised to keep each other informed of any new developments.

After putting down the phone, Alan sat back in the chair, his hands locked behind his head. He tried to find reasons for Rhonda not revealing her plans to start the magazine. He could understand the worry about the job. But they were more than just colleagues, or so he thought.

I thought we meant more to each other than that. How could she keep something this important from me? Maybe I'm jumping the gun here. Maybe she's still thinking things through and when they're more firmed up in her mind, she'll tell me. But still, something like that you share with the one closest to you, even if it's still a dream.

So what makes you think you're the one closest to her? Hmm? taunted a nasty voice.

Oh hell, Alan replied to himself. *I don't know. I don't know what to think—what to feel.*

Just then Rhonda stuck her head around the adjoining door.

"Just wanted to remind you, I'm leaving early today," she said.

It was long moments before Alan responded. "OK. See yuh tomorrow, then."

"Are you OK?" Rhonda asked noting the hands behind the head and the lost expression on Alan's face.

"Yeah. I'm alright," Alan responded after some hesitation.

"You don't sound too sure. Anyway, I'm in a rush. See yuh tomorrow." Rhonda left.

The following day Alan received a call from Dave Rivers, the literary agent handling Rhonda's anthology. He had found a publisher to print Rhonda's anthology and the contract looked very good. Despite the feelings of hurt he had toward Rhonda right then he was happy for her and couldn't wait to tell her the good news.

"Could you come in here?" Alan asked when Rhonda answered his call.

His tone was ambiguous. Rhonda couldn't quite tell if something was wrong. She'd learned to dread going into his office when he used those words.

When Rhonda entered, Alan could see from the set of her shoulders and the light in her eyes that she was ready for battle if necessary. *Why must she always be on defensive with me? Am I that terrible?*

She looked pretty, but business-like in the navy blue skirt suit and white shirt she was wearing. He noticed she was wearing a bow tie, again—this time a red one. *The woman has a fetish for those things*, he thought humorously.

"Sit down. . . please, " Alan said seriously, adding the "please" as a deliberate afterthought. Then he fixed her with the meanest look he could summon and said, " I have something here that involves you. . ." He stopped deliberately.

He watched as she moved her hands from her lap to grip the arms of the chair. She sat up ramrod straight.

"I am. . ." He stopped ominously. "I am very proud of you, you're going to get your poems published," he finished in a rush.

The information took a few seconds to sink it. Alan's face, still serious, was at odds with the good news. But she noticed that a tiny smile he was trying desperately to hide tugged at the corners of his mouth. Then she leapt forward and took his neck in her hands in mock strangulation.

"You son of a . . .You teasing me, right, misleading me?"

Alan started laughing. She started shaking the head between her hands. She joined him in laughter.

"Yuh choking me," he croaked between the mirth.

"I haven't even started yet, mister."

"Yuh serious? They really gon' publish them?" she asked joyfully, yet skeptically, fearful she may have misunderstood him.

"Yes. Yes. . .Let go!"

"No. . .I could kiss you," she said happily.

"Please do," he replied, caught up in her joy and a pleasure of his own.

And Rhonda did, lightly, her hands still on his neck. The warmth of his lips teased her. Again she kissed him, helplessly. Suddenly, his right hand snaked up and gripped her neck firmly, pulling her farther across the desk. Anyone coming into the room would have been shocked not only by the editors kissing but also by the picture of Rhonda, half-exposed, across Alan's desk. His mouth attacked hers greedily. He couldn't get enough of her warm sweetness. The sharp shrill of the telephone made her jump; Rhonda reluctantly broke the kiss.

"Thank you, thank you, thank you," she whispered, punctuating her gratitude with a kiss to his nose, a cheek, his irresistible lips. She backed out from the room, leaving him to answer his phone.

He had never seen her so happy, so excited. It made him doubly sad that she couldn't trust him enough to tell him of her plans. He decided, however, not to disclose his knowledge of the venture. He was going to let her come to him with the information in her own time.

Rhonda returned to her desk. Sitting, staring into space with a grin on her face, she knew it would be extremely difficult to concentrate on her work for the rest of the day.

"Let's celebrate with dinner tonight."

Alan's voice brought her from out of space. He had stuck his head through her door to issue the invitation.

"OK," she smiled.

I really love that smile, Alan thought as he returned to his desk.

❧ ❧ ❧ ❧

When Rhonda came downstairs around nine o'clock, Alan was leaning against his car waiting patiently. Around him people and cars moved back and forth in the mild summer night. He watched as she took the steps slowly, the tail of the dress switching from side to side. He took in her black stockinged feet and the thin straps of the black shoes she wore. The neck of the yellow dress with black tulips was cut in a wide V with a broad collar laying demurely on the shoulders down to the chest. A row of big black buttons ran down the front from the chest to the hem. A cluster of tiny yellow flowers studded her ears. When she reached him, he pulled her close and kissed her on the cheek. Then he reached into the tiny pocket of his off-white silk jacket and took out an ivory rose, specially cut for her. He stuck it in her hair on the left side and smiled at his masterpiece.

"You really like to see me with flowers in my hair, don't you?" she asked smiling.

"Yeah. . .One of my favorite fantasies is making love to you on a field of sweet-smelling red roses. I haven't figured out what to do with the thorns yet though." Alan said softly, pulling her back into the circle of his arms.

"Well, until you figure that out, I'll pass, thank you." Rhonda touched his lips lightly with a fingertip and moved to climb into the car.

Dinner was wonderful. They both let their barriers down and enjoyed the seafood. They went to the restaurant they had gone to for their first dinner date. Alan couldn't help comparing Rhonda then to Rhonda now. She had changed in many ways and he had gotten to know her. Even more surprisingly, he had grown to love her.

What am I waiting on to tell her? he groaned in frustration.

"So, tell me everything, " Rhonda demanded after they had satisfied their appetites.

"There's nothing to tell."

"Do I have to do any reorganizing or anything?"

"Not yet anyway. They have editors looking over the work

now, but I don't think you'll have to do much more. I worked on it thoroughly."

"Yuh think we should have approached Michael with it?"

"I thought of that. But TradeWinds couldn't have given us the kind of deal we have; they would have wanted more control. " Alan shrugged.

"Are you sure I don't have to do anything on it?" Rhonda persisted, insecure.

"Rhonda, relax. Let's talk 'bout something else before you drive me crazy."

"But I can't think 'bout nothing else," she whined.

"Try."

"What's Nadine to you?" Rhonda blurted out suddenly.

Rhonda hadn't meant to ask him about the woman then, it just slipped out. But lately she had been thinking about their relationship and wondered just how involved Alan was with her. He never talked about Nadine and she never had the courage to really question him. But she had to know. It had become almost a burning obsession. *So what if I am picking up some of his bad habits, prying into people's business. It was bound to happen; we see each other almost everyday.*

Alan rocked back in the rattan throne and cupping his chin with his hand, a forefinger touching his nose, he looked Rhonda straight in the eyes. She was looking back at him a strange expression on her face: a slightly embarrassed smile attempted to soften the serious intent, but it wasn't working. There was more to the question than idle curiosity; he felt it in his gut.

"A friend," Alan said gravely. He thought back to Tuesday night when Nadine called him, stranded on the Turnpike, her car broken down. It was about ten o'clock and the rain was pouring, but he had driven out to New Jersey without hesitation. In the car, on the way back, they had patched up their friendship. She was really just a friend.

Rhonda placed her elbows on the table, laced her fingers and with her chin resting on her hands, she popped her next question.

"Are you lovers?"

A slight frown creased her eyebrows, her lips drew together tightly.

Alan moved forward to rest his arms on the table. He leaned toward her, His eyes travelled from her tense lips to the wary look in her eyes.

"Not since you," he whispered. "Why?"

He watched as Rhonda expelled a small puff of air from her lungs. She was a lot more tense than he thought. Something serious was going down. He only prayed she would let him in on it. He had his suspicions, but he couldn't rely on them totally.

Rhonda sat back in the chair and lowered her eyes to the plates filled with discarded lobster shell, the half-eaten bread and cheese, the platter with pickled vegetables, the crumbs and bits of food littering the table.

"Just curious, that's all. . . Do you think you'll sleep with her again?"

Rhonda waited, her stomach knotted. It was a very personal question, she knew. And she probably didn't even have the right to ask it. But she had to know, and the fact that he was her boss didn't figure into it at all. It was completely forgotten.

Alan took a while before he answered Rhonda. If he told her he'd broken off with Nadine where would it put him? He felt naked, vulnerable.

I should forget about my ego, he thought. *I'm always up-front. I shouldn't stop now. And she's the last person I want to mislead or deceive. But, Oh God. What if she realizes just how much she means to me? What if she sees how much power she has over me? What then?*

"No. I broke off with her the night of the bus ride."

"Good." Rhonda said, a smile lighting up her entire face. *Good. Good,* Rhonda thought. *I don't have anything to worry about. I think.*

"That bit of news seems to have made you happy," Alan said, somewhat shyly.

"Now can I ask what this third degree was about? " Alan continued slowly, punctuating every word.

"Oh. Nothing. Nothing important." Rhonda toyed with a piece of pickled carrot sitting on a small silver platter.

"Think we can handle dessert tonight?" Rhonda added perkily, changing the topic.

"You getting away with murder, yuh know," Alan said, smiling.

"Oh yeah. . . Wuh yuh think we should order, ice cream?" Rhonda smiled into his eyes with wide-eyed innocence, refusing to tell him anything.

She couldn't hide her burst of happiness even if someone had paid her, and a softening glow radiated her face. *Soon I'll be able to tell him,* she decided. *I just need more time to work things out in my head and get Caribbean Woman started.*

You may lose him by then, stupid, insisted her nagging conscience. *But what if he doesn't love me? Then what? I can't afford to have my head all screwed up now. Too much at stake.*

What could he do? There was nothing he could. *I can't force Rhonda to tell me why she was asking all those questions. She is obviously curious about my love life. . . Definitely pleased I broke up with Nadine. But what if I add up one and one and got twenty? You know what, leave it alone. Just relax and enjoy the evening.*

"OK. Let's have some chocolate ice cream." Alan announced.

"Goodie. My favorite." Rhonda rubbed her hands in glee, a big grin showing her teeth.

"I know. That's why I suggested it."

They ate dessert quietly. When they resumed talking it was about *West Indian World*—the magazine was never far from their thoughts. They had a special affection for the publication. Alan was telling Rhonda his idea for the special section they wanted to do on famous Caribbean women for the January issue. It was the perfect opening for Rhonda. He watched closely to see her reaction. Twice she opened her mouth to say something and decided against. He was almost sure it had to do with her plans, but she never said a word.

She's holding back for some reason, Alan thought as he tried to squelch his annoyance. *Have patience, relax. Why is she holding back?*

At about twelve o'clock they left the restaurant. Sleepy from the food and wine, Rhonda leaned back against the seat with her eyes closed and let the cool summer breeze lull her into a semi-conscious state. You could feel a slight chill in the air, a signal that fall was approaching. Rhonda wasn't looking forward to winter. She never did. Many times she asked herself what she was doing in this cold, hard place, but always found some reason why she couldn't just pick up and leave: First it had been graduate school, and then it was *West Indian World*. Now she wasn't so sure. She was ready to leave. She would come yearly as required for a resident, but she didn't think she would be staying any real length of time.

Rhonda drifted off into sleep. Occasionally, Alan would take a peek at the woman peacefully sitting next to him and his heart filled with joy. Who would think he would fall in love with a "Bajan gal." He could hear Eddie teasing him with things like "Trini, take yuh meat out muh rice," or "Callaloo versus coo-coo," lines from two famous calypsos.

It's just as well. I don't think I could have made it with a Trini woman, they mouth too hot, he smiled at his silly musings. But he knew Rhonda had a mouth on her when she was ready. If they managed to work it out, it wouldn't be all sugar and spice.

When Alan pulled up outside Rhonda's apartment building Rhonda was still asleep. He shook her awake and she turned and smiled at him sleepily.

"Are we home?" she asked.

"Yes, sleepy head. Let's go."

At the front door of her apartment, Alan drew Rhonda to him and wrapped his hands tightly around her.

"I'm really proud of you. The anthology is some good writing." He rocked her gently.

"I couldn't have finished it without you. Thank you very much." Rhonda's voice was muffled, her face buried in his neck.

They remained quiet, gently rocking each other for long moments. She felt so good in arms, fitted so snugly to his body. He hadn't wanted another woman as much as he wanted Rhonda since that first taste of her. He wasn't a womanizer, but he was no monk either. He had to have her tonight. It had been much too long.

"Rhonda?" Alan called softly, taking her by shoulders and pulling her out of his neck.

Rhonda raised her head reluctantly. She was afraid her wanton need for him would show in her eyes. It did. It was too strong to master. He saw the hunger and the sight made every muscle in his body tighten, almost painfully.

"Oh, baby," he sighed, hugging her tightly once more.

Taking her face in his hands, he looked into her eyes, showing her the depth of his desire. His eyes told her all the things he was going to do to her, way into the wee hours of the morning. Then his hands began to spread the message. There was no escape tonight. She knew that, and there wasn't a bone in her body that wished to escape anything that this man wanted to do to her. She wanted to do things to him that she had been only dreaming and fantasizing about.

Alan lowered his lips and began the sweet torture. He inhaled her breath, spicy with wine and her own scent. It was intoxicating. He bit her lower lip, gently, then sucked its warm softness. Rhonda whimpered her pleasure, pulling Alan closer to her. She kissed his mouth the same way, but more forcibly. That action was another chip off his self control, so he broke the kiss with difficulty. Rhonda was wrapped around him like a vine.

"Rhonda, calm down. . . Not here. Not at the door," Alan soothed.

"Why not?" she sighed against his lips.

"Because. . ." The words got lost in Rhonda's mouth. She had enslaved him once more.

Reaching down, he grabbed her buttocks and lifted her bodily up around him. Rhonda wrapped feet and arms around Alan, attacking his delicious mouth again and again. In moments, Alan released his grip on her, easing her body down his slowly. She wasn't light, and he was no body builder.

"Let's go inside. We'll be more comfortable." he said, running his hands up and down her arms.

"OK, but hurry, please," she begged softly.

"No. I won't hurry. We're going to make love all night," Alan stated softly.

A tremor ran through her at his words. Would she be able to control herself and make the loving last? She doubted it. But she would die sweetly, trying.

He took her to the couch and told her to sit, he'd be right back.

"Oh, and turn on the Quiet Storm," he added, throwing the words over his shoulders on his way to her bedroom.

Rhonda slipped off her shoes, got up, put them next to couch and turned on the lamps. She walked over to the stereo her mother had given to her recently. Harold had complained it was ancient and Deborah should throw it out or give it away. He already had one for their new home. Rhonda turned on the radio at WBLS, in time to hear the soft rushing waves of the Quiet Storm jingle.

The man is uncanny, she thought, and smiled wistfully at his hidden romantic nature. She walked into the kitchen and poured two glasses of wine. With her stockinged feet curled under her, Rhonda sat sipping wine and waiting for Alan.

Just when she began to wonder vaguely what he was doing, Alan came from her bedroom clothed in her long-sleeve white terry robe and armed with a comforter, a sheet, and two pillows. When Rhonda made an attempt to help him, he shook his head, no. Alan made up their bed on the floor in front of the couch.

He sat down on the floor, and extending his hand, indicated that she should join him. Before she did, she handed him the glass of wine.

"I'd like to make a toast. . . a toast to a soon-to-be-celebrity."

Rhonda chuckled at his nonsense.

"To Rhonda, poet, and shortly, lover."

They touched glasses. The chink of the crystal meeting was a sharp sound against the background of soft music. The toast completed, Alan took the glasses, placed them on the lamp tables and returned to Rhonda.

"Now, I'm going to make you mine. . . in places you've never dreamed could belong to someone," Alan announced in a low, silky tone.

Kneeling back on his heels next to her, Alan stared to undress Rhonda from the ears down.

"I want nothing in my way," he added, taking the earrings from delicate lobes.

The picture of Alan's big hands awkwardly removing tiny earrings from her little ears made her laugh softly. The laugh turned to a gasp suddenly when he bent his head and flickered a warm, wet tongue along the edge of each ear. Alan ran a trail of soft licks, nibbles and kisses across her neck. He stopped his branding temporarily and started work on the buttons on the front of the dress.

Did I choose this dress subconsciously? Hmm... Talk about easy access. With her back firm against the couch and her eyes closed, Rhonda relaxed and gave Alan a soft, loving smile as he started unveiling her body.

Alan pushed the dress half way down Rhonda's arms and bending his head briefly savored the brown velvet of exposed shoulders. Though the temptation to linger and explore her upper body tugged him, Alan resisted and pushed the dress all the way down the arms. Rhonda uncuffed her wrists from the dress' hold and placed the palms of her hands flat on the floor at her sides. She shivered from the caress of the cool air against her heated, naked skin.

Rhonda's breasts, covered in black lace, jutted out proudly, and Alan swallowed the urge to immediately take them, lace and all into his mouth. He watched as her breasts rose, swelled and pushed against their confinement. He felt the same bursting within, so he set them free with hands that could barely contain their impatience.

Alan's hand trembled as he continued the unbuttoning. Rhonda's dress was pulled down her waist and gathered around her buttocks in a crumpled mass; further removal was slowed by a pair of ultra sheer pantyhose, and he frowned at their challenge. However, he had promised himself to go slowly tonight, and teased her restraint with his manual, sensual strip.

Rhonda opened her eyes and noticed a sheen of perspiration on his upper lip as he reached for her waistline. Using her hands to brace herself, Rhonda lifted her rear off the floor so that he could slip her pantyhose down her thighs. She felt no shame or discomfort as he boldly surveyed her body.

Alan watched Rhonda languidly sitting before him and knew that he would never tire of loving that body. The dark honey hue of her skin was caught and softened by the muted yellow light of the lamps. Alan's eyes travelled downwards observing her slender limbs, thicker thighs and broad hips. His gaze returned to her face. He knew in moments his hands would rove almost frenziedly over that short black cottony hair as he sampled her lips again and again. Rhonda's dark brown eyes looked black in the semi-darkness, and they glistened intensely. He could feel himself being sucked into their depths. The nostrils of her small nose widened ever so slightly with each deep breath she took. Her wide full mouth opened slightly and he wanted to reach over and place the tip of his tongue in the tiny hole the lips made. *I'm losing myself just looking at this woman.*

Alan firmly suggested Rhonda lie down and ensured her comfort before kneeling at her feet. He had all night and he intended to use the time to savor every nuance, every sensual cranny of the ambrosia of her body. He raised a foot and gently kissed her instep—flickering his tongue rapidly back and forth over its sensitive skin. Her leg jerked and a sharp thrill shot up its length straight to her abdomen. The core of her contracted almost painfully, and she moaned her delight. Trailing a firm tongue up the sole of her foot to her toes, he took each one slowly and individually into the cavern of his mouth. Taking his time, Alan repeated the entire process on her other foot.

Opening her eyes to slowly watch his open enjoyment of her body, Rhonda was struck by the loving, sexy nature and intent of his acts. Alan reminded Rhonda of lion grooming its mate, his action neither subservient nor unmanly; instead each stroke, each lick, kiss, and caress was that of a mate tending to his female.

Alan ran his tongue over Rhonda's body, working his way up from the ankles. He bypassed all her key zones, saving his ultimate pleasure for later. The coolness of the air against the wet spots made her shiver, but a heat from within caused flashes to alternate with the chills. She thought she was going to die. The sensations were almost painful, almost unbearable, but oh, so sweet.

"Alan," she moaned when he finally closed his mouth over her right breast.

"Alan. . . What are you doing to me?" she gasped.

"Just relax baby. I won't hurt you," he assured her.

She wasn't worried about pain, just extreme bliss. She didn't know a body could tingle so. Every hair on her skin felt raised. Rhonda reached out and started caressing his shoulders, his arms, his back. Her touch triggered a series of tremors throughout his body. What was it about this woman that made him want to lose himself completely within her? Rhonda writhed beneath him so erotically that he was tempted to abandon the slow seduction of her senses, and plunge his hard length deep within her warmth.

Alan travelled downwards again, running his tongue between her breasts to her navel, where he stayed, toying and stabbing. Each jab in its center brought a fresh ripple over her abdomen.

Momentarily, Alan left her navel for more lush pastures. The pungent, sea-like scent of her beckoned and trapped him. He had to taste her. At his tongue's intimate touch, Rhonda body lurched and her scream pierced the air.

Alan lost himself in the salty-sweet savor of Rhonda, loving the varying textures of silk and smooth pliant flesh, the smell of her. He had to grip her hips to restrain her thrashing, and time and time again she cried out. Soon, her body mellowed and absorbed his homage. She reached down and gripping his head pulled him closer, much closer.

Alan reached up and claimed Rhonda's wrists as she begged for release. She freed his head and he eased his way back up her body.

Laying on top of her, he bent his head to kiss her lips lightly. She felt his manhood, insistent, wet against her thigh. The essence of her on his mouth was ambrosia, serving as an aphrodisiac to already heightened senses. Rhonda kissed him hungrily and reached down to guide him into her. Alan's firm grip held her hand. He released her mouth.

"No risks, this time," he said.

He attempted to get up, but Rhonda hooked a leg around his, stopping him.

"It's OK. I'm prepared, too."

He resumed his position. This time he did the guiding. The penetration was his undoing. A sharp hiss, followed by a loud groan defined heaven. The rush of heat that met him was sweet ecstasy.

Oh God. *This is good, so good*, he thought. And as Rhonda wrapped both legs around his hips, he cried out, "Yes. Yes."

They both gave and received pleasures that neither knew existed. A ride that had started out slow, savory, became swift, hard. Both Alan and Rhonda gave themselves up to the rocking rhythm that brought them closer and closer to the climax of absolute excitement, that point when all else was null, void. The simultaneous paroxysm of pure delight and satisfaction left them weak, trembling, in awe of nature's blessing of absolute union.

Later as they laid hugging under the sheet he had thrown over them, Alan set free his song.

"I love you," he said.

When he got no response, felt not even a twitch, he called her name softly. He received no answer. Rhonda had fallen asleep. He chuckled silently, uncertain if he was relieved or disappointed, but he acknowledged a certain peace with himself. It was free— expressed into the open air. And even though she hadn't heard him, he was relieved.

Alan woke Rhonda thirty minutes later. He was showered, dressed and ready to go. The temptation to stay the night was strong and it took almost super human efforts to rouse himself and take a shower. In the past, leaving a woman after a night of pleasure was never a problem. He needed the familiarity of his own sheets to relax and fall asleep and he never met anyone before who even came close to eliminating this idiosyncrasy of his. But he sensed that sleeping with Rhonda would be a lot more pleasing than sleeping alone ever was. Now, the problem wasn't the inability to fall asleep comfortably, but whether he should encroach on some unspoken rule between them. Given Rhonda's independence and her private nature, he felt he needed permission, some indication from her that it was alright to spend the night. The one time he had innocently made a remark about falling asleep in her apartment she had all but jumped out of her skin. So rather than tempt any demons within her he had forced himself into the shower.

"Hmm, you smell nice," Rhonda yawned, stretching her limp arms. "When did you do all that? What time is it?"

"Now which one do you want me to respond to first?" Alan chuckled. "Come on. Get up and lock your door."

Rhonda stood and wrapped the brown-and-white stripped sheet around her body, sari style. At the door, Alan reached for her and kissed her on the nose.

"I have a question for you," he said, rocking her body from side to side.

"You always have a question for me." Rhonda shot back, teasing.

"Wuh you think about marriage?"

"In two sentences or less?" she asked with raised brows, humoring him.

"Yep."

"Ah. . . Marriage is an honorable institution that people should not take lightly or enter into unless they're in love and totally committed to making it work. . . What do yuh think? Not bad eh? I did it in one sentence," Rhonda teased.

"All jokes aside, is that what you really believe?" Alan asked, his voice grave, his eyes solemn.

"Seriously?" she asked, no longer smiling.

"Yes. Seriously."

"Yes. That's what I really believe. . .Why?

"Ah. Nothing. Nothing important. . .Remember that line, hmmm? Goodnight."

"But you can't do that." she said, desperately curious now.

"Oh yeah. Watch me," Alan grinned.

Alan reached over kissed her on the nose once more, unlocked the door and left, throwing "Bye," over his shoulders.

Leaning behind the closed door for a moment, Rhonda wondered at the question, and his earnest need for a serious answer—from her.

Maybe it has something to do with the illegitimacy article, she considered. *It can't be nothing else. He's never once said anything about loving me, so it can't have anything to do with me. You know, I really ought to pin him down and find out what he feels. I know I love him, but I don't want to just go along and have him think that we are casually having an affair. There has to be more to it than this. Yeah. As soon as I get a chance, I'll demand to know his intentions.*

Rhonda smiled at her gusto and pulled her body from the door. She walked into the living room, half dragging the sheet around her, and stood for a moment watching the ruffled makeshift bed.

His intentions are wonderful, whispered a reassuring voice. *You know that. Do you really want to scare him away and end beautiful nights like this? Hmmm?*

Yes, she replied to her own question. *Yes, because I need to know. Losing him is a chance I'll have to take.*

Rhonda picked up a pillow and hugging it close, she sniffed for any lingering scent of him. *Huhhhh. Oh well, I guess I'd better go to bed.*

"Well, Mr. Pillow, it's just you and me tonight, as always." Rhonda said aloud.

Rhonda tucked the pillow securely under her left arm, unwrapped the sheet from her body with the other, and threw it on the couch. She then gathered up the comforter and the second pillow and threw them on the couch as well. *I'll deal with you tomorrow.*

Pulling the pillow carrying Alan's fragrance from under her arm, Rhonda sank her face into its softness, and while breathing in deeply, made her way to the bedroom.

CHAPTER ❧ THIRTEEN

*I*t was Friday night and Rhonda was on her way to her mother's house for dinner, again. She had already eaten there twice for the week. The Bentleys had moved into their new home, so Deborah was still in her proud-homeowner phase.

"All this new found love is going to make me fat," Rhonda grumbled as she got dressed in a peach cotton skirt and top. Tonight she and her mother would be alone; Harold was working late.

When Rhonda arrived, dinner was already laid out—with candles. Her mother looked pretty in a baggy pair of black pants and a short-sleeved green blouse. Low-hanging gold fish hung from her ears, adding that special touch to a face made more bold by hair severely secured in the back.

"Ma this is the first time Harold has worked late in weeks. I can't replace him. I'm sorry," Rhonda teased her mother.

" Oh shush. . . I just feel a little festive, that's all. Besides candles add a special touch to a meal. And I think we're worth it, so be quiet." Deborah said, brushing aside her daughter's teasing with a sweeping hand.

There still remained a slight reserve between the two women—it was understandable for years of resentment couldn't be wiped out overnight. But there was a lightness between them, a sense of relief.

Encouraged by the mood and the comfortable atmosphere during dinner, Rhonda decided to test fate and ask her mother some questions about her father. The burning urgency to know had faded when she recently came to terms with his abandonment. Now she approached the subject with it mere curiosity and an genuine interest in a mother's first love.

"Ma, how come you never married my father?" Rhonda asked warily.

Deborah raised her head from the plate in front of her and fixed Rhonda with a searching gaze. She wanted to make sure what she saw in the eyes was as innocent as the tone. It was and she relaxed. Although Deborah didn't relish talking about Frank Garfield and her past, she would—just for her daughter's sake. She owed it to Rhonda.

"Oh, I don't know. We just never got around to it I guess. We wanted to have a good old-fashion wedding but we didn't have the money. Then you came and it was more important to find a house and settle in. And then everything else took priority: taking care of you, paying bills," Deborah's voice trailed off.

"Were you in love with each other?" Rhonda asked quietly, her chin resting on her hands on the table.

Deborah laughed softly and her eyes glimmered with the good memories.

"Yes. Very much. Frank just had to smile at me and I was of no use to myself."

"Then, why the other women, Ma? Why are men like that?" Rhonda, asked urgently.

"Ah girl, if I could answer that one, I would probably still be with him. But I can't. Men fool around for all kinds of reasons and half the time they don't know why themselves." Sadness and regret tinged Deborah's voice.

"Why didn't Daddy come to see me?"

Deborah was moved by the plaintiff cry of the little girl hidden within the grown woman seated before her. Where her father was concerned, she would always be just a wounded child.

"Shame I guess. Plus he must have found out about the piece of wood I had waiting for his behind if he set foot cross my door," Deborah chuckled—she had put a lot of the old resentment to rest.

"Would you really have hit him?" Rhonda asked.

"The way I felt at the time, who knows? Maybe." Deborah responded, shaking her head.

"Yuh know, it so important for a woman to be strong, self-sufficient . . . to have self esteem. Yuh never know what life 'gon dish out. And if you don't have that. . . then look out. . . .trouble, and worse yet if you have to mind children on yuh own," Deborah continued. Her eyes were lost in time, thinking of the past, envisioning a younger, more vulnerable woman who had dug deep and found the strength to survive.

Rhonda sat quietly, absorbing her mother's musings. *If only we had done this all along, maybe I would not feel so confused right now.*

"So, " Deborah clapped her hands suddenly, making Rhonda jump. "This is what love does to you, huh, make you pump your mother with all kinds of questions?" Deborah smiled knowingly.

"Wuh you talking 'bout Ma?" Rhonda asked, her eyes lowered.

"Oh don't pretend with me. Tell me 'bout Alan," Deborah demanded.

"Who says I have a relationship with Alan?" Rhonda asked shyly. Visions of she and Alan making love stirred in her head.

"Don't try to sidestep me—I saw the way you two were dancin' at the wedding. Not to mention you couldn't wait to leave with the man. Shame," Deborah laughed at her daughter's discomfort.

"So how was it?" Deborah asked impishly, taking delight in Rhonda's shocked expression.

This new side to Ma is pretty unnerving, she thought, while shaking her head. Sandra was the only one she shared all her innermost thoughts with. She definitely couldn't see herself giving her mother a blow-by-blow of her nights with Alan.

"You don't have to answer. If your eyes got any bigger, they would be saucers," Deborah laughed heartily.

"Any body who finances my little girl's dream like Alan is doing must have something going," Deborah continued.

Rhonda got a sick sinking feeling in her stomach. "Ma, what are you saying?" She wasn't prepared for the answer.

"Don't try to hide it from me. I know all 'bout Alan supplying the money for *Caribbean Woman*, even though you didn't tell me that little tidbit," Deborah announced, quite happy with herself.

Rhonda sat back in shock. She lost her appetite instantly and felt as if she would bring up what she had already eaten.

"Alan is backing me?" she asked, her face tightening almost painfully.

"Don't look so shock... You mean you didn't know?" Deborah took in Rhonda's sick pallor.

Rhonda shook her head, no. Now it was Deborah's turn to experience that sick feeling: Harold was going to kill her for her big mouth.

"I didn't know it was supposed to be a secret. Harold said he didn't have all the money so he decided to ask Alan. He knew Alan wouldn't turn him down if he had it. I'm sorry. I thought you knew." She, too, lost her appetite. *Harold can't be angry because he didn't say I was supposed to keep quiet about it,* Deborah rationalized.

"How dare he do this," Rhonda muttered angrily.

"Calm down, Rhonda. It ain't a crime to help someone you care about," Deborah said, trying to keep her daughter from exploding.

"It has nothing to do with care. And who gave him the right to stick his nose in my business? This time he gone too far. Always questioning, always probing. Now he wants to take over the one thing that means the world to me." Rhonda got up and started to pace the floor.

"I don't understand why you so mad. He only trying to help. That kind of work you want to do takes a lot of money. I certainly can't help you. It's just a loan... C'mon eat... You ain't wasting my good food." Deborah tried in vain to sidetrack Rhonda.

"I'm not hungry," Rhonda, sat down again and blew out her fury through tight lips.

"C'mon try to eat," Deborah implored. "Yuh making a mountain outta a mole hill."

The evening was ruined. They both knew that. Picking at their food, Rhonda and Deborah tried to talk about other things to pass the time. The house was coming along fine; they were working on renovating the basement. Sheila and Sonia had decided to stay through winter. Sheila wanted to see how Sonia would adjust to living to New York, and had even enrolled her in a local school temporarily. Sheila still wasn't sure she wanted a permanent switch for both of them.

After Rhonda got home from dinner, she sat in her living room thinking about the information her mother had revealed. It was unusual for her to curl up in a robe on the couch, but because of Alan Rhonda could not find any peace of mind. She was livid. No matter how Rhonda tried to think coherently, her emotions got in the way.

She kept envisioning Alan's face as she mentally railed at him for all the injustices of the past few months: *You came and took the job I wanted, the job I busted my butt for. OK. I learned to live with that. Now you want to take over the only thing I have left. This is my dream, my magazine. You can't own it just like that. Why, oh why did Harold have to tell you. And why did you try to take control behind my back?*

Rhonda had already transferred the $30,000 she'd received from Harold, or rather Alan, and $15,000 from her savings into her account in Barbados. She had already gotten a real estate agent to work on locating a small office. She had written letters to writers, artists, photographers and advertisers, people she had renewed contact with when she was in Barbados covering the Musical Sun Splash.

Rhonda decided, irrational or not, she had had it with everything. She was quitting her job immediately.

As a matter of fact, she decided, *I'm cleaning out my office tomorrow. To hell with this crap. It's time I got things moving. I'm tired of waiting around for the right time. As for Mr. Hussein...hmm... I don't even think I could look at him right now.*

With her mind firmly made up Rhonda went to sleep. Alan haunted her dreams and twice she cried out, waking herself.

ε✿ ε✿ ε✿ ε✿

Alan was in bright spirits as he walked in the front door of TradeWinds Enterprises, whistling as he weaved through a series of desks and cubicles on the way to his office. He was looking forward to seeing Rhonda whom he hadn't spoken to all weekend. He had tried calling her, but for some reason, she was apparently out on both days. When he tried at twelve o'clock on Sunday, he was puzzled for it was unusual for her to be out on that night. He knew she hated going anywhere on a Sunday, unless she was going to be back home early. She needed a full night's sleep in order to deal with work on a Monday morning. He had teased her, calling her weird. Monday is just like any other day in the week, he had said. No, she had replied. Monday is punishment, torture for a crime you didn't commit. He had laughed at her definition.

Sitting down at his desk, the lighthearted whistle slowly died on his lips. There was a white envelope with his name and the words, "Personal and Confidential," scrawled on the front in Rhonda's handwriting.

This wasn't here when I left Friday. What is it? he asked himself as he slit open the envelope.

It had Monday's date on it, was addressed to him, and read: "Effective today, I, Rhonda Baptiste, am resigning from my position as assistant managing editor. Personal problems that need my immediate attention make it impossible for me to continue working here at this time. I've enjoyed working with you and I've learned a great deal about publishing from you. I apologize for the suddenness of this resignation, but it couldn't be helped. Thank you for giving me the opportunity to work with you."

Alan reached up, and grabbing the knot of the gray tie, yanked it from his collar. He felt an urgent need for air. He couldn't breathe. He got up, almost knocking the chair down and stormed into Rhonda's office. He checked the drawers—they had been cleaned out. He checked her closet—there were no personal items there.

He went back to his office and sat down heavily; the chair groaning its complaint. He picked up the letter and read it once again, then he tore it up and threw in the garbage. His eyes glistened in their fury, the jawline's telltale muscle beginning to throb.

She can't do this, he thought dejectedly. *She can't just up and quit like this without warning, and not have the decency to tell me to my face. No. You don't do that. Not after all we've been to each other.*

Alan reached for the phone and dialed Rhonda's home number. There was no answer. Periodically throughout the day he tried without success. He didn't know how he made it through the day. By eleven o'clock, the whispered word around the office was to stay away from Alan Hussein, so no one crossed his path unless he or she absolutely had to. The demon inside him was aroused and he was short tempered with even the breeze.

᠀ ᠀ ᠀ ᠀

When Rhonda pulled up behind the black car with the man leaning against its door her immediate impulse was to reverse and drive away—far away. But this confrontation was unavoidable and she had spent all day preparing for it. She had spent the day shopping for essential office supplies and some summer clothing. She had had a hard time finding the clothes because the fall and winter wardrobes were already on display. That's why she was late getting home.

She looked at her wrist. It was seven twenty. She wondered how long he had been there, waiting for her. *Looks like he came straight from work*, she thought noting the gray slacks and white shirt with opened collar and rolled up sleeves. He had witnessed her arrival but had shifted his gaze ahead of him, once he had confirmed it was she who had pulled up.

Rhonda got out of the car and went to the trunk to gather her bags. Laden with packages, she walked up to Alan and greeted him with her eyes. His stony glare cut across her like a sharp blade. It was going to be a rough evening.

She continued up the steps and he followed, noting in the midst of raw emotion that she looked enticing in the blue jeans and blue denim jacket she wore.

Rhonda set down her packages to get her keys for the door. When she turned to retrieve the bags, as her body leaned against the door, to keep it ajar, Alan already had taken them up and with his cold eyes indicated she should go in. She did and he followed her up the stairs. She felt his eyes like ice daggers piercing her back.

Oh Lord, she prayed, *help me through this one. I know it's not going to be easy.*

Inside, Rhonda went immediately to the bathroom to wash her hands. It was a habit. She looked up at her face in the medicine cabinet's mirror—same face, just a little tense around the eyes; her lips trembled slightly. The sight of Alan had extinguished the gnawing hunger from her stomach, and she hadn't eaten all day.

When Rhonda returned to the living room, Alan rose from the couch to face her. The lamps were on, the room bathed in soft yellow light. Alan dug his hands deep into his pant's side pockets. He felt he had to put them away or they might shake her, or worse, desperately pull her to him. He couldn't afford the latter. He needed a clear head to deal with her tonight. For long moments, they stared at each other, not knowing how to start or who should start.

For some reason, despite the determined set to her lips and shoulders, Rhonda looked lost, vulnerable. But Alan couldn't be sure if that was what he wanted to see or if it was really so. He decided to make the first move.

"When did you decide all this?" His voice was husky, raw.

"Friday night," Rhonda responded. There was no denying the slight tremor in her voice. Alan was the coldest she had ever seen him—his entire body was curved from marble, still, hard.

"Why didn't you call me or come over? Don't you think I deserve to hear something like that from you directly?" he asked, the heat of anger creeping into his voice.

"I thought it was best to do it that way." Rhonda turned around from the force of his emotions.

The grip on her shoulder was firm. It hurt, slightly. Alan turned her back around.

"Best for who? Huh? Do you know how I felt when I read your little note this morning? No warning, nothing." he said harshly.

Rhonda was silent, trapped. Up this close, there was no escaping his hold or the fury in his brown eyes. She could see the velvet webs and they looked as if they were moving and stretching.

"You know we had work up to here," Alan indicated, with a hand to the chin. "And you quit without notice. And you call yourself a professional?" he continued, louder.

For long moments Rhonda was silent. He was right. She had put him in a very bad position. But she had to make a move.

"I'm sorry, but they won't have any trouble getting someone to help you out till they replace me. In fact, I could recommend a very good temp," Rhonda said, moving away from his touch.

"Forget the blasted temp. What about me?... No. No... Forget about me. You obviously didn't give a damn about me... What brought this on?" Alan asked, his voice lowered by the time he got to the question, his brows furrowed. He was beginning to lose control. If he continued on that irate course, God knows what would be said.

"I found out about the money for *Caribbean Woman*," Rhonda replied. Her lips curled downwards and the initial anger she had felt when she first heard the news from her mother returned, in spades.

"Ah," he said, nodding.

"Who gave you the right to meddle in my affairs?" she blasted.
"Meddle. Is that what it is? Meddle?" he returned.
"Yes. Haven't you done enough damage. First you come in and take over my job. Yes. My job. It should have been mine. I worked hard for that position. Now you want to come and take over my magazine. No way."
Alan shook his head. He couldn't believe that she saw him that way, as someone taking something that belonged to her.
"I thought you had gotten over that nonsense with the job. Look, I gave you the money because I thought you had an excellent idea. It had nothing to do with wanting to take over anything, " Alan grated, his hands returning to his pockets.
"Then why the sneakiness, the underhand maneuvering?" Rhonda sneered.
"You don't talk to me about sneakiness. When did you plan to tell me, huh? When the first issue was printed?" Alan's voice rose a fraction.
"I was going to tell you when I was ready. On my time." Rhonda emphasized jabbing her chest with a forefinger.
"Oh I see. Your time. So wuh happen to common decency, courtesy? After what we've been to each other, I don't deserve that?" Alan asked, with some plaintiveness creeping into his voice.
"This had nothing to do with you and I. It's about me, my personal plans to create something. And I did plan to tell you," she stressed, with a stronger voice, hands gesticulating.
"OK. Fine, fine," Alan said with raised hands. "You were going to tell me; I found out before you did. Now what? You quit your job. Now what's the next move, or is that none of my business, too?" Alan crossed his hands on his chest.
"I don't want your money," Rhonda announced, folding her arms across her chest as well.
"What?" he asked, the anger started to boil within him again. His hands dropped to his sides.
"I don't want your charity. . . loan. . . or whatever it is. I don't want it."

"Now yuh being stupid," Alan responded, in disgust.

"I don't care. I'll get it somewhere else." Rhonda turned her back to him, away from the blistering sheen of his eyes.

"You don't turn yuh back on me," Alan turned her to face him for the second time, his face contorted, ugly with his ire.

"Why are you so defensive about every damn thing? You act as if somebody always out to hurt you, take advantage of you. Not every man is like your father, yuh know." he said fiercely.

"What my father got to do with this?" Rhonda returned.

"Everything. You walk around with this warped idea in your head that all men the same, no blasted good."

"You don't know what yuh talking 'bout," Rhonda responded, not as convincing as she would have liked to sound. He had a point and she knew it.

"You know I do. If you would stop being so stubborn and look at what in front of you, you'd know yuh being ridiculous," Alan said harshly, clearly showing his impatience and the disappointment he was feeling.

"You can believe what you want. It doesn't change the way I feel."

"If this really means that much to you then you shouldn't care where you get the money." Alan continued.

"I don't want your money," Rhonda hissed, through clenched teeth.

"Goddamit woman, I gave you the money because I love you. I want you to succeed. I didn't give it to you because it made me feel like some big man. I love you," Alan declared angrily, shaking Rhonda.

Alan watched as the shock of his declaration sunk in. Rhonda's face creased and her lips tightened with the intensity of her emotions. She was startled, confused, and it showed. Unshed tears formed and brightened her eyes. It seemed as if what he said pained her to the core.

Alan released her, his hands tiredly falling to his sides.

"Do what you want. I don't care," he whispered. Then he turned and walked out the door.

Rhonda stood paralyzed for long moments. When she could force movement into her body, she sat down in one corner of the couch and curled her body into a tight ball.

ᢞ ᢞ ᢞ ᢞ

Downstairs, Alan sat in his car frozen in immobility, his back upright against the seat, his eyes staring straight ahead. *I have never met a more hardened woman. That damn stubborn pride is going to destroy her if she don't watch herself, he* fumed. Anger churned around inside him like a whirlpool.

Alan turned and looked out towards the building, past the activity on the street, his mind travelling to the upstairs living room, reliving the scene of moments ago. He forced himself to unclench the fists resting on his thighs.

He knew she was going to be upset when she found out about the money, but he had planned by then to have declared his love. He hadn't allowed himself to face the possibility that she might not return his feelings. There was something there, he was sure of it, and if it wasn't undying love then he would have worked on it. Now he wasn't so sure. The way she treated him with the resignation was so brutal, cold.

She doe*sn't care about me,* he concluded. *If she did, there's no way she could have resigned like that. No way.*

Are you so sure your pride isn't getting in the way, Hussein? inquired his inner devil's advocate.

Put yourself in her shoes. You know the kind of mentality you're dealing with, the scars of her childhood. She's an independent woman who has supported and taken care of herself most of her life. She's carving out her space and you're trying to take the knife from her.

Alright, alright, when you look at it from that angle, maybe. But why can't she see that I was only trying to help?

Because you never talked to her about it. You just went in and took over. You're the first man she's been involved with since her fiance died. And face it, you're not an easy man to like, far less love. You're demanding, impatient, and you have a nasty temper, one you know you have to learn to control. And though you don't delve into them too often, you have a few scars of your own. Growing up without both your parents might not have had as strong an effect on you as it did Rhonda, but it did have some effect. Why yuh think you've been avoiding a serious relationship all this time? You're scared, scared to love too fast, too deeply. And you definitely don't want to have any children until you're absolutely sure of the woman and the strength of the relationship.

"The joke is really on me, isn't it?" Alan said out loud, dryly, humorlessly.

So what are you going to do now?

I don't know. I really don't know. Give it some time, I guess. Just give it some time.

ۿ ۿ ۿ ۿ

Slowly Rhonda uncurled her body. She stretched out her cramped limbs and tried to pull herself together. She didn't know how long she had sat there, too shaken to even cry. At least that might have brought some release. But all she felt was a dry ache inside.

He loves me. It's what I wondered about, wanted to know. So how come I'm not jumping up and down with joy. Why do I feel so stunned, so choked up with fear? Yuh know, Rhonda, you should have really gone to see that shrink a long time ago. Yuh ain't right in the head.

Alan's angry declaration of love played in her mind's eye. She could see his face, twisted, raw with the depth of his feelings. His eyes never looked more brilliant, alive with the mixed emotions he was undergoing. It seemed as if loving her was a dull pain, something he couldn't stop.

Rhonda pulled her feet back up into the couch and wrapped her hands around them. Her abdomen tightened with the vision of Alan.

What am I going to do with this love? It's every woman's dream to have a man love her like this. I've always fantasized about it. But now that I have it, I don't know how to handle it. Should I call him? I don't know. I guess I did hurt him with the way I resigned and by refusing to accept the money. But it was the only way I could do that. I just want to go in there and get Caribbean Woman *off the ground. It's the only thing that can make me whole right now.*

Rhonda tried to communicate her feeling towards an imaginary Alan: *It has nothing to do with you. It's something I have to do for me. And you're right, I shouldn't let pride slow me down. I will accept that money and I'll make us both proud, you'll see. Just let me do this, please. If you really love me, be patient and let me do this my way. And please, please be there when I'm ready to face you, when I can accept you and be the type of woman you deserve. Oh Alan, I do love you. Please don't let this evening ruin your love for me.*

CHAPTER ❧ FOURTEEN

*R*honda stepped off a plane at Grantley Adams International Airport Wednesday morning at eleven o'clock. The sun was almost blinding in its brilliance, its warmth pure heaven against her naked arms. The short-sleeve royal blue dress had been an excellent buy: comfortable, attractive and under fifteen dollars. One good thing about leaving New York in October: she wouldn't be facing the fast approaching fall and winter, and that in itself was reason for her to clap hands in glee.

But she didn't really feel joyful. She hadn't said good-bye to Alan. She had picked up the phone to call him twice and had driven by his house on Tuesday night before she left, but she couldn't drum up the courage to face him. She didn't know what she could say. I love you? It didn't seem enough. It couldn't make the lingering doubts disappear.

Sandra was at the airport as promised. But this time the excitement of Rhonda's last arrival was missing. Instead, Sandra greeted her with solemn eyes.

"Hey, kiddo, why the sour face?" Rhonda asked, hugging her dear friend.

"You didn't sound that great when you called. I was worried."

"Well, stop your worrying right now. I'm OK." Rhonda patted Sandra's shoulder reassuringly.

"Nice cut—are you losing weight?" Rhonda commented on Sandra's stylish short hair cut and a slightly smaller figure.

"Thanks. And yes, I lost seven pounds. Seeing you all nice and slim the last time made me get really serious about losing some weight," Sandra replied.

"Good for you. Now, how's my little man doing?" Rhonda inquired about Shawn.

"Oh, the same ole' pain in the neck, but adorable anyway. I swear that little boy is something else. But don't worry, your turn will come," Sandra laughed, shaking her head like an old sage.

The women left the airport, walking close together. Rhonda slung her free hand across her friend's shoulders, unknowingly conveying a need for human warmth and comfort.

Sandra knew Rhonda almost as well as she knew herself. They had grown up together, and were inseparable in their young years. Rhonda's move to America had been a painful one to accept, but they had kept in touch. She knew her friend was hurting; something had happened to erase the smile that sprung so easily to those full lips and dull the glimmering mischief of those dark brown eyes. And although she was tempted to probe, she sensed Rhonda's need for quiet support. This wasn't time for any analysis. In fact, it would probably be days before her friend would open up and share her feelings.

≈ ≈ ≈ ≈

The first week of Rhonda's return to Barbados was a time of healing. She spent everyday at the beach, mostly with Shawn, whom she took with her after school. He made no demands on her and was quite happy playing in the light peach sand on his own. She was losing weight because she had little appetite, but she felt one hundred percent better than she did when she had first arrived. She purged herself of her doubts and insecurities and renewed her faith in her abilities. Sandra had talked her into going to evening prayers at a nearby Anglican church and she was glad she'd gone. It had been spiritually uplifting. Rhonda fully accepted her feelings for Alan. She loved him deeply and did trust him as much as was humanly possible; there was finally the strength to reject her mother's teachings about men. They might have been true for some men but not Alan. Being forced to acknowledge this latest revelation was frightening because she missed him terribly, but still wasn't ready to face him as yet.

Caribbean Woman was her priority now. During the upcoming weeks, Rhonda poured all her energy into making her dream a reality. Meetings with bankers, advertisers, printers, and writers, sapped her mental and physical strength.

Deborah had signed over ownership of their home in Barbados to Rhonda, and with the house as collateral Rhonda was able to get a $50,000 loan to supplement the funds she already had. She used some of the money to buy two computers, office equipment and furnishings for the small two room office her agent had found near the public library in Bridgetown.

She hired an artist, an editor and an assistant. Monica Springer, (the assistant) fresh from college, was as energetic and enthusiastic as Rhonda was at that age. She hadn't the time or inclination to retrained an already conditioned person and it was important that she had immediate rapport with her right-hand man. Together, the small staff set the wheels of *Caribbean Woman* in motion.

They had no problems getting writers. Ads in the leading newspapers, magazines and word of mouth spread the news like wild fire. Men and women sent in articles on everything from marriage and sex to cooking and gardening. Photographers and artists saw the chance to display their work as a lucky break. Advertisers, quick to enhance their image and stimulate sales, leapt at the golden opportunity Rhonda offered, and although her rates were pretty steep, they knew the woman was creating something hot.

In addition to the customary favorites—health, people, current events, business, sexuality, cuisine, interior design—Rhonda added two main departments: one on education and the other on the history of African peoples. Two short stories and a section for poetry were a definite in each monthly issue.

The 150-page magazine was a slick four-color representation of women's concerns throughout the Caribbean. The cover was immediately catching. Bold and graceful, the logo, designed in two columns, ran down the left side in sleek letters; its background colored in graded rich tints of brown, indicative of the varying shades of black women's skin. The hue of the logo's letters changed according to the color scheme for the issue. Photographs of beautiful women, celebrities and non-celebrities, were scheduled to grace the cover each month, while bold banners offered tantalizing peeks into the contents of each issue.

The days and nights were long and grueling. She tried to push thoughts and the yearning for Alan far, far away. At times, it was impossible to resist temptation, and she would break down and call Harold for any word on him. He was alive and alright; that much she found out. But what she really wanted to know, she couldn't ask: *Does he still love me? Will he want me when I'm ready to give myself to him?*

At other times, she succeeded in keeping the need for him at bay. But it was only because by the time she got home she was often too exhausted to do anything but collapse on the bed. Rhonda didn't think a body could survive on two or three hours sleep nightly but hers did. She knew this tolerance was short-lived and it was only a matter of time before lowered resistance to illness and rapid weight lost told her so.

Two-and-a-half months after Rhonda arrived, the first issue was put to bed and so was Rhonda, by a livid Sandra. Rhonda had a 104-degree temperature, a tremendous headache, body aches and chills. After giving Rhonda flu medication and covering her with two blankets to ward off the chills, she left the room in a huff.

"What are you trying to do—kill yourself?" Sandra asked Rhonda angrily.

Too weak to even attempt an answer, Rhonda had turned watery, sick eyes on Sandra, pleading for comfort. *No yelling, please—my head can't take it,* they seemed to say.

This was the way Alan found Rhonda late that Friday night.

ᕞ ᕞ ᕞ ᕞ

Time. That's what you said, isn't it? Give it time. Alan frowned as he desperately tried to counsel patience to an impatient nature.

Time for what? How many times are you going to pick up that phone and put it down again? You've done it at least six times in the past two weeks alone.

Alan laid on the black leather couch in the den with his hands behind his head. Staring into space, he tried to reason with himself. More than two months had gone by and he was nowhere nearer to reconciling himself to life without Rhonda.

For a long time he buried himself in the work she had left him to handle alone. With the aid of a temp and a copyeditor, Alan managed to survive the madness of the two months he had given Ramdeen to find replacements for both Rhonda and himself. *West Indian World* wasn't the same with her gone. She haunted the place, making it extra difficult to work throughout the day. Sometimes he thought he could smell her perfume and would pick up a folder or book he imagined she had once held and put it to his nostrils in order to sniff for any lingering scent. Other times, he thought she called his name and he would look up expecting to see her tan legs and suit-clad figure at the adjoining door. He missed trying to guess which bow tie she would be wearing.

The nights were the hardest. He would lie there for hours reliving the nights they made love. He could almost feel and taste those pliant lips. He would clench his hands, stopping the restless caress of the sheets, as he imagined them moving slowly over her warm, smooth skin, and ruffling those black cottony curls that laid close to her skull. It had been unusual, the sensation of grasping that small head in his hands without locks and strands of hair getting in the way. He had felt like he held her life in hands; she was small and helpless like a tiny bird in an open palm. *Dear God, Rhonda it's hell without you. I miss you so damn much.* He would end up rolling over to pound the pillow in frustration. Rhonda frequented Alan's dreams as well and there was some measure of relief, and even joy while the vivid pictures played on the curtain of his subconscious. In the dreams she would come to him, to express her sorrow over the wasted time. She would reach out and touch his cheek, whispering her love for him; he would gather her into his arms and tenderly shower her with loving.

After these consistently bittersweet nights, he survived the ordeal of the lonely days by making frequent calls to Harold to find out how Rhonda was doing. He didn't need to be told that she was working like a maniac trying to prove herself—that was the way his stubborn lady operated. But she didn't have to prove herself to him. He knew all he needed to know about her.

"All I want is your love," he whispered, "that's all."

Once Harold lost patience with him and told him quite clearly what he thought of the whole situation.

"Alan, yuh driving me crazy with all these phone calls. Why don't you hop on a plane and go down there to see how she's doing for yourself?" Harold had yelled in exasperation.

"I can't do that," he had replied, gravely, not bothered by Harold's annoyance.

"Why the hell not? You're obviously nuts over the woman. Go down there and settle this nonsense. Time is precious. Don't wait till you get my age to find out," Harold declared.

Alan was silent.

"Yuh know between the two of you calling to find out about each other, my gray hair increase ten times."

"Yuh mean she's been asking about me?" His heart had leapt with the hope that maybe he was wrong about her feelings for him.

"Yes. Just as many times as you've asked about her. Does that make you feel any better?"

"A little. Thanks for being patient with me, Harold," he had said in a voice clearly brightened.

"No problem. Just hurry up and take care of business." Harold returned.

He had almost booked a flight the day after that conversation, but the fear of rejection had surfaced, curbing the initial enthusiasm. Now as he laid in his cold bed recalling the conversation, he knew Harold was right. He was wasting precious time existing in limbo like this. He had to find out once and for all where he stood with her so he could get on with life.

This is really ridiculous. It has gone on long enough. Either she loves me and wants to marry me or she doesn't. And the sooner I find out, the better it will be for all of us.

With that firm resolution in his mind, Alan got up and went to bed and for the first time in the two-and-a-half months enjoyed a sound night's sleep.

🥜 🥜 🥜 🥜

When Sandra angrily cracked her door to answer the persistent visitor knocking at twelve-thirty in the morning, she saw a tall handsome man with a hard decisive face. A black suitcase stood at his feet.

"Goodnight. I'm sorry to disturb you so late, but I have to see Rhonda. She was my assistant, back in New York. It's urgent that I talk to her," Alan requested in a courteous but determined voice.

It is urgent alright, Sandra thought. *This is the real reason Rhonda fled New York. . . hinting vaguely about some Trinidadian man she worked with. Hogwash. This is the first time in all the years we've been friends that she's kept stuff from me. Now I see why. Feel those powerful vibes. My poor friend probably didn't know what hit her.*

Sandra opened the door wider and stepped aside and let Alan in.

"Hi. I'm Sandra," she introduced herself and extended her right hand.

Alan shook it briefly. "Hello. I'm Alan Hussein. Can I see her?" His only concern was Rhonda and though the light-skinned woman he had heard so much about was fixing him with a curious stare, he didn't dwell on it.

"I have no objections and Rhonda isn't in a position to object," Sandra replied.

"What do you mean?" he asked, alarm causing the words to come out loud and hard.

"I'll show you," she said, leading him toward the rear of the house. He quickly catalogued the large mahogany chairs with cushions covered in a floral design and the multi-colored square area rug that sat in the center of the room. The wooden walls were painted a soft pink.

Sandra opened the door to a room painted rich cream and Alan's eyes immediately focused on the curled body beneath the gray blankets on the double bed with a dark wooden head board. A sharp chill ran the length of his body and his belly instantly contracted with fear. He swallowed the space to her bed in long quick strides, forcing his brain to think, not panic. Rhonda's head was completely covered and he eased the blanket back, careful not to disturb her. She was asleep, her thin face, pale. Her forehead was banded with a white scarf. And once his brain had started functioning again, he picked up the distinct odor of Vicks and Limacol and other home remedies for influenza. He covered her head again and joined Sandra hovering outside the bedroom door.

"She has the flu doesn't she?" he asked softly, while closing the door.

"Yes, a bad case of it and she's completely exhausted, among other things," Sandra explained.

"What other things?" he asked, brows wrinkled.

"I have a feeling you already know the answer to that," Sandra said a little tartly.

He looked at Sandra puzzled for a moment, not quite sure of what she was getting at. He sensed she was accusing him of something, her dark brown eyes gazing directly into his.

"What took you so long? You should have known that if you left it up to her it would take a lot longer to straighten out," Sandra said, lapping thick arms across her chest.

"I wanted to be sure. Even now I still have doubts about what she feels," he answered. He had nothing to hide; he couldn't hide if he wanted to. Her sharp piercing eyes missed little.

"Well, yuh still have to wait a little longer, as you can see. . . Where are you staying?" Sandra asked.

"I came straight from the airport," he said a little sheepishly.

Sandra picked up the unspoken plea for her hospitality. "You're welcome to bunk with my son for as long as you want. Luckily, there is an extra single bed in there.

Sandra settled Alan into Shawn's room and went off to her own room. Alan took a quick shower and changed into pajamas. He peeked at the little boy who looked so much like him when he was a boy. It was amazing, that curly hair and cinnamon skin. A cluster of toys laid outside the open chest already filled with more toys. Pictures and posters of animals of well-known cartoon characters lined the soft blue walls. Nothing like when he was growing up. He had made his toys from discarded bits of wood, milk cans, wooden spools from which he had unraveled the remaining thread—just about anything he could put his hands on. Alan shook in head in memory, a small smile softening his tired face.

Minutes later Alan crawled cautiously under the blankets next to Rhonda. Her skin felt like it was on fire. He snuggled close to her and she mumbled his name sleepily, deliriously. He answered, yes, but she didn't respond. She had no idea he was there.

Hours later, Alan awoke, drenched in sweat. He eased the scarf off her forehead, putting his palm to it and the back of his hand to her neck. She was still feverish, but not as much as before. He wanted to change their pajamas but didn't want to disturb her. The round white-face wooden clock on the wall read 6:30. He could survive another another half hour, but by then he would wake her to change if she wasn't already up. Alan ran his hands gently along her arms, sides and back; protruding, angular bones previously covered by yielding flesh. She'd lost a lot of weigh. *Oh baby, what have you been doing to yourself?* he thought in agony. Rhonda moved and nestled closer to him and soon he drifted into sleep again.

ع‍ا ع‍ا ع‍ا ع‍ا

Rhonda awoke to the weight of something across her waist. She opened her eyes slowly. Her heart leapt. Her eyes drank in the sight of him, face gentle in sleep, dark shadows under his eyes. His mouth slightly opened and showed a thin line of teeth. It was his arm resting on her waist that felt like lead.

Alan, you're really here? When did you come? she asked herself in disbelief, afraid that the burst of joy she felt would force its way past her raw, aching throat and explode in a piercing scream.

Alan stirred, his eyes flew open and met Rhonda's shining, stunned scrutiny. They stared at each other, feeling the months of loneliness melt away, taking in the changes in the other.

"I can't leave you alone for a minute, can I," he whispered.

At the sound of Alan's gentle teasing, Rhonda's eyes brimmed with tears that gradually overflowed and ran across the bridge of her small nose onto the pillow. With lips trembling and eyes tightly closed, Rhonda rocked with the emotion that overtook her. Quiet sobs shook her tightly curled body and she rasped over and over, "Alan, Alan, Alan." She didn't know the months of denial were so close to the surface.

"Shh. . . Shh. It's alright, baby; it's alright," Alan soothed, kissing her forehead, her nose, the salt-ravished cheeks. His hand stroked her hair, her face, her arms, not stopping in their quest to console her.

Rhonda grabbed the calming hand and cupped it to her face, her lips dry and feverish. Kissing the palms again and again, she cried, "I love you. . .I love you. . . I love you. I didn't know how to tell you. I'm sorry, so sorry." Her red, watery eyes pleaded for his understanding. She started crying again, her face wrenching in its grimace.

"Rhonda. It's alright, baby. It's alright. I'll never stop loving you. You are the woman I want to share the rest of my life with. Stop crying. It's alright."

She did eventually and he wiped and kissed away all traces of tears from her face.

"Yuh shouldn't be here in bed with me; yuh gon' get sick," Rhonda whispered hoarsely.

"I can't get any sicker," he replied, running a forefinger across her lips.

"Yuh right 'bout that one," she chuckled and then broke down into a fit of coughing.

"C'mon, yuh gotta get out of these wet clothes. Where yuh clean pajamas?" Alan sat up with his back half turned toward her, poised for movement.

"No," Rhonda said, pulling the blankets up to her neck.

"Yes. Let's go," he commanded.

"OK. But you have to leave the room."

"Now yuh being ridiculous. I know every hair on yuh body. You're too weak to stand. Let's go."

Rhonda sat up and pointed to dark wooden bureau to the side of the bed. Her head swam dizzily.

"Top middle drawer," she moaned and collapsed against the white sheets once more.

Alan climbed on the bed once again and peeled away Rhonda's damp clothing. He watched the outline of her ribs, the sunken brown belly and jutting pelvic bones. He shook his head sadly. He replaced the light blue pajamas with tiny blue flowers with a similar pair in red.

Rhonda's eyes were closed when he started to remove her pajamas and she kept them that way. She was hiding the pleasure his caring hands brought to her sensitive skin as he undressed and dressed her.

"Yuh can open yuh eyes now hussy," he teased.

She did, guiltily. He read her so very well.

"Now let's get you fed," he continued, getting up and walking over the lone wooden chair in the room. Rhonda watched as he quickly changed his red-stripped pajamas, replacing them with a pair of black cotton pants and a red T-shirt that he picked up from off the chair. Last night, he realized that he was going to need a change of clothing as soon he got up. To avoid disturbing the entire household, he had brought them and placed them in the chair before he went to bed.

Rhonda's eyes glued themselves to his lean, brown frame. *It looks like he lost a little weight too. But he still looks good*, she thought. She wanted to walk over and stop him from stepping into the pants because she wanted to renew her hand's intimate knowledge of that warm smooth back, those hairy thighs and chest, that black curly hair. Desire rose and knotted her already weakened belly. She ran a warm tongue over dry lips and forced away the longing for him. He threw her a quick glance and believing she was dozing slipped out of the room quietly.

When Alan returned a little later, he was laden with a tray and Shawn was in tow, still wearing his light blue pajamas. Seeing Rhonda was wide awake, he placed the tray on the bureau and helped her up against the head board before he got the tray again and placed it on her lap. Shawn watched quietly from a distance.

"Come here, poppet," she croaked, beckoning with her hand. Shawn did, slowly, his eyes filled with concern.

"When you gon' get better," Shawn asked, almost accusingly.

"Soon, very soon. I promise we'll go to the beach the first day I'm better," Rhonda said huskily.

"Uncle Alan say you stubborn, that is why you sick. Wuh is stubborn? Can I get sick from it, too?" Shawn asked with a five-year old's curiosity. He and Alan had obviously met and had instant rapport.

Alan, leaning against the bureau, hooted and Shawn scowled at him. Rhonda forced herself not to smile, knowing how serious Shawn was when he wanted to know or understand something.

"When Mommy tells you to do something over and over and you won't do it, you're stubborn. When you won't listen to Mommy, you're stubborn. OK?" Rhonda explained coarsely.

"So you got sick when you didn't listen to Uncle Alan," Shawn asked a frown marking his tiny brows.

"Not exactly. I got sick because I worked too hard and didn't get enough sleep. But if I had listened to Uncle Alan I wouldn't have had to work so hard."

Shawn still frowned, confused.

"Don't worry about, poppet. Auntie will be better soon. Now, go back to Mommy. I don't want you to caught my cold." Rhonda said.

Shawn left as quietly as he had come. He seemed subdued. Not for the first time, she mused about the absence of a father in his life. Patrick Braithwaite, Sandra's husband, had drowned in a fishing accident. And as Sandra put it, "I haven't met a man, man enough to father my child."

"Hey." Alan snapped his fingers. "Eat. Stop daydreaming." he came and sat down beside her.

Rhonda wasn't hungry and stared at the breakfast a long time before she started picking at it. She ate the orange and asked for another. She didn't want the hot cereal or tea. Alan took away the tray reluctantly, admonishing, "How yuh expect to get better if yuh don't eat?"

He returned with his breakfast and two oranges on a tray and sat down beside her.

"You ain't sick. How come you get breakfast in bed," she complained gruffly.

Alan ignored her and fed her figs of orange in between eating his meal of ham, eggs and toast.

Soon Rhonda felt the strain of her malaise and snuggled back under the covers. Alan kissed her forehead and left the room as soon as she fell asleep.

❧ ❧ ❧ ❧

Monica Springer didn't know how to take Alan Hussein when he purposely walked into the office of *Caribbean Woman* that Saturday morning. Though she was sorry Rhonda was ill and was very nervous about following Rhonda's instructions, she knew it was an ideal opportunity to prove herself.

He introduced himself, explaining his previous working relationship with Rhonda and his intention of giving her a hand while she was sick.

Rhonda had mentioned this Trinidadian editor briefly in editorial meetings, but she had never said he was so good-looking, Monica thought, observing the tight fit of blue jeans and black T-shirt.

Alan took in Monica's youthful appearance, his scrutiny going way beyond her slender dark-chocolate frame in a white pants and dark blue top, her dark brown eyes, full lips and lines of cornrows braided backwards from the prominent forehead. He wanted to make sure she was trustworthy, caring and dedicated. He wanted no other type messing with his woman's livelihood. He sensed he had nothing to worry about and immediately took charge.

He took in the frenzied chaos of the large room's contents. There was paper everywhere. He located Rhonda's desk immediately, but only because the stacks there were piled higher and there was some attempt at order in the arrangement. The artist's sloping table was the only spotless space in the entire room, save for a narrow path for walking.

He made his way over to Rhonda's desk and settled down with Monica next to him, notepad and pencil in hand.

Alan didn't make her feel inferior, but his thorough probing kept Monica on her toes. He made her feel very young, very inexperienced. Yet she wanted to gain his respect. He would be a valuable contact later on when she was ready to test her wings.

"Yuh sure you ain't forget anything?" he asked at the end of the grilling session.

"Yes, I'm sure," Monica answered timidly, getting up.

"Oh. I did forget something," she added moments, later, her hand to her mouth. "Rhonda said we have to call the printer and double check the stock of the paper. It wasn't the one she ordered."

"Did they start printing yet?"

"No. they're supposed to start this weekend," Monica replied.

Alan got on the phone immediately, praying that he was in time. He almost got into an argument with the printer and made a mental note to tell Rhonda to find another printer. The man was cocky and rude. In any case, Alan settled the minor dispute and approved the printing of the first issue on the paper Rhonda wanted.

Alan was amazed at the degree and amount of work Rhonda had put into *Caribbean Woman* in the time she had been in Barbados. He could see his mark in the layout and in some of the copy. He smiled. *She did learn a few things after all. This magazine is damn good.*

Going over the budget figures, he realized that her start-up capital had already been gobbled up and she needed more money quickly. He put a call to an old friend in banking to find out the procedures for transferring money from his account to Rhonda's as quickly as possible. Monday, he wanted to walk over to Rhonda's bank completely prepared.

Alan worked late into evening. It was exciting working at something new again, especially something as personal as this was. He called Sandra during the day to check on Rhonda, who was tired and congested, but no worse.

Monica in overhearing his conversations, realized that he was a lot more than a colleague of Rhonda's. The man cared deeply about her boss. She could hear it in his voice. She also discovered that she never wanted to get on his bad side, for she was almost sorry for the printer.

"Oh Monica, before you leave, could you get the editor and artist in here tomorrow. We need to clean this place up. Thanks." He raised his head from the stacks of paper in front of him to issue the request to a departing Monica. She returned to her desk and made the calls immediately.

Alan worked until twelve o'clock that evening and when he pulled up in Sandra's blue Escort about forty-five minutes later, the entire house was in darkness. He disliked the idea that he would have to wake Sandra up. But he didn't have to; she opened the door as soon as he walked up, noting the tiredness on his face when he got inside.

"How's she?" he asked, bypassing a hello to Sandra.

"Oh I'm doing fine, thank you. I had wonderful day teaching those little monsters."

"I'm sorry. Hi... How's she?" he chuckled, still bent on finding out how Rhonda was feeling.

"I can't win, can I? She's doing well, very well as a matter of fact. Must have something to do with the weather—what do you think?" she teased.

Alan laughed and went straight in to see Rhonda. She was asleep and he kissed the cool forehead and went off to the bathroom to take a shower before bunking down next to Shawn.

Alan was gone before Rhonda awoke at nine o'clock the following morning. She knew he was at *Caribbean Woman* again. The evening before Monica had called to update Rhonda on her progress and told her about the bulldozer effect of Alan's helping hand. In joy, she couldn't help telling Rhonda about Alan's call to the banker.

"I know I probably shouldn't be talking about his calls. But I'm so happy he's giving us some money. You know we need it desperately." Monica said, praying Rhonda would excuse her tactless behavior.

"No, you know you shouldn't repeat people's private conversations, but you're family and I guess I'll let it slide this time." Rhonda admonished.

"Thanks, I promise I'll watch it in the future." Monica said apologetically.

After hanging up the phone from talking to Monica, Rhonda laid back against the pillows, torn between exhilaration and defeat: *That man is determined to stick his nose in my business. What can I do? He's only doing it because he loves me. I better get use to it because he will be doing a lot of that in the name of love. Well, I am glad about the money— God knows how we were going to make it to the next issue.*

Rhonda sat up and did feel good enough to get up and leave the bedroom. She was sick of the bedroom and she was also determined to stay up as long as she could, so she could talk to Alan when he came home. After dinner with Sandra and Shawn, Rhonda stayed up until twelve o'clock watching television. Tired and defeated, she decided to go to bed. Alan didn't come home until two o'clock in the morning.

By 6:30 the following morning, Rhonda was dressed and sitting in the living room, in case Alan had any intention of leaving early without talking to her.

Alan didn't stir until 11:30. After having breakfast with Sandra and Shawn, who left at 8:15, Rhonda decided to treat Alan to breakfast in bed. *Poor man*, Rhonda sympathized, *he's so tired he can't even get up this morning.*

It must have been the smell of the coffee, because he got up within seconds of her entering.

She had never seen his wake-up face before and smiled at the tousled, red-eyed picture he presented.

"What's so funny?" he grumbled.

"You don't look that great in the morning," she laughed.

"I don't think you do either, but you love me anyway," he groaned, stretching his pajama-clad arms into the air.

"Well, here's your breakfast. And after you eat, we have to talk," Rhonda said firmly, sitting down on Shawn's bed.

"Let's talk now. I want to enjoy my breakfast," Alan replied, sitting up and crossing his arms against his chest.

"How are things at CW?' she asked, catching Alan off guard.

"CW, hmm. So that's what you call it. Easier than *Caribbean Woman*, that's for sure. Things are fine. Next question," he said.

"I hope you realize I intend to make the decisions at CW," Rhonda said, also lapping her hands across her chest.

"Of course. . . when you're on your feet again. But for now, I am," he announced, raising his dark eyebrows.

Rhonda got up suddenly and throwing Shawn's pillow hit Alan full in the face.

"Why did I have to fall in love with such a bossy man? You're impossible," she screamed.

Alan started laughing and threw the pillow back at her. It knocked her flat onto the bed and she stayed there because battling with Alan was sapping what little energy she had.

In the days ahead, Rhonda relaxed and let Alan run the magazine. In the evenings, they went over everything. And he did allow her to run the show. They talked shop and stayed away from discussing any personal plans for the future. Alan wanted to give Rhonda time to get her strength back before he attempted any kind of intimate probing.

Late that Sunday night, about a week after she was confined to bed, Rhonda decided she would return to work. Alan accepted the news and suggested they take a stroll on the beach. Rhonda agreed knowing that once she started work again, it would be a while she could enjoy her favorite past time. She went to her room for a light black jacket to put over the black T-shirt she wore with the calf-length black slacks. She asked Alan if he needed a jacket also, but he declined.

"I'm overheated as it is," he smiled devilishly, glancing down-wards at his navy blue knee-length shorts.

The drive to the beach was done in silence. The atmosphere in the car reminded Rhonda of the drive they had shared on the way home the first night they made love. Only now there was a sense of anticipation, no fear.

After parking, they left their shoes in the car and side-by-side walked along the beach. A full moon gave the night a soft, blue glow. The air was cool, caressing, carrying salty-fresh moisture on its wings. Blue-tinged sand provided a cushiony carpet for their bare feet and the sound of the rushing waves, a balm for their spirit. For a long time, the couple walked quietly, just holding hands, relishing the peace of their togetherness.

Suddenly Alan stopped; Rhonda turned to him questioningly.

Alan released her hand to tenderly grasp her face, softened and tinted by the moon's light.

"Rhonda. . .I love you and I want to marry you. Please say yes," he said huskily, almost pleadingly.

The rush of emotion Rhonda felt was indescribable. It sent tears to her eyes instantaneously.

"Did I say something wrong?" he asked fearfully.

"No." she said solemnly, looking into the spice-colored face that meant the world to her, delighting in the warmth of his hands on her cheeks.

"No, you won't marry me," he gulped.

"No, you didn't say anything wrong, silly." Rhonda smiled, releasing some of the tension that poured from him.

"I love you too. And I will marry you. . .on one condition," Rhonda said, reaching up to hold Alan's wrists.

"What's that?" Alan questioned in concern. She was unpredictable and he was threading on thin ice with this proposal stuff as it was.

"On the condition that we get married here on the beach. . . a small quiet wedding. It's one of my favorite fantasies." Rhonda explained.

"OK. But I have a condition for that condition." Alan responded.

"What," she laughed joyfully.

"That we spend our wedding night here on the beach, starting now." he said hoarsely. Already the blood was pumping rapidly through his veins.

"Are you crazy?' she asked.

"Yes. Totally bananas about you and I mean to have you *now*," he emphasized.

"We can't do that. What if somebody comes along?" Rhonda giggled, but she was genuinely skeptical.

"No buts. Let's get the blankets from the car?"

"You have blankets in the car?" she asked, stunned.

"You beginning to sound like a broken record, woman. Let's go."

Minutes later, after some tricking maneuvering, all clothing was removed and all protests were swept from Rhonda's lips as Alan bore down on her in reckless abandon. It was as if they were coming together for the first time. Only this time, mutual love and a declaration of that love ignited the passion and it sizzled out of control. It was a battle to see who could give the most pleasure, an entanglement of frenzied limbs, wet kisses and hot panting breaths.

Rhonda straddled Alan, restraining his arms and legs. The blanket fell off her shoulders, revealing erect nipples that protruded from breasts caught and painted by the moonlight.

"Calm down, my sweet," she panted. "I owe you one."

Alan just groaned. Rhonda flicked her tongue in an ear, across a cheek, into his mouth, down his neck and didn't stop flicking until she faced his manhood, throbbing, gleaming in the light. She lowered her head and Alan's entire body exploded. His piercing cry was captured and got lost in the sound of the rushing waves. He was hers completely.

EPILOGUE

"Alan, somebody is at the door. Could you get it? I'm in the bathroom," Rhonda yelled.

Alan who was in the yard helping little Kenny make his kite didn't hear Rhonda, and the persistent knocking made Rhonda hurriedly dry her skin and scamper into the bedroom to pull on a white cotton dress.

She opened the door and Deborah and Harold stood beaming at her.

"Surprise," her mother said softly.

"Ma," Rhonda screamed, rushing forward to envelope her mother in a warm hug. Deborah squeezed her daughter to her body tightly, while unshed tears stung her eyes. Grinning widely, Rhonda left her mother and reached over to hug Harold too.

"Well. Don't keep us at the door. Let's go in," Deborah grumbled, happily.

The women went inside, leaving Harold to handle the heavy suitcases.

"Where's my little man?" Deborah said, looking towards the rear of the house. Deborah didn't notice Rhonda had repainted the room since she visited the Husseins in Barbados a year ago.

The soft peach walls were the perfect background for the wicker chairs with black-and-white-stripped cushions.

"He's outside with his father," Rhonda said.

Rhonda followed Deborah to the back door and watched joyfully from the doorway as Deborah greeted her six-year-old grandson.

"Hi there, little man," she called, after giving Alan a brief wave of the hand.

"Grandma," Kenneth squealed, running to his grandmother as fast as his little legs could take him.

"Careful, careful," Deborah warned as she prepared her body for the shock of his greeting. Deborah gathered up her favorite bundle of love, hugging and kissing the skinny brown-skinned boy who had his father's flared nostrils and cinnamon complexion and his mother's kinky hair. His huge dark brown eyes shone in excitement.

"Grandma, grandma, come see my kite. Daddy helping me make a kite. Come see."

Alan watching his wife at the door, noticed the strained look on her face as Deborah went off to see the famous kite. He knew joy and regret were at war within her. He walked up to Rhonda, put an arm around her shoulders and kissed her at the side of her forehead.

"Just think: He'll be getting ten times what you got because she'll be trying to make up for what she didn't give you. And doesn't that help ease the pain, make you happy?"

"Yes. It does... But still I wish..." Rhonda moaned huskily.

"No. Let it go. She has more than made up these last six years. Kenny will grow up with so much love he wouldn't know what to do with it. I'm not going anywhere. This little family unit of ours is breaking that chain," Alan said solemnly.

"In case I haven't told you lately, Alan Hussein, I love you." Rhonda turned and hugging Alan kissed him loudly on the lips.

"You may want to change that statement when I tell you what I did," Alan said, warily.

"What did you do?" Rhonda was skeptical that maybe he wasn't teasing.

"I located your father," Alan said watching his wife's expression closely.

Rhonda was silent for long moments. She couldn't describe what she felt to anyone, but underneath it all, curiosity reigned.

"Why not? It's about time the man faced his responsibility. I'm ready, I think. . ." Rhonda said smiling into her husband's light-brown eyes.

ка ка ка ка

GLOSSARY

Ackee: A fruit that grows in clusters on trees. Its skin is green and its center is a seed covered with orange pink pulp that is both sweet and sour to the taste. The ackee, so called in Barbados, is called *chennette* in Trinidad and is known by various names in other islands. The Jamaican ackee is a totally different fruit used primarily in cooking.

Breadfruit: A large round vegetable that grows on trees. Its skin is green with small circular patterns and its flesh is creamy white, solid, and starchy.

Callaloo: A dish made from the leaves of the dasheen, okras, and seasonings that is very popular in Trinidad. In Jamaica, spinach is sometimes called callaloo.

Calypso: A type of music indigenous of the West Indies whose tempo can be either fast or slow with a heavily syncopated rhythm. The songs sang by calypsonians usually satirize social, economic, and political life.

Coo-coo: A dish made from cooked cornmeal and okras that is usually served with fish steamed in a rich sauce. It is extremely popular in Barbados.

Dasheen: A ground vegetable that grows in damp swampy areas. Its leaves are used in callaloo.

Dashiki: A brightly colored loose-fitting pullover garment usually worn by people of African descent.

Durex: A brand of prophylactics.

Guava cheese: A soft sweet candy made from the guava fruit.

Guinness Stout: A brand of dark, malty ale called stout.

Jep (Jack Spaniard) : A wasp whose sting is extremely painful. When irritated, the Jep or Jack Spaniard, as it is also called, usually raises the rear end of its abdomen high in the air.

Jimmy Cliff: The Jamaican actor who starred in the movie, *The Harder They Come.*

Lime/liming: To have a good time visiting with friends, or to"hang out."

Mauby: A cold beverage made from the bark of the mauby tree that is flavored with sugar and extracts. It has a very bitter aftertaste.

Pigeon peas: The seeds of a leguminous plant that grows on small trees.

Pelau: A dish made of rice, peas and vegetables cooked in stewed chicken or beef.

Plait: A braid. The term "plait" is more commonly used in the Caribbean.

Plantain: A starchy fruit similar to the banana that is bigger and is usually steamed or fried either green or ripe before it's eaten.

Pony comb: A round clasp or barrette for holding a woman's hair in place.

Quiet Storm: A popular musical program on a radio station in New York (WBLS) featuring ballads, jazz, and classics by black singers and musicians.

Rastas: The shortened term for Rastafarian. Rastafarianism is an indigenous African-based religious sect that has its roots in the belief in the divinity of the late Haile Selassie of Ethopia. Rastas wear their hair long in uncut, uncombed mountainous curls called dreadlocks. Although they tend to look fierce, they are gentle in belief and practice. True rastas shun the values of the modern society and live off the land. They eat only vegetarian foods and smoke marijuana as a part of their religious beliefs.

Reggae: A popular type of music of Jamaican origin whose tempo is slow and hypnotic and whose rhythm is moderately syncopated.

Roti: A dish in which curried meat or shrimp and vegetables are wrapped and served in covering made of flour, spilt peas and other spices that is cooked on an oiled iron griddle (baking stone). Roti is East Indian in origin.

Salt fish: Dried, salted cod fish.

Spouge (spooge): A type of music that combines the rhythm and beat of calypso and reggae. Spouge is primarily sung and played in Barbados.

Steelband: A band of musicians whose instruments are primarily steelpans.

Steelpan: A musical instrument made from the tops of oil drums and whose origin is Trinidad and Tobago. These pans are tuned to key by extensive hammering.

Sweet bread: A loaf of bread made from grated coconut, sugar and spices. Sometimes raisins and other fruits are added.

Tamarind: A tropical leguminous tree. Its fruits has an acid brown pulp and seeds that are dark brown, almost black.

Tamarind whip: A stem from the tamarind tree often used to flog recalcitrant children in the Caribbean.

The Harder They Come: A Jamaican movie produced in 1972 by Vista Film Production. Jimmy Cliff, the famous Jamaican singer and actor played in the leading role. It's the story of a young man who moves from the country to the city in search of fame and fortune.

Threading: A term commonly used in Barbados and Trinidad and Tobago that means copulation and is used in relation to the mating habits of poultry.

University of the West Indies: An institution of higher learning that presently has three campuses in the West Indies: Cave Hill in Barbados; Mona Campus in Jamaica; and St. Augustine in Trinidad and Tobago.

WLIB: A black-owned radio station based in New York that serves the African American and Caribbean communities. WLIB is a favorite among West Indians not only because it provides reports of happenings in the Caribbean but also because the station plays calypso and reggae on a regular basis.

Yam: A starchy tuberous root, whose flesh is usually white, that is common in tropical areas. It is not to be confused with the orange-

fleshed root that is called a yam in the United States—West
Indians call this a sweet potato.

ﺏﺏﺏ ﺏﺏﺏ

·&· ·&· ·&· ·&·

Dear Reader:

We hope that you have enjoyed *Island Magic* by Loraine Barnett, just as much as we have enjoyed working with her.

We are very proud of this series featuring black women in love. As the months go on, and as we expand and enlarge the dimensions of this fresh approach to romantic fiction, we hope that you will not only greet **Romance In Black** with welcoming hearts, but it is also our hope that MARRON PUBLISHERS will be included in and warmed by this embrace.

For the convenience of our readers, subscriptions are available for those who wish to receive both **Romance In Black** releases quarterly. A discount of up to 25% is offered to those who decide to participate in our special "family" service. This service also entitles you to a free three- or six-month subscription to **Dark Secrets,** our new bimonthly newsletter showcasing contemporary short stories and poetry.

Should you decided to write Loraine Barnett, or wish to receive further information on any of MARRON PUBLISHERS' publications, please contact: MARRON PUBLISHERS, P.O. Box 756, Yonkers, NY 10703. Or call 1-800-766-0499 for fast subscription service.

Marquita Guerra

Marquita Guerra
Publisher

Sharon A. Ortiz

Sharon A. Ortiz
Publisher

P.S. New writers—sharpen your pencils! Guidelines for the **Romance in Black** series are available at your request.

·&· ·&· ·&· ·&·

ROMANCE IN **BLACK**

Island Magic by Loraine Barnett

Follow Rhonda Baptiste and Alan Hussein, assistant editor and managing editor of *West Indian World* magazine, from their exciting meeting on a subway platform to the development of their mutual respect and love. The action surrounding these two lovers is played out in New York and Barbados.

Love Signals by Margie Walker

Patrice Mason, the general manager of a Houston radio station, and Lawrence Woodson, Vice President of Banneker University, clash over an anti-apartheid concert sponsored by KHVY Radio. As bomb threats and pranks jeopardize the project, Patrice wonders if Lawrence is yet another distortion in her world, or is the attraction a viable love signal.

Posters of RIB covers are available for purchase. For details, contact: MARRON PUBLISHERS, P.O. Box 756, Yonkers, NY 10703.

------------------------------- ✂ -------------------------------

ROMANCE IN **BLACK**

☐ *Island Magic* $8 ☐ Six months $25 ☐ One year $45
☐ *Love Signals* $8   (4 Copies)   (8 copies)
    Plus 3 free issues   Plus 6 free issues
    of Dark Secrets   of Dark Secrets

☐ Maybe. Please place me on mailing list.

☐ Payment Enclosed   ☐ Bill me

NAME _____

ADDRESS _____

CITY _____ STATE _____ ZIP _____

PLEASE ALLOW TWO TO FOUR WEEKS FOR DELIVERY

Call 1-800-766-0499 to claim your free T-shirt or leather bookmark when you refer a friend.

------------------------------- ✂ -------------------------------

DARK
S E C R E T S

Let MARRON PUBLISHERS stimulate your visual and literary senses. Subscribe to this refreshing bimonthly newsletter designed to appease your craving for a finely crafted short story or an inspiring poem. Explore the vast dimensions of love, the intricacies of family relationships, or the complexities of the human and ethnic experience.

You'll not only enjoy the works of our upcoming writers, but share the visions of many talented artists as you view **Dark Secret's** original illustrations and photography. And for you aspiring writers, MARRON's bulletins featuring resource organizations, seminars, lectures, and workshops will keep you informed, updated, and motivated.

Share in America's growing awareness of its vast cultural diversity—join our family of readers!

Oh, and remember: **Dark Secrets** is free to **Romance In Black** subscribers!

---------------------------- ✂ ----------------------------

DARK
S E C R E T S

☐ YES   ☐ One Issue $3   ☐ One year $15   ☐ Two years $29
                                           (6 Issues)   (12 Issues)

☐ Maybe. Please place me on mailing list;
   or mail a free copy to :

☐ Payment Enclosed   ☐ Bill me

NAME ——————————————————————————

ADDRESS ————————————————————————

CITY ———————————— STATE ———————— ZIP ————

PLEASE ALLOW TWO TO FOUR WEEKS FOR DELIVERY

Call 1-800-766-0499 to claim your free T-shirt or leather bookmark when you refer a friend.

---------------------------- ✂ ----------------------------